GOSPEL FEVER

*A Novel About America's Most Beloved
TV Evangelist*

FRANK G. SLAUGHTER

Doubleday & Company, Inc., Garden City, New York
1980

The situations and characters in this novel are entirely the products of the author's imagination. Except for a few well-known individuals in today's evangelical movement, it is an accident if the name of any living person appears.

ISBN: 0-385-15308-2
Library of Congress Catalog Card Number: 79-6094

GOSPEL FEVER

Chapter One

"SHUT THAT DOOR!" MIKE D'AGOSTINO JERKED HIS HEAD AROUND, when a blast of warm spring air struck the back of his neck as he squatted in front of the slightly elevated stage upon which stood the set of the Logos Club.

As director on the set for the three television cameras facing it, part of Mike's job was to see that no one entered the studio during the final seconds before a broadcast as well as while the actual program was in progress. His angry expression turned to startled wonder, however, and he whistled softly before nodding to Lee Steadman, who stood in front of Camera One beside the piano where Jim Cates sat ready to start the five-times-weekly broadcast of the Club theme song.

"Take a look at what just blew in, Lee," Mike said sotto voce.

Lee's quick glance toward the studio door told him the brief interruption had been caused by a strikingly lovely girl. She had slipped into the studio and was now being seated by one of the hostesses in the front row of the visitors' gallery overlooking the stage. He had time only for a glance, however, for Mike began the regular cadence of the prebroadcast countdown and Lee tensed himself for the cue that launched the opening signature song of every Logos Club broadcast.

It was the time of the day Lee loved most, the electric moment before the red eye of Camera One, its broad lens reflecting his own image, winked into brilliance, indicating the picture being taken was also going out over the air. Beyond the slightly elevated stage bearing the set of the Logos Club, the studio audience—limited strictly to fifty by the seating capacity of the gallery—had been shepherded fifteen minutes earlier into comfortable theater-type seats. Fresh from a brief period of mood creation and instructions by one of the volunteer hostesses in what was called the "Prayer Chamber," they waited eagerly now for the program of "Brother Tim" Douglas and his Logos Club to begin.

The studio audience was always a select one, made up largely of those who, during the five-year existence of the most widely broadcast daily religious television and radio program in the world, had contracted to donate a minimum of twenty dollars monthly to the support of the Logos Club. The Club itself, in turn, was the most important part of the Christian Broadcast Center, largest organization in what was often referred to as the "Electric Church."

So named because in Christian theology the Greek word *Logos* was traditionally defined as the "Word of God," the Club's program sessions were ninety minutes long. Emanating live from the Center at Weston, South Carolina, to more than a dozen TV stations, and by satellite or videotape to hundreds more all over the world simultaneously, Logos Club programs were also broadcast by radio, bringing the total number of out-lets to more than a thousand cities.

An inch over six feet, his body honed to physical perfection by a five-mile run four mornings a week, Lee Steadman could have posed for a cigarette advertisement—except that he didn't smoke. Dark-eyed and clear-skinned, dressed casually in gray slacks, an open-throated blue sport shirt and dark blue blazer, he waited patiently for the signal from Mike D'Agostino. Behind Lee on a platform of two steps stood six handsome young men and women in white, the vocal backup group trained by Lee known as the Gospel Troubadours.

"Stand by! Ten seconds!" The calm voice of Henry Waterford came through the studio loudspeakers from the control room with its glass front overlooking both stage and set.

An electronic genius, Waterford had kept the station equipment in operation since the early years, when the paucity of funds had made its continued existence questionable from

broadcast to broadcast. With a bank of switches and monitors before him—one for each of the cameras facing the set below—Waterford could control both picture and voice being flung from the tall framework of the antenna outside the Center.

Beamed by a network of microwave towers, the programs were received by the stations scattered over the southeastern United States that broadcast the Logos Club live at the same moment each day. Simultaneously, too, the electronic miracles of both videotape and audiotape recorded the activities on the stage below for later use through the worldwide network managed by the Center's own syndication department.

"Tape rolling!" Mike D'Agostino announced.

In a bank of a dozen seats beside the gallery, the twelve counselors for today's program—products of the Club's intensive training course in religious counseling—waited for the red light at the base of the telephone on the desk before each of them to indicate an incoming call. Beside each counselor's phone was a pad of printed forms on which to scribble questions and requests. Each caller's name and address were carefully recorded too, swelling the Center's mailing list, the ranks of the faithful from whom came a daily flood of checks and currency.

Occasionally, the counselors provided the most exciting part of a morning broadcast, when the anguished voice of a troubled individual about to commit murder or some other crime came on the line. At such times, an alert counselor could press a second button beside the telephone, causing a red light just offstage to glow. A warning signal would also be sounded while the call was switched to the tiny white earphone worn always during the broadcast by Alex Porcher—the Logos Club's counterpart of the Johnny Carson "Tonight Show"'s Ed McMahon, upon which the daily broadcast was patterned. Alerted immediately, Alex must decide whether the call should be switched to the studio loudspeakers, interrupting the interview or song in progress and cueing Tim Douglas in on the emergency.

Because of these occasionally dramatic interruptions, the founder of the program was able to promise that any question needing an immediate personal answer would be heard. And lest the low-voiced conversation between callers and counselors be picked up by the microphones on the stage, a plate-glass wall separated them, giving complete visibility both to the counselors and to those upon the set that occupied most of the stage.

Like the broadcast itself, the set, too, was low-key and almost austere in its simplicity, consisting of a sofa and two comfortable chairs. The chair occupied by Alex Porcher was also connected to a switch by means of which he could bypass the control room and channel the voice of a caller into the main loudspeaker system of the studio. At the back of the stage, a large screen and a rear projection setup allowed infinite variations in the set background. Above it, and out of camera range, a large monitor screen gave a continuous picture of the scene being broadcast but without the sound, which could be heard in the studio or over the loudspeaker system when a film was being shown.

"Five seconds!"

With upraised hand Mike D'Agostino, one earphone pushed up so he could hear what was being said on the set, as well as receiving instructions from the control room, began to count off the seconds. Lee Steadman glanced instinctively at the Tele-PrompTer beneath Camera One to make sure it was ready with the first words of the opening song. Printed in extra-large type on a long paper strip, the TelePrompTer would unroll at a synchronized reading speed, keeping the lyrics of the song Lee was singing always before him.

"Two!" The word brought a sudden hush to the entire studio.

"One! Applause!" Mike's hand came down and, as the spectators obeyed, pianist Jim Cates struck the opening chord of the song with which every Logos Club broadcast began.

"He's Alive!" Lee's vibrant baritone turned the lyrics into a paean of joy while, behind him, the Gospel Troubadours—mostly voice majors from nearby Weston University—broke into sound, along with the drums, rhythm guitar, and keyboard making up the rest of the small combo.

The thirteen-hundredth broadcast of Brother Tim Douglas'

Logos Club, most widely heard religious television and radio program in the world, had begun.

II

As the final words of the song died away amid a burst of applause from the gallery, Alex Porcher moved toward the set from the wing at the right where, behind the wall of glass, he had been talking to Cornelia Douglas, Tim's wife. Straightening his tie and glancing into a nearby mirror strategically placed for just that purpose, Alex moved confidently into position before Camera Three, to another burst of applause from the audience.

Porcher was nearly fifty, but the darkening effect achieved by the hairdresser who ministered to him twice weekly kept any telltale gray from showing in the rich waves of his hair. Pancake makeup also took away any shine of perspiration produced by the heat of the studio lights from his face. His shirt a pale blue, the widely knotted tie a bright red, the suit a ministerial black with every crease perfect, Alex was a very handsome and virile man, as well as the epitome of the successful minister of the gospel and one of the few conventional religious figures in the entire program.

Moving to the platform where the Gospel Troubadours stood, Lee Steadman saw Cornelia Douglas—affectionately known as Neeley to the studio staff—smile and lift her hand with thumb and forefinger joined in a circle of approval. The two had been good friends since Lee had joined the staff of the Center while still a junior majoring in music at Weston University. Now, one year away from his graduate degree in religion and sacred music, his strong baritone, plus the combo and the Troubadours under his direction, had made the musical part of the broadcasts almost as well known as its now world-famous master of ceremonies, "Brother Tim" Douglas.

Besides the opening, "He's Alive!" two production numbers and two solos were allotted to music during the ninety minutes

of the broadcasts. One was always an old-time hymn, which
Lee loved. The second was usually a swinging, hand-clapping
gospel-rock tune that brought young audiences to their feet,
when the Troubadours and the combo gave concerts in nearby
cities and towns of North and South Carolina. The rest of the
musical selections varied but were usually rhythm tunes that
were becoming more and more popular with both young and
old.

Both Weston University and the new Gospel Broadcast Center, built by Tim Douglas on the grounds of the defunct UHF
TV station he and Neeley had bought with a minimum of cash
and a maximum of faith 5½ years ago, were located in the
western foothills of South Carolina in the shadow of the Great
Smoky Mountains. The station and studio had been little more
than junk when Tim, seeking an outlet for his new concept of
a TV gospel program, had come upon the area. The location,
however, was breathtaking. A promontory overlooking a man-
made lake in the foothills of the Smokies allowed a view across
2 miles of water to the peaks of the southern range of the Ap-
palachian chain that stretched from northern Maine almost to
the Gulf of Mexico.

Camera Three winked into life and Alex Porcher's features,
lit by a beatific smile, appeared on the large monitor located
above the stage. At the same moment, Neeley Douglas glanced
at the clipboard she carried in her left hand and clicked the
stopwatch in her right. Always attentive to detail, she observed
each broadcast from the sidelines, signaling to Mike D'Agostino when the interviews ran short or long so he, in turn, could
give a covert hand signal to Tim and Alex that the pace of
questions and answers needed to be slowed or speeded up.

If Tim Douglas, known world over as "Brother Tim," was
the light that shone most brightly from the busy Gospel Broadcast Center, Neeley was the Keeper of the Light. A human dynamo, she furnished much of the Center's nonelectric energy,
although rarely seen on the cameras of the Logos Club. Only
five feet tall, with a compact, wiry body and sandy hair curled
in such riotous confusion that it had to be cut short weekly to
keep it out of her way, Neeley had a freckled face, bright eyes

that were astonishingly green in color, and a gamin grin that
endeared her to everybody.

On the small glass viewing screen at the back of Camera
Three, Alex had begun to speak, his voice with its Carolina accent like warm syrup.

"My name is Alex Porcher," he announced with just the
right touch of humility and pride. "Today it is my pleasure to
welcome you, whether in some farflung corner of the world or
here in the studio audience at Weston, South Carolina, to the
thirteen-hundredth broadcast of the Logos Club."

On cue, Camera Two, its lens directed toward the audience,
panned the rows of eager faces in the visitors' gallery rapidly
and smoothly, pausing for an instant to center on the girl who
had arrived late at the studio. The color camera confirmed Lee
Steadman's first brief impression that she was astonishingly
lovely, with reddish-gold hair, blue eyes, and a complexion that,
obviously natural, was near perfection.

Suddenly conscious of her own face looking back at her from
the large monitor screen behind the set, the girl blushed and
smiled a little self-consciously. An instant later, Henry Waterford's command of "Take Three" sounded in the control room
above, and Alex Porcher was again on the monitor, his voice
pouring across the narrow aisle separating the gallery from the
stage.

"Now let us give a big welcome to the host of the Logos
Club," Alex announced, his voice rising almost to a shout in
the traditional manner of introducing the star of any television
show—"Brother Tim Douglas!"

Smiling warmly, Tim came down a ramp from the left wing
behind the musicians. "To God be the glory!" he cried in the
voice of a loved one greeting a loved one, and the gallery stood
up on the cue of an upswept hand from Mike D'Agostino—just
as they had been instructed in the prayer room by the day's
hostess.

Not having been coached before, the girl who'd arrived late
scrambled to her feet a second later, but the applause was so
deafening that no one noticed the delay. At the same moment
Lee Steadman, facing her and the other visitors from his place
beside the piano, saw come into her eyes the familiar glaze he'd

seen so often in women both young and old, when first assailed by the boyish and, he was thoroughly convinced, really sincere charm of Tim Douglas.

III

Only five-eight and a bit more stocky than he'd been at the first of the thirteen hundred broadcasts five years ago, Brother Tim and his famous half-deprecating grin were known in popular religious broadcasting the world over even better than Johnny Carson in his own commercial field. Although only forty-five, Tim Douglas had let the normal sprinkling of gray remain in his hair. It, plus his bright-colored sports jacket and open-collared shirt with blue slacks, gave him a somewhat rumpled appearance, just like—his millions of admirers loved to say—the "guy next door."

Tim stumbled a little at the foot of the ramp, calling attention to his loafers and bright-colored socks. Catching himself, he chuckled and said, "Old Satan's always waiting to trip me—" bringing down the house.

"Good morning, Alex, and a big Hallelujah to the Lord for the day." Tim moved across the stage to grip the hand of his slightly taller cohost before taking a seat at the end of the sofa. Then turning to face the camera, Tim added on the same happy confidential note, "Wherever you are, friends and partners in Christ, I wish you could be here this fine spring morning. The dogwoods are in bloom outside the studio, and the morning sun falling on the lake makes it shine like a mirror reflecting the glory of God."

"Glory Hallelujah! Praise the Lord!" Alex's shout boomed from the loudspeakers as Tim's face, covered now by Camera Two, which had been turned away from the audience, loomed large on the monitor screen.

On cue, as he'd done hundreds of times before, Lee Steadman lifted his voice in the thrilling beat of the second of the two opening songs, supported by the singers and the combo.

"God is greater!" the opening phrase boomed out, closing ten bars later with the rousing final climax, "God is here—today!"

"Glory Hallelujah!" Tim echoed happily.

Spoken by other lips, the words would have seemed almost banal, the stock chant of the professional evangelist, practiced and delivered in a voice pregnant with the illusion of deep emotion. Not so when coming from Tim Douglas, however. Something about the deprecating smile, the somewhat rumpled clothing and the warm voice with its hint of a southern accent betraying his West Virginia birthplace gave an effect of honesty, of natural emotion and gratitude to Higher Authority for even the crumbs from the heavenly table.

While Lee and the six-member Troubadour team were singing, Tim settled comfortably at the end of the sofa, his favorite position during the interviews that were the major part of every program. As the music died away, the girls of the singing group —all wearing white dresses with blue ribbons in their hair—and the men likewise in white suits, sank to the floor of the ramp by which Tim Douglas had come onstage, and Lee moved to join them.

"Thank you, Lee." Leaning forward, as if he were confiding a secret to the listeners, Tim added, "Those of you who follow the regular programs of the Logos Club know Lee Steadman to be a highly talented musician with a God-given voice, plus the ability to train others in songs of praise. Now he is preparing himself for his own special ministry in the service of God by continuing his studies at the School of Religion and Sacred Music at Weston University.

"Long ago, the Son of God taught us, when we prayed, to go into our closet and be shut away there with God," Tim continued. "However, that was before the miracle of electronics made it possible to teach others, often thousands of miles away, the truth of the sacrifice made on that hill called Golgotha. I like to think of this studio as our own private closet where we can pray to God in secret, yet broadcast His message to the rest of the world."

As the applause following Brother Tim's brief introductory monologue died away, Alex turned to the wing where Neeley

Douglas stood. A tall, well-dressed and startlingly handsome man, in spite of his numerical age of sixty-odd, was beside her.

"Folks," Alex confided to the studio audience and the millions who would eventually see the picture or hear the words on tape, "we have a great honor and a particular privilege today to present to you the special guest of the Logos Club. Now the leading character in the inspiring television series 'Melton's Mountain,' he is also author of a best-selling autobiography depicting his life before, by God's Grace, he was 'born again.'

"*Satan Made Me Do It* is the title and here is the author himself. Will you welcome Walter Lincoln?"

The actor strode across the stage to be greeted by Alex, Tim and a wave of applause from the gallery before being ushered ceremoniously to a seat on the sofa next to Tim. Meanwhile, Alex leaned forward to clip a small microphone on Lincoln's tie.

"I read your book last night, Mr. Lincoln." Tim opened the interview with his characteristic chuckle. "You must have really had to struggle to win your way out of the morass of sin Satan was threatening to drown you in. And particularly to get his talons out of your flesh."

"It wasn't easy," Lincoln admitted, as Henry Waterford switched the picture on the large monitor back of the set to a group shot of the three men.

"I know many famous people are reluctant to recite the details of how they were 'born again,'" Tim continued, "but would you mind telling us about your own particular experience?"

"Well"—the actor hesitated momentarily—"it's sort of embarrassing."

"I know—but you and the television series you have brought to a place in the top ten shows—against some pretty sleazy competition, I must admit—are important in the fight against sin."

"It's not *that* I'm embarrassed about," Lincoln confessed. "In fact, I'm very proud of the image we've helped create on 'Melton's Mountain' of how much good can be found in everyday people. I could talk your ear off on that subject—"

"Keep it to sixty minutes, please," Tim said in a mock plea.

"It's just that I was shown the way to Christ by another evangelist—who's a competitor of yours—Billy Graham."

"Billy and I aren't in competition when it comes to fighting the Devil," Tim assured him. "You see, we have the same Boss."

A wave of laughter rippled through the audience on cue from Alex.

"It happened one night when I was being considered for a film about an evangelist," said Lincoln.

"Not Elmer Gantry, I hope," Tim interrupted.

"No, Burt Lancaster got that one. To tell the truth, I don't even remember the title of the script," the actor continued. "Dr. Graham was holding a crusade in Los Angeles at the time and I dropped in one night, trying to get an idea of how to play the part, if I got it. You see, I had reached something of a low tide in my life and was much troubled."

"Most rebels against Satan's wiles are deeply troubled when their souls are in the throes of the final struggle to see the light," Tim assured him.

"I know that now but I didn't then," Lincoln admitted. "I was sorely disturbed by Dr. Graham's sermon that night. When he gave the invitation, I wanted—more than I ever remember wanting anything else in my life—to get up and go down the aisle."

"Writers used to call it 'taking the sawdust trail,' because old-time tent-show evangelists like Billy Sunday put sawdust in the aisles," Alex interposed. "The ground sometimes got pretty wet in those tents with the summer rains and the sawdust helped to keep the aisles from being turned into mudholes."

"Like I was saying," Lincoln continued, "that night in Los Angeles, I felt a strong urge to get up and go down the aisle, but it was as if two powerful hands were on my shoulders, shoving me down in my seat. Then suddenly I felt a surge of power I'd never known before; in fact, it was so strong that I shot right out of the seat like a rocket."

"Glory Hallelujah!" Alex Porcher exclaimed. "Praise the Lord!"

"Amen!" Brother Tim added.

"I guess the other people going down that aisle thought I was possessed or something—"

"Actually, you'd been *de*possessed or *un*possessed by the power of the Holy Spirit, freeing you from the clutches of Satan," Tim assured him.

"Anyway, I went tearing down that aisle and threw myself down before the platform—ruining a three-hundred-dollar suit."

"But you were saved and that's worth ruining even a *five*-hundred-dollar suit," said Tim. "Not that I ever possessed one, mind you."

A ripple of amusement came from the audience.

"I knew then that whether I got the part of the evangelist or not really didn't matter anymore," said Walter Lincoln. "The important thing was that the Devil had been forced to let me go. A week later a TV producer called to ask if I'd read the script of 'Melton's Mountain'—and you know what's happened since."

"The Lord set your feet straight in the Way," Tim assured him. "And the Devil was forced to erase you from his list of slaves."

The interview, mainly dealing with Lincoln's much-publicized romantic image in earlier days, continued until a sign from Neeley, standing with her clipboard and stopwatch in the wings, warned that only a few minutes of time remained.

"It has been a great inspiration for us all to hear the story of how you were saved, Walter," said Tim warmly, as he stood up and shook hands once again with the famous guest. "Even though our network of religious stations is in competition with the commercial channels, we can wish you well with 'Melton's Mountain' and with the sales of your book;" Camera Two's lens zeroed in on a poster advertising the book at the same moment that Tim lifted a copy from the arm of the sofa to show the title, *Satan Made Me Do It*.

Chapter Two

In the control room, a small fixed camera transmitted the emblem of the station and the religious network, while Walter Lincoln was ushered from the stage by Alex Porcher to another round of applause from the studio audience. As the opening title of a fifteen-minute film made on Tim's recent visit to Ghana appeared on the monitor, the evangelist left the set and joined Neeley in the wing at the right side of the stage, accepting the steaming cup of coffee she handed him. The studio crew, too, used this brief period of release from the tension of a live broadcast to cluster around an offstage coffee urn while Tim's recorded voice poured from the loudspeakers, narrating the film.

"How'd it go?" Tim asked his diminutive wife.

"The audience loved it, especially the lecher bit before he ruined that three-hundred-dollar suit." She softened the impact of the words with an affectionate punch at Tim's beltline, where an incipient paunch was threatening to become real.

"Are you insinuating that Walter Lincoln's a fake?" Tim Douglas' tone was serious, knowing Neeley's instinct for uncovering a publicity gimmick was well-nigh infallible.

"I was just implying that the earthily humorous preacher of 'Melton's Mountain' was 'born again' conveniently close to becoming the star of a TV series aping 'The Waltons' and 'Little House on the Prairie,'" she said. "The scuttlebutt says the series is losing out in the ratings to what you so colorfully described as 'sleazy' programs. *Satan Made Me Do It* was in the remainder stacks on the booksellers' shelves at half price three months after hardcover publication, too, and the first paperback run was only sixty thousand, peanuts in the 'as told to' slot. Without those six glamorous females advertised as Walter's onetime mistresses on the jacket cover, the book would be even more of a dud on the bookstands than it already is."

"Why did you schedule him, then?"

"His publisher insisted and we get a lot of very good author interviews from him. Besides, Lincoln's already been on Pat Robertson's '700 Club' and Jim Bakker's 'PTL,' plus a lot of others among what's coming to be known in the trade as the 'Born Again Circuit'—"

"Lincoln's series has real impact," Tim insisted. "You can't deny that."

"I don't, having watched it enough times when my darling husband was off raising money by personal appearances to keep the CBC network on the air. The message of hope is always in the series, but you can thank the scriptwriters—not Walter Lincoln—for that."

"Why are you always trying to cut me down to size?" Tim asked somewhat petulantly.

"Because I love the size you really are—which, even if you don't like it, is really a lot more human than even the one you manage to project over the tubes." She stood on tiptoes to kiss his cheek. "Just keep on being God's gift to popular religion on television, darling, and leave the practical details to your adoring, but very pragmatic, wife."

"I suppose you're building up to another argument against the weekend evangelistic crusades I'm planning," he said.

"You *could* say that. I don't deny that I'd be happy if you'd just spend a weekend with Aggie and me occasionally."

"Christ's work must go on."

"But does even the Master want you to risk your health with so little gain for the Kingdom? I was talking by telephone to the pastor of one of the biggest Presbyterian churches in Asheville yesterday, arranging for your next crusade. Do you want to hear what he told me?"

"Judging from what you've been telling me, I'm not sure I do."

"Well, you're going to hear it anyway, either now or some other time."

"Give it to me *now*, then."

"When a famous evangelist—who shall be nameless—last conducted one of his well-publicized crusades in Asheville, how many members do you suppose joined the leading Presbyterian church there afterward?"

"I don't think I even want to hear."

"Not one, and I've known this pastor long enough to be sure he would tell me the truth."

"That's just another proof that Satan is in this world, actively working against us."

"Which reminds me," said Neeley. "Did you have to play up the Devil bit so strongly when you were interviewing Walter Lincoln just now? I freely admit that a force of evil is at work in all of us; there've even been times when I was a bit jealous of those adoring females who follow you around whenever you're out of my sight."

"You know you don't have any reason to be jealous."

"I'd better not have; I'm not redheaded for nothing. But I do remember that you didn't play up the Lucifer side so heavily before Alex joined the show."

"Most people believe in a finite Satan."

"Maybe not as many as you think. If you're planning to bear down with the Billy Graham scare technique on the weekend crusades, I'm voting against it."

"We're also offering sinners the forgiving love of Jesus Christ and the sacrifice of His Body."

"While threatening them if they don't accept? That doesn't fit the concept in my book of a Father who loved even the sinful world enough to let His Son die for it."

"What do you want me to do then?"

"What you were doing in the beginning, when we were working with young people back in Airmont while you were in the seminary. Stick to your own impulses and don't imitate anybody else in the evangelism business."

"We were a lot happier back then, weren't we?" Tim's tone was wistful.

"We can be again, if you stick to the TV Club broadcasts, where not even Johnny Carson can hold a candle to you in your field. Leave sawdust-trail evangelism to the specialists, darling. Go on setting the example of a loving and forgiving Father, instead of clobbering poor sinners over the head with threats of roasting in Hell forever."

"Two minutes!" Henry Waterford's warning voice came over the second set of loudspeakers for the ears of the television crew alone. "Get ready for the hymn, Lee."

"You've got a better record of converts with TV alone than traditional evangelists." Neeley gave her husband a shove toward the stage. "Go out there and turn on the boyish charm when you announce Lee's hymn. I need to find out where your next guest got sidetracked to."

"You don't expect a No-Show, do you?" Tim asked on a note of alarm.

"Nothing so drastic. She's new to TV and, human nature being physiologically fallible, I know just where to find her—in the Ladies' Room."

II

As it happened, the second interview in the Logos Club program scheduled that morning had to be postponed. During the showing of the film, the counselors at the telephones had been busy taking calls, writing down on the notepads beside their telephones the requests Tim and Alex would try to answer during the final moments of the ninety-minute program.

As Lee threw away his coffee cup preparatory to joining Jim Cates at the piano for his next song, Lee saw one of the counselors pick up her phone and suddenly stiffen. When her finger reached the emergency button beside the phone, the red warning light on the wall in the wing flashed on and the buzzer beneath it sounded, indicating a particularly dramatic call that might need to be switched into the broadcasting system. Alex Porcher saw it, too, from where he had been talking to one of the girls in the Gospel Troubadours.

"Emergency!" he shouted as he raced to the empty set and punched a button on the side of his chair, switching the call into the studio loudspeaker system. Tim followed but, even before one of the crew managed to reach his camera, which had been idle a moment before, the distraught voice of a girl sounded from the loudspeakers.

"Brother Tim!" she sobbed. "I want Brother Tim!"

As Tim settled into one of the chairs on the set, the operator, who had now reached his camera, swung it to face him, and the red light showing that it was in action glowed. At the same instant, the closing scenes of the film on the monitor were replaced by Tim's face instead of the usual station and network logo. Leaning forward intently, he held up the small lapel microphone he'd taken off before leaving the set but hadn't had time to clip back in place when the sudden call came.

"This is Brother Tim Douglas," the evangelist answered. "How can I help you?"

"I can see you now on my TV set." The woman was sobbing. "I just took sleeping pills to kill myself but now I want to live. Pray God not to let me die."

"I'll pray with you." Tim was following the routine emergency procedure developed to cope with just such a crisis. "Jesus will not let you die, if you ask Him for a miracle. We will pray for that together."

Designed to seize the attention of the caller, the request would hopefully keep her on the telephone long enough for the call to be traced and one of the emergency squads assigned to several fire stations throughout the city dispatched directly to the scene.

"God won't forgive one who takes his own life." The slurring of the words suggested that whatever drug the caller had taken was beginning to dull her senses. "It's the unpardonable sin."

"Jesus will save you!" Tim's voice was warm and friendly. "Whoever you are and wherever you are, I want to help you. Jesus wants to help you."

"Tell God to help me, Tim." The voice rose in a last desperate plea but the words were barely distinguishable now, as the drug appeared to be taking hold upon the caller's senses, slowing her capacity for understandable speech. "You talk so much about the power Jesus gives you," she whispered brokenly. "Why can't you command the drug to leave my body?"

"Pray with me, then. Speak the words after me," he begged and, without waiting for an answer, began to pray: "Almighty God, I ask you to help this soul in her time of torment. Send the healing power of your Son to save her from the unforgivable sin of taking her own life as we pray together in Jesus' own words: 'Our Father who art in Heaven . . .'"

Somehow the slurred voice on the phone managed to follow the words of the prayer, sobbing and breaking down at times. A sharp sound and a sudden stop in the flow of words toward the end of the prayer warned that she had dropped the receiver, but Tim still prayed. Seconds later, the faint anguished voice sounded again, indicating that she had picked up the telephone without breaking the connection and once again her own sobbing prayer followed Tim's soothing voice.

Glancing up at the monitor, Lee saw the gripping picture of Tim Douglas leaning over the microphone in his hand, his head almost buried in his arms as he prayed into the microphone. The same picture was being broadcast to the cities where microwave towers instantly received both picture and sound, relaying it to thousands of viewers and listeners. In the studio audience, too, every eye was fixed upon the dramatic scene, when Neeley's voice came through on the studio loudspeakers, low so as not to interfere with Tim's microphone but still audible.

"The call has been traced and an emergency squad is on its way," she assured the studio audience—and Tim. Then raising her voice a little louder just to be sure he could hear, she added, "The dispatcher says to please keep her talking as long as you can. The energy she's using will help burn up the drug she took and give them more time to get there."

"Who is she?" Lee heard Alex ask Neeley. "Does anyone know yet?"

Offstage, Neeley shook her head. "They only have the location of the phone but that's all they need for the emergency medical squad to reach her."

"Whoever you are, the Lord Jesus doesn't want you to die," Tim was assuring the distant caller. "He died for us both and if you take your own life now, you make His sacrifice worthless."

"I called you for a miracle but you failed me." The agony in the distant voice tore at the hearts of the listeners, just as it was obviously tearing at the heart of the man the woman was accusing of failing her.

Drops of sweat had popped out on Tim's forehead, although the studio was air conditioned. No one could watch him—as thousands were doing across the country and eventually around the world—without realizing the agony he was going through in a desperate attempt to save the life of a woman he did not know and could not see.

"O God! Hear the voice that cries for help to you and your Son through me!" Tim begged in a tone that emotion and strain had reduced almost to a whisper. "Pour out your healing Grace and give her the miracle of life, wherever she may be."

The crash of the falling telephone struck the ears of those in the studio like the sound of a metal gong struck by a hammer, which they realized could very well mark the end of a life. For a long, suspense-filled moment, silence gripped the studio, broken only by Tim's hoarse whispering voice, still praying on for the miracle that, it seemed now, was not to come.

Then another sound was heard through the distant phone, presumably still hanging from its cord after the girl dropped it the second time. It was the faint whine of a siren, growing louder as its source raced toward the dying woman. Moments later the voice of a technician from the medical emergency squad could be heard, though muffled, as through the door of an apartment.

"Miss Halliday, let us in." When there was no answer, a crash was audible as the emergency squad broke down the door.

For a long moment then, while Tim continued to pray, only crisp phrases spoken by members of the team as they worked and, finally, a retching sound could be heard. Then the calm voice of the fireman in charge of the group suddenly boomed out of the studio loudspeakers.

"This is Sergeant Polter of the emergency squad, Dr. Douglas," he said. "She must have swallowed half a bottle of Seconal capsules; they're scattered all over the bathroom floor so we can't be sure just how many she got, but it was enough to put her out. She ought to be okay, though; her vital signs are good and we're pumping her stomach now. When we finish, we'll start an IV before taking her to the hospital."

"Thank God! Thank God!" was Tim's fervent reply.

"Hallelujah, Brother Tim. You've wrought another miracle!" Alex shouted as the listeners in the gallery broke into a crescendo of applause.

"Lee!" Mike D'Agostino's voice was low but urgent. "Neeley says start the next song."

Lee didn't question the order to change the schedule, certain that it had come from the small microphone Neeley used to keep in touch with Henry Waterford in the control room and thence to Mike's earphones.

"Right!" Lee glanced up at the large monitor above the rear projection screen at the back of the set.

The cameras were still fixed on Tim, who was now slumped over in his chair, exhausted from the strain of keeping the woman the emergency-squad technician had called Miss Halliday talking and awake until help could reach her. In response to Mike's command, Camera One had swung its huge lens on Lee and at his signal, the Troubadours stood up quickly, arranging themselves into position.

As Lee stepped up beside the piano, Jim Cates began playing "Jesus Was There All The Time" and the first line of the song began to move on the TelePrompTer. Lee himself was momentarily startled by the words for, almost as if by some miraculous precognition, he had chosen for today's program nearly a week ago the most appropriate song for the scene just recorded by the cameras.

It began with the words:

> A lifetime ago a young girl alone
> Stood quietly thinking of grief she had known,
> I know what she felt like, I know the cause.
> The girl I speak of is who I was.

Unable to face what life seemed to be
There seemed to be nothing important to me,
Nothing to look for and nothing to find,
*No one close to ease my mind.**

The rhythm increased tempo as Lee and the other singers swung into the chorus:

But Jesus was there all the time,
Waiting to open the door,
Forgiveness has always been mine
A new life and, oh, so much more.

Several more verses followed, each ending with the words *"But Jesus was there all the time."*

When the song was finished, a thunder of applause came from the gallery with no urging from Mike D'Agostino.

"Thank you, Lee," said Alex when the cameras swung back to the main set. "Surely God must have known Brother Tim would be given the opportunity to save the life of that distraught girl and made you select that wonderful song."

"I'm sure He did," said Lee—and meant every word.

The program ended a few minutes later and Tim and Alex went down from the stage to shake hands with the departing audience as usual.

"Any news from the hospital?" Tim called over his shoulder to where Neeley was talking on the telephone.

"Henry's been talking to them on Line Two," she replied.

"The girl's okay." Henry Waterford's voice came from the control room over the studio loudspeakers. "She's in the hospital and they've given her a stimulant to combat the effects of the drug. They report that she's already beginning to wake up."

"Thank God!" said Tim Douglas fervently. "Thank God for saving her—"

"Jesus used you as His agent," Alex interposed smoothly. "*That* was the real miracle."

"Be sure and have Lee check on a girl who was supposed to be here this morning to audition for Alice Turner's place," Tim told Neeley as he returned from saying good-by to the studio audience at the end of the program. "I've forgotten her father's name but he's on the Board of Trustees and she's a student at Weston. A seat was supposed to be reserved for her but I don't know whether she got here or not."

"She made it, but just barely," said Neeley. "I'd be willing to bet that's her still sitting at the end of the first row."

"Good! Remind me to write her father, whether Lee chooses her or not."

"I think he's almost decided on another girl," said Neeley, "but he can see how this one sounds."

Alice Turner, one of the original members of the Gospel Troubadours besides Lee Steadman, their founder and director, was married to a senior seminary student at Weston's School of Religion. She'd been with the group as lead soprano for nearly four years but, with a husband about to graduate from the School of Religion and already appointed assistant minister in a large Florida congregation, they had decided to start their family. Alice was eight months pregnant now and the cameras were having to be raised for shots of the Troubadours so as not to emphasize the swelling outline of her offspring *in utero*.

"If I were in Lee's place, I'd stake a claim on that one, even if she can't sing a note," Neeley added. "She's a knockout; reminds me of Evie Tornquist."

"If she can sing half as well as Evie, the Logos Club will have another star."

III

Once or twice while he was singing the final song, Lee had glanced at the girl in the first row. Her face had come alive with the music and he could see by the rise and fall of one nylon-clad knee that her foot was beating time to the rhythm. Her eyes, too, were glowing with a familiar light he'd seen in those of thousands of young people who made up the major portion of the audiences when he and the Troubadours—plus a larger combo formed by adding several rhythm instruments— gave concerts over weekends away from Weston.

The program finished, Lee made his way to the wings where Neeley Douglas was still standing.

"Did you see that girl sitting at the end of the first row in the gallery?" she asked.

"The one who came in late?"

"You saw her, all right."

Lee laughed. "I hope I'm not so old already that I'd fail to notice something like that. You don't happen to know her name, do you?"

Neeley glanced at the clipboard she was carrying. "It's Ravenal, Tracy Ravenal. Tim had a call from her father in Lankashire yesterday. He's on the Board of Trustees for the Center and owns textile mills up that way. The family's been a liberal supporter of the Center since we started broadcasting."

"Don't tell me his daughter would like to audition; I've been up to my ears in girls for the past week." Lee's voice took on a note of sarcasm. "Those small-town Jenny Linds—even when they're as beautiful as that one is—can hit more clinkers than you'll ever hear in Grand Ole Opry. Besides, I've just about decided on another girl to replace Alice."

"What about the redhead I heard you auditioning a few nights ago after the Troubadours finished rehearsing?"

"Miss McCauley?"

"I didn't get the name but she's built for the part. Sopranos are supposed to be tall and willowy, aren't they?"

"Sometimes."

"Had experience in gospel-rock, hasn't she?"

"More rock than gospel, but she's had experience, all right. Invited me into her apartment for a drink when I took her home."

"Knowing you, I'd say she was wasting her time—and liquor."

"She didn't waste any; I turned down the invitation. Made it perfectly clear, too, that if I choose her, it will be because she sings better than the rest of those I've auditioned."

"Does she?"

"Yes, but not as well as I would like. We need someone who can do solos and even a duet occasionally."

"With you? I'd like that."

"So would I but I haven't found a girl yet who'd fill the bill."

"Don't take somebody you're not satisfied with, just because Alice's time is near. We can always pick songs that don't need a clear high soprano, while you're looking for the perfect choice."

"I'm beginning to believe there isn't such a thing in these parts. Well, here I go with this one, for better or worse."

Crossing the stage, Lee stopped beside the girl he'd been discussing. She had stayed in her seat when the rest of the audience rushed down to shake hands with Alex and Tim.

"Miss Ravenal?" he asked.

"Why, yes." He was sure the look of surprise in the violet eyes was genuine. "How did you know me?"

"Your father called Brother Tim yesterday—"

"That's my dad!" It was an expression of proud exasperation. "He thinks he can handle everything."

"Including your life, I imagine."

"As much as he can. All he told me on the phone was that he particularly wanted me to be here for this broadcast—and I almost didn't make it because the bus was late."

"Your father asked Brother Tim if you might audition to replace one of the Troubadours who is being forced to leave the show."

"A victim of motherhood, from the looks of it."

"*Touché.*" Lee had lost his aversion at being used—as he had been used before by Tim and Neeley to satisfy requests from regular contributors to the activities of the Gospel Broadcast Center. "Alice Turner is not only our lead soprano, she's also the wife of a good friend. He'll graduate in June and become assistant minister of a large Presbyterian church in Florida."

"Believe me, I didn't mean to be derisive." Her quick concern for the possibly suggestive aspect of what she had said seemed genuine.

"I'm sure you didn't. We're all very proud of Alice and Ron

and wish them well, even though it means losing a fine voice. May I ask you a question, Miss Ravenal?"

"Of course. The name is Tracy, by the way; I'm a third-year student in fine arts at the university."

"Third year and I haven't noticed you before?"

She laughed. "I spent the first two years at the community college in Lankashire, my hometown. They have a fine music department there. Last year, I studied abroad."

"That accounts for my not seeing you but, now that you're here, would you be willing to audition for a spot with the Gospel Troubadours?"

"I'm not sure about making voice a career." A serious light had come into the violet eyes. "I only came this morning to please my dad."

Tim Douglas had been taking a telephone call offstage and, on the way to his office, came by where Lee and Tracy Ravenal were standing at the corner of the stage near the piano. Lee reached out and touched Tim's arm.

"This is Tracy Ravenal, Tim," he said, but when the evangelist looked momentarily blank, realized that Tim must have forgotten all about the call from the girl's father and quickly added, "You promised her father over the phone that you would have me audition her for Alice's part."

"Oh yes!" Tim's charm was immediately at its full. "I hope you enjoyed the broadcast, Miss Ravenal. It was far more exciting this morning than usual."

"I did!" The hitherto coolly assured young woman had suddenly turned into a blushing, stammering girl—an effect Lee had noted more than once when Tim Douglas turned his infectious charm upon young people. "It was all marvelous! Just marvelous!"

"Your father is a trustee and one of the regular supporters of the Logos Club," said Tim.

"My mother was even more so," said Tracy Ravenal. "She watched every morning until her death two years ago."

"Miss Ravenal isn't sure she wants to audition for the Troubadours, Tim," Lee interrupted, as anxious now to get the girl to try out as he'd been tempted to evade the chore, when talking to Neeley immediately after the end of the program.

"You must do what the Master tells you is His purpose for you, but I hope you'll give us a try." Tim was still holding the girl's hand, a fact of which neither seemed conscious at the moment. "We need a new voice very badly, Miss Ravenal. If Lee accepts you to take Alice's place, you'll find him a skilled and very conscientious instructor."

Suddenly conscious that he'd been holding Tracy's hand, Tim gave it a second perfunctory shake and added, "Please give Lee at least a chance to listen to you and by all means give your father my regards."

"I'll call him tonight," she promised, as Tim crossed the now empty stage to where Neeley was waiting to consult him.

"Well?" Lee asked.

"He's wonderful, isn't he?" With an effort she brought her attention back to the present. "So courtly and so charming, yet so dedicated."

"That's a pretty good description of Brother Tim," Lee agreed. "What's more important, everything about him is natural and sincere."

"Oh I'm sure of that. You can tell it from his voice and the look in his eyes." •

"We all love Tim—and Neeley, too. She's something special in her own right."

"I couldn't see her very well through the plate-glass partition." Tracy Ravenal's tone was back to normal now. "She appears to be very attractive."

"Even more so, when you get to know her. About the audition? Anything particular you want to sing?"

"Whatever you'd like—that I already know," she answered as he moved to the piano bench. "I'm not very good at sight reading."

"Suppose you run the scales first." His skilled fingers rippled the keyboard. "By the way, what's your approximate range?"

"I can reach D over high C without much trouble."

"Good! That's Alice Turner's range, too, and exactly what we need. Start whenever you like."

Lee listened intently as she sang the scales—which she did very effectively and clearly. High C didn't seem to bother her at all and her D was still pure and true, with no *vibrato*. Listening, he could not repress a thrill of satisfaction—and hope. Tracy Ravenal was a natural lyric soprano and, he suspected strongly, exactly what he needed to fill the soon-to-be-empty slot in the Gospel Troubadours—provided she could sing with a group as well as she did solo.

"You have a beautiful voice," he told her. "It appears to be God-given to be so pure. Have you thought about opera?"

"I'm afraid the discipline would be too much for me," she confessed. "I like tennis, riding, swimming, and waterskiing too well to ever spend all the hours of practice it takes to make an opera singer. What about you? I've never heard a finer baritone."

"I'm in my third year at the School of Religion, after graduating with a masters in vocal and instrumental music from Weston. Are you ready to try a song, or would you rather stick to vocal exercises?"

"I sang 'In the Garden' with the chapel choir a few Sundays ago. You know, the hymn that begins: 'I come to the garden alone, while the dew is still on the roses.'"

"It's one of my favorites among the old time hymns," said Lee. "I think I still remember the music. Let's give it a try anyway."

"All right, but if I forget a word or two, don't be upset."

"If you do, just hum the notes." Lee's fingers moved over the keyboard and, when he switched to the first notes, she began to sing effortlessly, continuing until the hymn was finished and he took his hands from the piano keys.

"You're very good," he told her sincerely. "Have you done much group singing? Quartets and the like?"

Tracy Ravenal shook her head, making her hair shimmer like gold in a ray of sunlight pouring through a window high up on the wall behind the stage and the Club set.

"No, I have not done much group singing. My father had a heart attack right after I graduated from high school. I'd been accepted at Duke but I stayed home and as I said went to Lankashire Community College for two years. They have a very fine music department."

"Did you come directly from there to Weston?"

"I then got a case of wanderlust and spent a year in Switzerland at the University of Geneva. I'm afraid I wasted most of the time traveling and skiing, though—until I got bored and came back home to enroll here at Weston."

"Are you familiar with Evie Tornquist's records?"

"No, I'm afraid not," she confessed.

"She's tops in the gospel-rock field. The song we sang in the last third of the Club broadcast this morning—'If Heaven Never Was Promised to Me'—is from a popular Tornquist album called 'Mirror.' "

"It was beautiful but I could tell from listening this morning that all of you are experts," she said doubtfully. "Isn't what you call gospel-rock difficult compared to conventional religious music?"

"Not really—only more natural. The rhythm carries you on." He had a sudden inspiration. "We're going to rehearse here at the Center tonight around seven o'clock for a group of concerts the Troubadours, along with a larger combo, are booked for two weekends from now, at Georgia State University in Atlanta. Another girl will also be auditioning, so why not drop by tonight and just listen during the rehearsal and audition. Then you and I can practice rhythm singing afterward. Alice will be here and can give you a lot of pointers."

Tracy Ravenal still looked doubtful. "Dad won't let me have a car until I finish my first year at Weston—he thinks I wasted the year in Geneva. Is there a bus between the university and the Center at that time of night?"

"There is, but you won't need to ride it. I'm picking up Alice about a quarter to seven and can easily go by your dormitory and get you. Or do you live in a sorority house?"

"I'm Tri-Delt but I live in Hubbard—sixteen."

"I usually stop for a pizza after the rehearsal ends at eight-thirty. Can you be out that late?"

"Till twelve."

"I'll get you home long before midnight," he promised. "Oh yes, I've got that Evie Tornquist album I mentioned in my office. I'll lend it to you so you can listen to some real professional gospel rhythms before I pick you up this evening."

"That would be fine," she said. "Dad gave me a stereo for making the dean's list the first semester."

"We'll stop by my office on the way out and I'll get the album for you." He looked at his watch. "The next bus leaves for the campus at twelve-fifteen, so you can just make it. I'd take you myself but the campus activities booking officer at Georgia State promised to call me here at twelve-thirty."

IV

Neeley Douglas came into Lee's small office at the Gospel Broadcast Center just as he was hanging up the telephone—after assuring the assistant director of campus activities at Georgia State that the Gospel Troubadours would be in Atlanta as scheduled.

"I couldn't help overhearing part of your audition this morning," said Neeley. "The Ravenal girl has a beautiful voice."

"One of the loveliest I ever heard. All she has to do now is prove she can sing in harmony with the rest of the group and the job will be hers."

"What about the redhead—Miss McCauley?"

"I'll have a chance to compare them both tonight at the rehearsal for the concerts at Atlanta. Tracy Ravenal is coming with Alice and myself."

Neeley chuckled. "Sounds like you don't mean to let this one get away. I suppose the fact that she's stunning, with that red-gold hair and marvelous figure, has nothing to do with your obvious interest in her."

"Just pray that she can sing as well in a group as she does alone."

"And if she can't?"

"Either way, I've an idea I'll be hanging around Hubbard sixteen a lot."

"You don't usually go off the deep end for people you've never seen before, like Tim tends to do," Neeley observed. "He believes everybody is exactly what they appear to be on the surface."

"Tracy Ravenal has star quality. Did you hear her singing a few minutes ago?"

"A little. What I heard sounded very good indeed."

"Better than good. I'd be willing to bet that with a little training she could do the 'Bell Song' from *Lakmé* and never miss a note."

"She certainly seems to have rung *your* chimes, darling, and that's something I never saw or heard any other girl do." Neeley's eyebrows rose in twin question marks. "In case you don't know it, being an outlander, the name Ravenal in South Carolina means oldest family, breeding, society at the highest levels, and money—lots of money."

"Incidentally, she's ga-ga over Tim."

"What woman who's met him, either in person or seen him on the tube, isn't—including yours truly?" Neeley said with the gamin grin that made everybody at the Center love her. "In fact, he's so perfect I sometimes feel like it's a sin to go to bed with him at night."

Chapter Three

IT WAS AFTER ONE WHEN LEE STOPPED AT THE SANDWICH SHOP across the street from the sprawling expanse of University Hospital before going on to his two-o'clock class in comparative religion.

One entire side of North Avenue was taken up by the main hospital building, along with the newer structure housing the faculty clinic. Leased from the hospital, it was operated by a privately organized medical group whose number included most of the doctors holding top teaching positions at the medical school.

A single booth in the usually busy lunchroom happened to be vacant and Lee slipped into it, rather than take one of the rows of seats in front of the counter.

"What'll it be, Reverend?" Mabel, the buxom waitress and often short-order cook, called from behind the counter.

"A burger, fries and coffee. You know how I like 'em."

"I sure do—after five years."

Lee's first two years of college had been spent at the University of West Virginia in Morgantown. He had transferred to the highly regarded Fine Arts Department of Weston, when Neeley and Tim Douglas—formerly pastor of a church in Lee's hometown of Airmont, West Virginia—had come to Weston to begin their radio and later TV broadcast activities.

Lee had sung in the choir of Tim's church in West Virginia, so he was a natural choice for the position of music director for the fledgling Gospel Broadcast Center, at that time practically

limited to the five-times-weekly broadcasts of the Logos Club.
He had occupied that position all during his undergraduate
days at Weston and now while doing graduate work in the
School of Religion.

Being in the graduate school, Lee could occupy a small
efficiency unit in the faculty apartments facing the entire end
of the block looking west on Weston Boulevard, not far from its
intersection with North Avenue where the hospital and clinic
buildings were located. And with the lunchroom so handy, he
often dropped in there for a quick breakfast, if he had an early
class before the start of the Logos Club broadcast, when coming home at night after a rehearsal, and occasionally before his
first afternoon class.

As a smiling Mabel was placing Lee's order on the table in
the booth, a tall young man wearing the long white coat that
identified him both as doctor and teacher came through the
door. Seeing Lee eating alone, Dr. Art Michaels slipped into
the other seat.

"Give me what the Reverend here is eating, Mabel," he said.

"Sure, Dr. Michaels. Coming up."

"How's the Electric Church, God's gift to the airwaves, coming along?" Michaels asked while he waited for his food.

Like Lee, Art Michaels had come from a small Tennessee
town. After college and the Medical School at Johns Hopkins,
he had accepted a psychiatry residency at Weston University
Hospital. Two years after completing the residency, he was already an assistant professor of psychiatry in the Medical School
and highly regarded as the brightest young man in the department. He and Lee had been friends ever since Lee had transferred from Morgantown to Weston and they'd discovered a
mutual interest in early-morning running.

"Full steam ahead," said Lee as Mabel brought a cup of
coffee to Art Michaels and refilled his own cup. "You know
Tim and Neeley."

"Dynamos, both of them. Brother Tim could have made a
fortune giving Dale Carnegie courses to ambitious Jaycees."

"You should have heard the Reverend here on the Logos
Club this mornin', Dr. Michaels," said Mabel. "He was really
singin' his head off."

"Do you listen to the Club broadcasts, Mabel?" Lee asked.

"Every chance I get when we don't have many customers, like this mornin'. What was the name of that piece the Troubadours sang, Reverend?"

" 'If Heaven Never Was Promised to Me.' "

"That's the prettiest song I ever heard, 'specially with that slow beat. There wasn't nobody in here 'cept me and Lou, the counterman, and you'd've died to see the way him 'n' me was discoin' while you was singin'."

"Maybe you ought to teach the studio audience to disco, Lee," said Art Michaels. "It would make your show the talk of the country and might even do them a lot of good."

"By the way, Mabel," said Lee, "which do you like better—the old hymns or the gospel-rock songs we sing?"

"The rhythm ones, of course," Mabel said without hesitation. "When I was a girl back on the farm in Carolina, we had to go to church twice on Sunday and to a prayer meetin' every Wednesday night. The old hymns are sweet—we didn't have anythin' else to sing besides them then—but the new ones have got a real message besides the beat."

"You write some songs yourself besides just singing, don't you, Lee?" Art Michaels asked.

"A few, but I'm not really what you'd call a gospel songwriter. All my spare time between Club broadcasts and classes is used up arranging songs for the Troubadours."

"We're two of a kind." Michaels tackled the savory hamburger. "I've been working overtime on biofeedback and holistic medicine."

"Whatever they are," said Lee. "Why don't you let the residents do the routine work? I remember how you used to gripe about the attending physicians bagging all the best cases."

"Speaking of attendings, I had another offer from the faculty clinic last week," said Michaels.

"How much this time?"

"Fifty thousand a year, clear of all expenses—plus the right to conduct three two-hour clinics in holistic medicine a week at the Medical School."

"That's the second time you've used that word in two minutes. Mind telling me what it means?"

"That would take an hour but the medical dictionary defines it as 'relating to the conception of man as a functioning whole.'"

"Religion's been doing that since the world began," said Lee. "When the soul is separated from the body, you're dead."

"Holistic medicine says a sick soul can *make* a sick body. A doctor needs to consider both of them, as well as the environment, before he can really cure disease, whether it appears to be purely mental or purely physical. For example, an executive who's tense because he's afraid of losing his job to a younger man often develops a stomach ulcer. You can treat him with a drug called Cimetidine and heal his ulcer. But unless you also heal the ulcer of fear that's eating away at his emotions—"

"The soul?"

"Maybe, I try to steer clear of theology," said Art Michaels. "The fact remains that unless you treat the fear ulcer, you can never heal the stomach ulcer permanently."

"Sounds fascinating."

"That simple concept is going to revolutionize medicine one of these days. I've been pressing for my own section of maybe ten beds on one of the psychiatric wards to experiment with some methods of treatment I'd like to try."

"The next thing you know, you'll be turning into a faith healer."

"God forbid! I've seen too many people, who were supposed to have been cured by faith healers, lose their faith when the disease returned. They usually end up on psychiatrists' couches if they escape turning into the medical cripples who wander from doctor to doctor and clinic to clinic, looking for the cure of a particular condition that can only come from the whole person instead of a diseased organ."

"If holistic medicine is so simple, why haven't I heard of it before?" Lee asked.

"Because not many people, medical or otherwise, know what it's all about and, more important, have a flexible enough mind to try. One of the first was Dr. Adolf Meyer. He started teaching holistic medicine at Johns Hopkins a long time ago but made the mistake of calling it 'psychobiological integration.' Practically nobody among the students could spell it, much less understand what it was all about, so only a few doctors really practiced it."

"Does anybody know now?"

"Sure. All Adolf Meyer said was that doctors needed to treat the person who has the illness rather than just the illness itself, as most doctors did then and more than half are doing now. Working from the holistic viewpoint, you can often pin down the trigger point that set off the trouble in the beginning. When you do, it's usually not even near the spot where the pain is."

"I suppose that means in the cerebrum?"

"Mostly. Close to 80 per cent of the people who consult a doctor have psychosomatic complications. More often than not, it's the whole picture."

"That's all Tim claims to do in his healing ministry—"

"You don't believe he really cures people who just watch him on the TV screen, do you?"

"We've got thousands of letters on file at the Center saying just that," said Lee. "Tim doesn't really claim to heal by faith alone though. He admits that such people are usually sick because they're suffering from a feeling of unworthiness and guilt about sin. The repressed desire to let Jesus take over their lives, plus the fear that they'll lose a lot of the things they think they enjoy and need if they yield, generate the wrong kind of psychic energy."

"That, at least, I can understand," Art Michaels conceded.

"Tim believes knowing—and trusting—someone who really loves his fellow man—not just claims to—can help the sick find a new channel for the emotional energy they've been using up in physical symptoms," Lee continued. "Once they get rid of doubt, fear, indecision and guilt by putting their trust in Jesus, they can see what the emotional diseases they've created within themselves are doing. Knowing that, they can stop contracting their heart arteries, causing disturbances in the stomach, or whatever else is happening to their bodies."

"If what you're saying is true," said Michaels, "your Brother Tim is doing something pretty close to what I want to do with this new concept of holistic medicine—except for one thing."

"What's that?"

"I'm trying to do it scientifically, with procedures like bio-feedback, hypnosis, even drugs that free the body briefly from the tyranny of the mind and the emotions. Tim Douglas, on the other hand, seeks to cure by assuring the sick person that his troubles are all tied up with evil influences in his mind, maybe even the Devil. That way he literally scares the hell out of the sick man."

"Does it matter much what method you use, so long as people are made well?"

"To me it matters a hell of a lot. When I get through treating a patient he really knows he's cured. What's even more important, he's convinced that letting his emotions get tied up in a knot again is going to bring back the sickness."

"Isn't it a lot simpler for the sinner just to throw off his burden of sin and turn to Jesus—the way Tim shows them how to do?"

"That's a cop-out, Lee! And copping out on a problem or a responsibility doesn't cure anybody of an ulcer that's eating away deep inside his mind as well as in his stomach. He may manage to kid himself for a while that he can shift the burden of his own conflicts to somebody who died nearly two thousand years ago, crucified because of a revolt against Rome—"

"Or as a sacrifice for the sins of mankind?"

"Heaping the sins of the world on one historical person is a cop-out, too."

"Six years or so ago when I was taking my first course in psychology up at Morgantown, I'd have agreed with you," Lee conceded. "But I've spent the last four years with a man who comes about as close as anyone can today to living according to the principles Jesus of Nazareth set down. Tim Douglas is just an example in his own right, of course, because the real Jesus Christ is everywhere—"

"You don't believe that, Lee! Neither does Brother Tim."

"Yes, he does, Dr. Michaels." Mabel had been listening to every word. "Just turn your TV to the Logos Club any mornin' and listen to the Reverend here sing the openin' song."

"What does that—"

"That song's titled, 'He's Alive!' If you don't believe it yourself by the time he gets through, I'll treat you to a hamburger and coffee here every day for a year."

"That's an offer I could hardly resist, Mabel," said Michaels. "You're on."

"Too bad you didn't hear the Logos Club broadcast this mornin'," said the waitress. "If you could have heard Brother Tim Douglas talkin' that poor girl out of committin' suicide—"

"Suicide?" Michaels' interest was immediately aroused. "What time was that?"

"Around eleven o'clock a woman called the studio to say she'd swallowed a lot of Seconals and begged Brother Tim to save her," Lee explained. "Tim talked to her and prayed over her long enough for the emergency squad to get there. They pumped her stomach out and took her to the hospital. I'm telling you, it was one of the most dramatic things I've ever seen."

"My ward supervisor called me about eleven-thirty and reported that an attempted-suicide case had been admitted," said Michaels. "We have a policy of hospitalizing any attempted suicides—who reach the emergency room alive—for a few days until the effects of the drug washed out of the stomach have pretty well subsided. They're put on psychiatry so we can try to stop them from trying again. What was this one's name?"

"Hal—Halliday, as I remember it," said Lee. "The sergeant of the emergency squad called her that before they broke down the door of her room to get in."

"That's the one. They'd pumped her stomach before they brought her to the emergency room. My chief nurse reported that she was in no danger, but was raising holy hell about the stomach pump. For which I don't blame her, so I ordered some paraldehyde to keep her quiet until I could see her after a seminar this afternoon."

Lee had a sudden inspiration. "Do you think I could talk to her after my last class today? Most of those cases we get on the Club program are over the long-distance telephone and we never see them face to face."

"Sure," said Art. "But why?"

"A lot of people who heard the program today would like a report on what happened later. After I talk to Miss Halliday, I can report to Tim and he can use it in his monologue tomorrow morning."

"And maybe brag a little—if it was a bona fide suicide try and he saved her? I don't blame him." The psychiatrist had been scribbling on a prescription pad and now tore off the sheet and handed it to Lee. "There's a pass that will get you into the psychiatric ward."

II

Lee's last class didn't finish until four. As he was walking toward the hospital, he met Tracy Ravenal, on the way from the music building to her dormitory, with a folder of sheet music under her arm.

"What are you doing in this part of the campus?" she asked. "The School of Religion is at the other end."

"I'm on the way to the hospital to talk to the girl who tried to commit suicide this morning. She's under observation in one of the psychiatry wards and I thought somebody from the Center should follow her up, if only to report on the Logos Club tomorrow morning."

She gave him a long, thoughtful look as they walked along. "Your real reason was because you wanted to see whether she needs more help, wasn't it?"

"I plead guilty," said Lee, and grinned. "When I was a little boy, I was always bringing home sick kittens."

"So was I. Could I go to the hospital with you?"

"Sure, if you want to. My pass doesn't say how many people it covers."

III

It was a little after four-thirty when Lee and Tracy stopped at the nurses' station on the open psychiatric ward, where they'd been told at the information desk downstairs that Desire Halliday was a patient.

"Come in," a somewhat hoarse feminine voice answered when Lee knocked on the door. "Don't bring me any of that damned foul-tastin' stuff, though, or I'll spit it right in your face. Imagine!! Giving me paraldehyde, just like I was a real nut or something."

The woman on the bed appeared to be older than she'd seemed when her anguished voice had come over the loud-speakers in the studio that morning. But that, Lee reminded himself, could be because the emergency squad had used a stomach pump rather vigorously on her some 5½ hours ago.

"Who are you?" the patient demanded warily.

"My name is Lee Steadman and this is Miss Tracy Ravenal. We're from the Logos Club."

"I talked to Brother Tim on the telephone during the broadcast this morning and he saved my life."

"We were at the broadcast and came by to ask whether the Center can do anything else for you," Lee told her.

"Just hand over the rest of my five hundred so I can get the hell out of here before the damned nurses poison me."

Startled, Lee looked at Tracy, who seemed even more stunned, but the effect on the patient was even more dramatic.

"You didn't come here with the money, did you?" Desire Halliday demanded.

"I'm sorry," said Lee. "We don't have the least idea what you're talking about."

"Who offered to pay you?" Tracy asked.

"None of your damned business." Desire Halliday started to laugh, a raucous sound, that ended in a fit of coughing. "So you two are just a couple of bleeding hearts that felt sorry for a fellow human and came to see whether you could help?"

"That's one way of putting it," Lee admitted.

"Well, go back and tell your Brother Tim I'll be fine, just fine."

"Just now you said something about being paid five hundred dollars—"

"Did I?" the blonde snapped. "Well, I was out of my head if I did. That damn foul stuff the nurse gave me while I was too

woozy to know what was happening has everything in my mind
goin' haywire. As soon as I can walk straight, I'll sign myself
out of here. *Me* in a nut ward?" Again the raucous laugh ended
in a fit of coughing. "All I did was have a fight with my gentle-
man friend and decide to kill myself—only he ain't worth killing or killing yourself for. Anyway, I went down to the drugstore and got me a bottle of downers—"

"Seconal?"

"Or whatever. You can buy 'em by the hundreds, if you
know where to go. I dropped the bottle in the bathroom at the
hotel when I was measurin' 'em out and wasn't sure how many
I took. Then I got scared and, when I saw a telephone number
on the TV screen offering people help and talking about Jesus,
I dialed it."

"That's the counseling number," said Lee. "It's a direct line
to the studio."

"You were there, so you know what happened."

"Except who's supposed to pay you five hundred dollars for
faking the suicide call," said Lee sharply, hoping to anger her
into revealing details.

"Faking?" the woman demanded angrily. "I never said nothing about faking."

"You *did* say you were to be paid."

"I told you I can't think with that stuff in me," Desire
Halliday's voice had risen to a shout of indignation. "You got
no right to come in here accusing me of something wrong. Just
get the hell out of here and tell Brother Tim he can go—!" The
obscenity that followed made Lee wish he hadn't brought
Tracy, who had spoken only once after they came into the
room.

"Mr. Steadman!" It was the charge nurse standing in the
partially opened doorway. "We really can't have you getting
our patients excited. It's very much against the rules."

"We're going," said Lee. "Good-by, Miss Halliday."

"Good-by—and don't ever let me see you or your goddamned
Brother Tim again. All I got out of this whole thing was a
stomach tube and a sore throat; nobody told me anything
about that." She turned suddenly toward the wall where a bed-

side table stood with glasses and a water pitcher. "Now get out before I throw something."

"I'm sorry," Lee told the charge nurse as they were leaving. "We didn't mean to get her so upset."

"She's been raising Cain ever since they brought her up from emergency, except for the two hours she was asleep from the paraldehyde Dr. Michaels ordered," said the nurse. "Even so, for the paraldehyde to have had such a short effect, I'd say she hadn't absorbed much of that Seconal she claims to have taken."

"Sounds like you think she was faking."

"With patients on this ward you never know." The nurse shrugged. "If she really did take enough Seconal to be in danger, she should still be out cold. It's absorbed rather quickly from an empty stomach."

Lee had a sudden thought. "Do attempted-suicide patients often act the way Miss Halliday has been doing?"

"None I ever saw—and I've been in charge of this ward for ten years."

"Thank you. You've been very helpful."

"Turnabout's fair play," said the nurse with a warm smile. "You and your vocal group have given me many hours of pleasure."

Outside the hospital, Tracy Ravenal asked, "What's this all about, anyway?"

"I wish I knew but I hope to find out. Until I do, though, mum's the word."

"Nobody could ever believe Brother Tim would pay a woman like that five hundred dollars to fake a suicide call." She hesitated, then added, "Would they?"

"Only those who want to."

"What does that mean?"

"What the newspapers call the 'Electric Church' is growing bigger every day and taking in more money through the mails. Already two main factions have emerged and are fighting for control of those dollars."

"That's terrible! When they're all supposed to teach that Jesus saves."

"Right now, Tim's on top because he appeals to the established churches and tries to steer his converts into church membership," Lee explained. "His theology is a lot more liberal, too, than that of the faith healers and strict fundamentalists, like Jake Schiller."

Tracy frowned. "I never heard of him. What does he do?"

"Jake was Tim's partner at the start of the Logos Club. Jake's quite handsome and women viewers loved him, as well as those who work at the Center—some of them a little too well from what I've heard."

"That's heresy—or something," she protested.

"Human nature is a better word. Being ambitious, Jake naturally worked to sabotage Tim in subtle ways, trying to get control of the Center."

"I guess I'm pretty naïve," Tracy conceded. "I don't understand what you're talking about."

"It happens all the time. Read the New Testament again and you'll find that the disciples John and James had their mother intercede with Jesus to place them on a higher plane than the rest."

"Judas even betrayed him for money, so I guess you're right at that."

"Getting back to Jake. He made the mistake of dipping into the till, so Tim finally fired him. He left, swearing to get even, and has been trying ever since."

"Where is he now?"

"In Atlanta. Started a faith-healing campaign in an abandoned tobacco warehouse and must be doing pretty well. A former roommate of mine in the School of Religion named Jeff Champion quit Weston in his second year and went to Atlanta. He works for Jake, and Jeff's a live wire. The last report I saw in *Evangelical News* said they were broadcasting three services a week over a network of nine TV stations and twenty-five radio outlets."

"How could anybody who knows Brother Tim believe anything bad about him?"

"A lot of TV evangelists envy Tim the success he's had with the Center but don't admit it. Instead they argue that his liberal theology and his helping local churches are threats to what they believe. With millions pouring into the TV churches by mail, competition for what Billy Graham calls 'the evangelical dollar' has become pretty fierce."

"My father's a trustee of the Center but I've never heard about any of this from him."

"Your father hasn't been very active lately but that can't be said of one faction among the trustees. Out of the dozen, I'd say four or five oppose practically everything Tim tries to do, simply because he refuses to go along with the strict fundamentalists in TV evangelism."

"What about Reverend Porcher?"

"Alex is a veteran of the faith-healing and fundamentalist movement; he was with the Kathryn Kuhlman healing team for several years. His views on religion are certainly far to the right of Tim's, but Alex was also smart enough to recognize a star and hook up with Tim after Jake left."

"Mind if I ask where you stand?"

"Not at all; I owe too much to Tim and Neeley ever to betray them. Besides, theologically, I'm even more liberal than Tim—about on a par with Neeley, I'd say." They had reached her dormitory and he stopped the car. "Shall I pick you up a little before seven?"

"After what we learned at the hospital and what you've just told me, I wonder whether I even want to start with the Troubadours."

"You'll like it," he promised. "Besides, you can do as I do, leave the preaching to Tim and Alex and concentrate on the music. Nobody can go wrong there."

Chapter Four

It was not quite seven when Lee and Tracy arrived at the Center for the rehearsal. Only about half of the Troubadours and the combo had arrived and neither had the redhead, Janice McCauley—who until this morning had been the leading candidate for Alice Turner's job.

"Would you like to watch Neeley's puppet show from the control room?" Lee asked. "She's taping it tonight."

When Tracy agreed, he led her upstairs and into the glass-walled room overlooking the stage of the main studio. There he introduced her to Ed Clayton, a graduate student in dramatics who was at the controls.

The set used in the Logos Club programs had been pushed to one side to make room for a boxlike set built in traditional Punch and Judy show style, with its small high windowlike stage. Two hand puppets, operated by puppeteers hidden in the bottom of the boxlike set, were engaged in an avid conversation with Neeley Douglas, who stood slightly to one side of the window-stage so as not to interfere with the view.

Only one lone observer was sitting in the gallery, a little girl who had Neeley's sandy hair, freckles and uptilted nose. She was watching the puppet show intently, laughing at the antics of the puppets.

"That's Agnes, Tim and Neeley's only child," Lee told Tracy. "Everybody calls her Aggie. She loves the puppet show and often comes to watch."

"She's cute—like her mother."

"And sharp; she's only ten and finishing the fifth grade. I'm her godfather," Lee added on a note of pride.

Two cameras were being used. One was centered on Neeley's mobile features as she conversed with the two puppets: a freckle-faced boy and a snooty-looking girl with long, pendant curls. They were sarcastically discussing a third, but as yet unseen, individual, and Neeley was scolding the two for the way they had apparently been treating the third. The pair in turn were busy defending themselves, the girl in a snappish high voice and the boy with a pronounced drawl.

"What show is this?" Tracy asked.

"Neeley tapes her own children's program Friday nights for showing on Saturday morning," Lee explained.

"She's very talented."

"More than just talented. Neeley writes the dialogue and stages the entire production. The puppeteers are a husband-and-wife team who teach in the Fine Arts Division of the university."

"How many programs does the Center put out?"

"I've no idea," he confessed. "It takes all my work time to keep up with the Logos Club."

"Fifteen," Ed Clayton volunteered. "We also do some of the dubbing for foreign versions of the Logos Club tapes and several other programs that go around the world by satellite. For dubbing, we use natives of the particular countries involved who are students or teachers here at the university."

"That's fantastic!" said Tracy. "Oh! Oh!" Another puppet—a black girl with plaited hair and a broad grin—had suddenly popped up above the bottom of the tiny stage and was talking now in a typical Catfish Row accent.

"That's Dinah." Clayton glanced up at the clock. "Here comes the punch line, right on time."

"I got an A in arithmetic," said Dinah. "What did you get, Mary?"

"A C," said the snooty white girl.

"I got a B-minus," said the freckle-faced boy puppet.

"Well," drawled the black girl, "we can't all be smart—and pretty, too."

The scene faded on the monitor, to raucous laughter from

the freckle-faced boy and the black girl, as well as the four in the control room.

"She really gave that holier-than-thou little girl her comeuppance," Lee chortled. "I told you Neeley was a genius."

The monitors went blank and, below them, Neeley was waiting for the puppeteers to emerge from behind the black cutout box of the set where they had worked.

Spying a group of the Troubadours and several of the combo lugging their instruments onto the far side of the stage, Lee said, "Let's go down to the set, Tracy. You haven't met Neeley yet, have you?"

"N—no."

"You'll love her; we all do. The puppeteers are an interesting couple, too. You might like to talk to them while we're getting set up on the other side of the stage."

"The tape's okay, Neeley," Ed Clayton called down to the set.

Descending the stairs from the control room, Lee escorted Tracy to the puppet show set, where Neeley and Aggie—a small version of her mother—were now talking to a young man and woman carrying an assortment of hand puppets.

"This is Tracy Ravenal, Neeley," he said. "I'm going to leave her with you while I round up the others so we can get started."

Neeley gave Tracy her hand and a warm smile. "When I was growing up, I prayed every night to be tall, beautiful and golden-haired like you, but I wound up a shrimp. Do you know the Potters, Don and Marie? And our daughter, Aggie?"

"Hi, Aggie," said Tracy. "Lee tells me you're way ahead of the other kids in school."

The little girl smiled. "Lee's nice. I'm going to marry him when I grow up."

"Oh?" Tracy was startled momentarily, then laughed. "Have you told him yet?"

Aggie shook her head. "I'm waiting for the right time. The love stories I read say you have to choose a very special moment."

"What stories do you read?" Tracy asked.

"None of that children's stuff," said Aggie on a note of disdain. "Mostly I like Regency novels, especially Barbara Cartland."

"She'd read Harold Robbins, if I'd let his books in the house," Neeley commented.

"I like Barbara Cartland, too," Tracy confided. "She was staying at the same hotel I was in on Lake Lucerne in Switzerland last year."

"Is she as beautiful as the pictures of her on the back covers of her books?" Aggie asked eagerly.

"Every bit," said Tracy. "And her jewels are gorgeous."

"I had my ears pierced last year, and Daddy's going to give me a pair of diamond earrings when I graduate from high school."

"Which could be any day now"—Neeley squeezed a small shoulder affectionately—"if the school authorities would let her skip more grades."

"Are you going to take Alice's place with the Troubadours, Miss Ravenal?" Aggie asked.

"Please call me Tracy. As for the Troubadours, we'll have to see."

"I'm sure Lee will choose you," said the precocious small redhead. "Mother told me when we were driving to the Center tonight that Lee was auditioning a new soprano with a lovely voice."

"Rock music isn't exactly my strong suit," Tracy confessed and turned to the puppeteers, who were packing up their equipment. "You're both very good," she told them. "I laughed at Dinah until my sides hurt."

"Dinah was Aggie's creation," Marie Potter assured her.

"She even writes a lot of the dialogue for me when I'm preparing the scripts." Neeley rumpled her daughter's curls with loving fingers.

"It almost breaks me up sometimes," Marie Potter admitted.

"I should think so," Tracy agreed. "Lee tells me you and your husband are on the faculty here at Weston?"

"Don teaches Renaissance history and I teach art appreciation," said Marie. "Puppet shows were so much a part of the Renaissance scene that we got interested and took up puppeteering as a hobby."

"Judging by what I saw from the control room, Mrs. Douglas," said Tracy, "the children must love your show—and adults, too."

"Call me Neeley, please; everybody does. Yes, it has a wide audience, considering the competition on commercial stations Saturday mornings. I got the idea when I saw Aggie watching an old rerun of Kukla, Fran and Ollie. I'd almost forgotten about them until then." Her arm went around Aggie's waist. "We'd better be going, child prodigy. The way you're growing, you'll soon be taller than your mother. Here's one Douglas who isn't going to be short. Tim always wanted to be tall but had to settle for five-nine."

"I met him this morning after the broadcast; he seems much taller than that." Tracy's voice had taken on a sudden note of abstraction that Neeley didn't fail to note, having heard it many times in the voices of young women meeting her husband for the first time.

"I guess he seems that way," she said, "because he's so much like a big brother, in love with the world and everyone in it. Sorry we can't stay to hear you sing, Tracy, but Aggie's coming down with a bug and I'd better take her home."

"I hope I don't disappoint Lee," Tracy told her. "He's given me a lot of encouragement. Even lent me an Evie Tornquist album to listen to this afternoon, but it's still a new field for me."

"Evie's a wonderful girl," said Neeley. "She's been on the Club program several times and stayed at our house when she was here. She gives concerts and records both here and abroad."

"That must be very rewarding."

"I'm sure it is. Lee has been urging us to let him take the Gospel Troubadours and the large combo on a European tour next summer or the summer after. A lot of the TV stations we broadcast on over there by satellite have asked to have the group. You may get to visit a lot of countries after you join them."

"You mean *if*, don't you, rather than *after?*"

"Not if you really want it to be *after*, my dear. One thing Tim has taught everyone here at the Center is that anybody who's in full partnership with the Lord is bound to succeed.

Sorry I can't stay for the rehearsal but Aggie came home from school complaining of a sore throat. I took her to the pediatrician just before coming to the studio. He made a culture and gave her penicillin but the housekeeper's away this weekend and I don't like to leave her alone, so I let her come to the taping."

"I'm better already," Aggie volunteered. "Laughing at the puppets helped my sore throat."

"I always heard that laughter was good for the soul," said Professor Potter. "No doubt it's good for the body as well."

"Tim left this afternoon in the company jet for Chicago," Neeley added. "The Association of Evangelical Broadcasters is having a meeting there and he's going to conduct a three-hour seminar tomorrow morning. Then he'll fly on to Washington to preach Sunday morning at the National Cathedral."

"That's quite an honor, isn't it?" Tracy asked.

"Tim thinks so, but he's got another purpose in mind. You know how he's usually doing two things at once, Tracy."

"I'd think you'd want to be with him in Washington," said Tracy.

If Neeley detected the faint note of criticism in the younger woman's voice, she didn't react to it. "Tim asked me, and if there'd been time, I would have gone, but I hadn't taped tomorrow morning's puppet show with the Potters, when Tim and Alex left for Chicago at noon. The Potters have classes until four o'clock so there wasn't any chance of taping the program earlier. Besides, when Aggie got sick, if I had gone with Tim I would have taken the first plane home anyway. Good night."

"I hope your throat is better in the morning, Aggie," Tracy called after them, but, when she turned back to Lee, her voice had taken on a critical note once more, when she added, "I wouldn't have let my husband speak in the National Cathedral and not be there."

Startled by her tone, Lee glanced at her face and saw that she was really angry at what she considered to be negligence on the part of Neeley Douglas. He started to speak in Neeley's defense, then thought better of it. He'd known the beautiful, tall girl beside him less than twelve hours but already he was more

attracted to her than he'd ever been to another. There was no
point, he decided, in getting off to a bad start by arguing with
her, especially when everything seemed to indicate that the
warmth and charm that made the Logos Club's master of ceremonies the world's most successful TV evangelist had already
put what the Center's work force often called "Tim's spell" on
her.

II

"Gang, I want you to meet Tracy Ravenal," Lee told the
assembled musicians when the rehearsal was about to start.
"She's a voice major at the university and auditioned after the
Club program this morning. I asked her to come by tonight
and sing with the group for a few minutes after the rehearsal."

"Hello," said Tracy and received a warm chorus of "hi's" and
"hello's" from the Troubadours, though not from a red-haired
girl sitting in the gallery.

"Tonight we're going to rehearse the entire program for the
concerts we'll be giving in Atlanta," Lee added, as Tracy made
her way to a seat in the gallery beside the girl already there.
"Does anybody have a conflict they know of yet?"

One of the rhythm guitarists added to the group for concerts
—an instructor in mathematics working on his doctorate—
wasn't certain. Fortunately, there were two rhythm guitars in
addition to the regular lead and the steel version of the same
instrument that could carry the rhythm along with the percus-
sions.

"My name's Janice McCauley," said the girl with red hair.
"Did he say you auditioned for the first time this morning?"

"Yes," said Tracy. "I didn't even know Lee was looking for a
soprano until I came to the Club broadcast today."

"Young people don't come very often. The audiences are
mostly older people."

"My father insisted that I come, but I didn't know why until
I got here," Tracy confessed.

"Your father arranged an audition for you?" Miss McCauley's tone was heavy with suspicion.

"Yes. He's on the Board of Trustees."

"So that's it," the other girl snapped. "What group have you been singing with?"

"Only the university choir." Tracy chose to ignore the slur. "And some musical productions at Lankashire Community College, where I was enrolled for two years."

"An amateur!" The other girl snorted derisively. "What made you think you could sing professionally?"

"Lee invited me to audition with the group tonight just like he did you." Tracy was irritated by Miss McCauley's questioning. "We've both got the same chance to be selected, so why can't you be a good sport about it?"

"Sport? With you the daughter of a trustee? A fat chance I'll have."

"I don't think Lee Steadman would let that influence him."

Miss McCauley laughed, but without humor. "He's got a job to do and he'll keep an eye on the main chance, just like everybody else."

Tracy felt a strong urge to walk out of the studio but, sensing that the other girl was baiting her in the hope of accomplishing just that, decided against it. At first, she hadn't particularly wanted the job of singing with the Gospel Troubadours, in spite of Lee's obvious enthusiasm after her audition this morning. But now that the redhead was making an issue of her father's influence, which she was quite certain would not sway Lee Steadman to the slightest degree, she determined to make her best effort to win.

The rehearsal started just then and Tracy ignored the ill-tempered Miss McCauley, concentrating on the beat of the music and the voice effects the group was producing. It opened with "He's Alive!" the theme song of the Logos Club, identifying the Troubadours with the most popular program being broadcast in what was rapidly coming to be known around the world as the "Electric Church." Next came "Four-feet-eleven," with which Tracy was familiar from the Evie Tornquist album Lee had lent her.

The lead for the song was taken by Kitty Lawson, the shortest girl in the group. Though not more than five feet at most, Kitty had an astonishingly vibrant alto voice which, with the combo and the rest of the group backing her up, made the whole studio seem to vibrate with its powerful beat. Like most gospel-rock, the words were ordinary, the secret of their success lying in the almost primitive rhythm of the music and the very evident sincerity and joy of the singers.

The first verse went:

> *I'm only four-feet-eleven, but I'm going to heaven,*
> *And that makes me feel ten feet tall.*
> *They say I'm not too strong but I've known all along,*
> *I've got the greatest power of all.*
> *He lifts me up, makes me shout*
> *Come to Jesus, that's what I'm all about.*
> *I'm only four-feet-eleven, but I'm going to heaven,*
> *And that makes me feel ten feet tall.**

Coming after the joyfulness of the rhythm song, Lee's solo version of "The Old Rugged Cross" not only gave breadth to the program but also an inspiring contrast. Next the group repeated "If Heaven Never Was Promised to Me," with Alice Turner in the solo part. Her lilting soprano and her obvious joy in the words, plus the backing of the other singers and the rhythm group had Tracy humming the rhythm softly.

The rehearsal for the two-hour concert took only about ninety minutes, and the clock said a quarter to nine when the last song was finished. It was an inspiring version of the "Te Deum" from Verdi's *Four Sacred Pieces*, using the Twentieth Century version by Vaughn Williams. With only the piano as accompaniment and Lee Steadman leading the entire company, it was an inspiring work, calculated to bring any audience to its feet cheering at the close.

"If you'll step down, Alice," said Lee when the Verdi ended, "we'll let Miss McCauley try her hand with 'If Heaven Never Was Promised to Me.' Ready, Miss McCauley?"

---

* Copyright © 1976, 1977 by Word Music, Inc. All rights reserved. International copyright secured. Used by permission.

"As ready as I'll ever be," the redhead said shortly as she left her seat in the gallery to take the place Alice Turner had vacated on the back row of the Troubadours. Alice moved into the gallery to sit beside Tracy.

"I'll never be able to do it the way you do," Tracy told her while Miss McCauley was taking her place.

"Lee made me rehearse the solo part at least a dozen times before he let me do it on one of the Club broadcasts," Alice assured her. "He's an absolute perfectionist when it comes to music."

The combo played the first two bars of the song as an introduction before the singer began. Listening closely to the vocal part, Tracy couldn't find anything wrong with the harmony and recognized that Miss McCauley must be far more experienced than she in group singing. When it came to the solo part, however, the difference between the other girl's voice and Alice Turner's was immediately apparent. The rich fullness of Alice's tone simply wasn't there.

"Thank you, Miss McCauley," said Lee when the song was finished and turned to the gallery. "Ready, Miss Ravenal?"

She nodded and descended the steps from the gallery to the stage. Once again the combo played the introduction and, when the lyrics began, Tracy found herself slipping easily into the rhythm and the harmony. Actually, she found herself enjoying the lovely song, caught up by the instruments, the voices all around her and, particularly, the beauty and meaning of the words.

When the solo part came, she found her voice responding effortlessly until the final lines:

> Living in a world of darkness,
> He brought me the light.*

There was a momentary pause, then the whole company gave Tracy a standing ovation that left her blushing and very

* From "If Heaven Never Was Promised to Me" by Andraé Crouch. Copyright © 1973 by Lexicon Music, Inc. (ASCAP). Used by special permission.

happy. Even Miss McCauley stopped to congratulate her before leaving.

"I take back all those nasty things I said about your father's influence," she told Tracy. "You've obviously won on your own and you deserve it."

III

Alice was tired, so Lee dropped her at the Turners' apartment. "How about waffles and coffee for a nightcap?" he asked Tracy.

"I've got a test in music theory Monday—"

"You could pass that in a breeze."

"Well, okay. I guess I can study for it over the weekend."

"So many things have happened so fast that I'm still sort of overwhelmed," Tracy said over their second cup of coffee. "Twelve hours ago I was hurrying through the Gospel Broadcast Center to get to the studio because Dad made me promise over the telephone that I would go."

"And not too happy even about the audition, as I remember from the look on your face," Lee commented.

"I wasn't—at first. Then everybody seemed to be enjoying themselves so much that I stopped feeling resentment at my father for pushing me."

"The Club broadcasts are always interesting," Lee assured her. "Besides, we get paid—as you will learn when you take over Alice's part. The Center not only pays us a salary for the Club programs, but also the net profit from ticket sales for our concerts away from Weston is split among members of the group, after paying for the gas the Center bus uses."

"What are you going to do after you get your graduate degree?" Tracy asked.

"Tim and Neeley want me to continue, at least for a while, as musical director for the Center, and I suppose I will. After all, I owe everything I've done so far to them."

"You really love them both, don't you?"

"Everybody at the Center does. They're two very special people."

"I'm beginning to see why." Once again he detected that hint of abstraction in her voice, as if she were thinking of something else.

"You tape the Club broadcast each morning for radio stations, too, don't you?" she asked suddenly.

"Yes. Why?"

"I was thinking that if I could borrow some tapes of previous programs, it would help me accustom myself to the music."

"The master tapes are on file at the Center," he told her. "Ed Clayton is on duty over the weekend and can easily make copies for you from the masters. How many do you want?"

"Maybe four or five different programs."

"No problem. I have to run down to Atlanta tomorrow to arrange the final details of the concerts but I'll be back Sunday afternoon. Shall I drop the tapes off at your dormitory on my way back?"

"I won't be free until after seven. The choir is responsible for the vesper services in the chapel on Sunday at six and I'm supposed to be the soloist."

"Wonderful! I'll come by the chapel early to hear you sing. What selection did the director assign you?"

" 'How Great Thou Art.' " She grimaced. "It's sung a lot at funerals."

"But still a very beautiful hymn." He leaned forward, gripped by a sudden sense of excitement. "Why don't you sing 'How Great Thou Art' as your solo when you're a guest on the Club program the first time there's an opening after we come back from Atlanta. Afterward, you and I and Tim can discuss the place rock-gospel music can have in TV and radio programs that draw upon charismatic experiences, as the Logos Club does."

"I've never been 'born again' the way they talk about it on the show," she demurred.

"Neither have I but I'm sure you know people who claim to have been. I'd like to hear your reaction to some of them—"

"I'm afraid it would be negative. That actor I heard on the broadcast this morning sounded like a fake to me."

"Neeley thought so, too, but your reaction to all this is just
the sort of topic Tim likes most for discussion. He'll jump at
the chance to put you on the show as a guest."

Tracy Ravenal suddenly started to laugh.

"Did I say something funny?" Lee asked.

"No—but you're so persuasive, I was thinking you should
have been a salesman."

"I was—with a plaque on the wall to prove it. The company
wanted me to stay on with their regular sales force but, while I
was trying to decide, Tim and Neeley called one night from
Weston. That was the end of my career as a salesman."

"Have you ever regretted the decision?"

"Never. Of course, my salary at the Center isn't anywhere
near what I'd have made on the sales force of that Bible
publishing company, but the other rewards"—he reached over
to cover her hand with his and she did not withdraw it—"like
discovering you—more than make up for the money I'm not
making."

Chapter Five

LEE WAS BUSY IN ATLANTA SUNDAY MORNING MAKING THE FINAL arrangements for the concerts at Georgia State University. He barely managed to catch the four-o'clock plane for Weston but did buy a copy of the Sunday *Journal-Constitution* as he came through the airport. When the plane was airborne for the brief flight to the Greenville-Spartanburg Airport that served Weston, he opened the paper and began to read. He'd gone no farther than the second page of the news section, however, when he came upon an article that captured his attention. The headline was: "EVANGELICAL BROADCASTERS CRITICIZE MOST FAMOUS MEMBER."

The dateline was yesterday and the location was Chicago. The rest was brief—and startling:

"Some 500 members of the Evangelical Broadcasters' Association convention at the Drake Hotel heard the most famous leader in what is called the Electric Church movement denounced as a religious liberal at the close of yesterday's session. Although religious fundamentalism generally characterizes this movement, 'Brother Tim' Douglas, whose Logos Club tops all others in membership throughout the world, barely escaped being censured by a majority of the convention members as a 'liberal.' The motion to censure, proposed by the Reverend Jacob Schiller of Atlanta, failed to gain a majority but a sharp split among the members was indicated when the motion failed by a vote of 190 to 225.

"In making the motion to censure, Reverend Schiller deliv-

ered a scathing denunciation of the most famous member of
the Electric Church. He claimed that Brother Tim fails to
avow the doctrines of biblical infallibility and other foundation
stones of fundamentalists in general and the TV preachers in
particular. The Reverend Douglas was not there to defend himself, having left after addressing the convention banquet Friday
night, to preach this morning at the National Cathedral in
Washington at the invitation of the President."

Lee's seatmate, a spare, angular woman with an outthrust
jaw and small, tight mouth, had been reading the article out of
the corner of her eye. When he started to tear out the part of
the page containing it, she said: "It's too bad that whole crowd
can't be driven off the air, especially the one that calls himself
Brother Tim."

"Why do you say that?" Lee asked.

"They're a bunch of swindlers, that's what they are. Taking
money from people who are too lazy to go to church on Sunday and using it to pay actors and former prostitutes to appear
on their programs."

"Are the guests paid?" Lee pretended ignorance.

"Of course they're paid," the woman said indignantly.
"Would you confess for free on television to doing a lot of
scandalous things decent people wouldn't think of doing?"

"Probably not," Lee admitted.

"You look like a clean-cut, decent young man. Are you a
Christian?"

"I certainly hope so."

"Do you belong to a church?"

"Yes. Back in Airmont, West Virginia, where I come from."

"Then you've got a vested interest in driving vultures like
Brother Tim off the air. Do you know the Episcopal Church
alone is losing fifteen members an hour?"

"Surely not to the 'Electric Church'?" Lee protested.

"Maybe not, but they're losing them just the same and so are
other denominations. Do you read the *Saturday Review*?"

"Occasionally."

"I read it religiously and I was so impressed with an article
dealing with those vultures that I clipped it out." She rum-

maged in her handbag and came up with a somewhat worn clipping pasted on a thin piece of cardboard.

"Listen to this," she said on a note of triumph. "The writer of the article is talking about people like Brother Tim: 'The message is one of pure fervor—good works are unnecessary, social action uncalled for—a video-induced adrenalin for the religious nervous system.' What do you think of that?"

"It's pretty strong stuff," Lee admitted. "From what the article I was just reading said, though, the leaders of the Electric Church criticized the Reverend Douglas for not preaching the same doctrine they did."

"Doctrine or no doctrine, he still leads people to take the easy way of watching sermons on TV instead of going to church. Do you know that the most popular among these TV programs takes in more money than the entire national budget of many denominations?"

"I've heard that," Lee admitted, wishing the woman would shut up so he could read the rest of the paper.

"You don't have to take my word for it," she said. "Church magazines all carry articles about the way these people are stealing money that ought to be used for foreign missions and other activities of the regular churches."

"You seem to be familiar with Brother Tim Douglas' programs," Lee observed. "Do you watch the Logos Club?"

"Watch it?" The woman stiffened into a picture of righteous indignation. "I wouldn't be caught dead looking at it."

"We are about to begin our descent for the Greenville-Spartanburg Airport," came the voice of a stewardess over the plane's public-address system. "Please see that your seat belts are fastened and your seats in the upright position with the tray tables closed."

While his seatmate busied herself following instructions, Lee folded the rest of the paper and stuck it in the pocket of his jacket. The two were among the last to leave the plane.

"Mr. Steadman!" the stewardess exclaimed with a warm smile. "I recognized you when you came aboard going to Atlanta yesterday morning but was so busy I didn't get to speak to you. I'm off tomorrow, so I'll be watching the Logos Club. What are you going to sing?"

"'If Heaven Never Was Promised to Me,' I believe," said Lee.

"It's one of my favorites. I'll make it a point to stay home and listen. Good-by."

As Lee started down the steps to the tarmac, he heard the woman who had been bending his ear since they'd left Atlanta, ask the stewardess: "Who is that young man? You seemed to know him."

"Lee Steadman is very famous, madame; I'm surprised you haven't heard of him. He's music director and lead singer on Brother Tim Douglas' Logos Club on TV."

Lee was halfway down the steps but still heard the woman's "humph!" and the sniff of disdain that followed.

II

It was a few minutes after six on Sunday evening when Lee slipped into the college chapel. He'd driven to Weston in the car he'd parked at the airport yesterday morning. The building was only about half filled and some two-dozen students making up the choir were robed and grouped in the stall back of the pulpit. A professor of homiletics from the School of Religion was at the lectern, reading from the Gospel of Mark. As the soloist, Tracy sat at the end of the first row in the choir—her bright hair and beauty making her stand out in any crowd.

The reading finished, the professor at the pulpit lectern led the congregation and the choir in a prayer, then stepped back to take one of the two chairs placed in front of the choir stall. As the organ started to play "How Great Thou Art," Tracy rose and, stepping down to the level of the pulpit, moved across to the rostrum in front of it while the organist finished playing the introduction to the hymn.

When she began to sing, Lee couldn't repress a sense of pride. Her voice was clear, the phrasing smooth and, with the help of the lectern microphone, filled the fairly large chapel. When she reached the closing phrase, *how great Thou art,* she chose the higher pitch, singing effortlessly until the last note died away.

"Beautifully done, Miss Ravenal," the professor complimented her when he returned to the pulpit for a short homily.

Afterward, the choir sang a more complicated selection from Handel's *Messiah*, directed by the professor of choral music with whom Lee had studied as an undergraduate. When the benediction ended the brief service, Lee saw that it was six forty-five.

The choir was leaving the chapel by the front and Lee made his way down the center aisle to meet Tracy, who smiled and took his arm when he reached her. "I was looking for you when the service started," she told him, "but I couldn't see you."

"I came in right after what must have been the first hymn, but I heard your solo. It was beautiful."

The professor who had directed the choir was passing and stopped to greet Lee. "I can echo those sentiments, Steadman," he said. "It's nice to see you again."

"Thank you, sir. The Troubadours are doing a concert in Atlanta in a couple of weeks. I got back from making the final arrangements just in time to hear Miss Ravenal sing."

Professor Stanley smiled. "In time to, or for the purpose of?"

"A little of both," Lee admitted. "Miss Ravenal is now a member of the group. She'll be doing solos for the morning Club performances and also during our concerts."

"He practically strong-armed me into the Gospel Troubadours, Dr. Stanley," Tracy explained. "I'd never done that kind of singing before."

"Lee was one of my best students but I still can't be sure I like the sort of thing he's doing now," the professor admitted. "When he first came to Weston and auditioned for my course, I thought of him as directing a large chorus, perhaps something like the Robert Shaw Chorale. I watch Tim Douglas' program occasionally, though, and I must admit that Lee gets a lot of harmony and some really fine musical effects out of that troupe."

"Thank you, sir," said Lee.

"You've got a fine addition to the Troubadours in Miss Ravenal," Professor Stanley continued. "I've rarely heard a so-prano who was able to reach the high notes with as much clarity as she does."

"Try to listen to the Club program sometime after she joins the Troubadours, sir. I think you'll admit then that even with a rock beat that was hardly ever heard in sacred music until the past five years or so, we manage to give an impression of dignity and inspiration fully as honest as that selection from the *Messiah* the choir sang just now."

"One of the things I always liked about you, Steadman, was your confidence in your own ability to meet challenges," said the professor in parting. "I've an idea you'll go a long way in popular religious music, and I wish you both well."

"You didn't tell me you were going to start me as Alice's replacement so soon," Tracy said accusingly as they came out of the chapel. "Are you sure I'm ready for it?"

"You will be by the end of the week. Had your dinner?"

"Not yet. I was too nervous about the solo to eat."

"I still get goosebumps every morning just before I begin the show with 'He's Alive!'" he confessed. "Where would you like to eat?"

"Nowhere—in this long white robe. Take me by the dormitory; while I run in and change, you can decide where we'll go."

While Lee was waiting in front of Hubbard House, the mobile telephone with which he'd equipped his car buzzed.

"I've a call for you, Mr. Steadman," said the mobile operator. "It's from Mrs. Douglas."

"Lee!" Neeley Douglas' voice sounded in his ear. "Are you busy?"

"I'm waiting in front of her dormitory for Tracy Ravenal to change dresses. She's been singing at vespers with the choir and we're going somewhere to eat."

"Sorry to interfere with a date, but fortunately you can take Tracy with you on what I want you to do and still have your dinner. Tim's due to land at the airport in the Center plane at eight-thirty, but I'm here at University Hospital with Aggie—"

"Nothing serious, I hope." The Douglases' ten-year-old daughter was a favorite of his.

"We don't know yet. I think I told you Friday that I'd taken her to the pediatrician with a sore throat, but he only gave her penicillin and sent her home. Her fever kept rising over the weekend, and late this afternoon she had a convulsion. Our pediatrician was out of town so I called your friend Dr. Michaels."

"I'm glad you could get him," said Lee.

"He had us meet him here at the hospital and immediately called in a pediatric neurologist, who's getting ready to do a spinal puncture."

"That sounds serious."

"They think she has encephalitis, Lee." Neeley's voice broke for the first time. "Please meet Tim and bring him directly to the hospital."

"I will," he promised. "And don't worry. With Art Michaels there, Aggie will have the best treatment she could get anywhere."

"I felt better the minute he took charge," Neeley admitted. "Don't tell Tim anything's wrong. We may have the report on the spinal puncture by the time he lands."

"If he isn't due until eight-thirty, Tracy and I will have time for a snack before he lands and will bring him straight there."

"You're a love, Lee. I knew I could rely on you. Good-by."

Tracy came down the walk as he was hanging up the phone. She'd changed into a sleeveless summer dress.

"I thought I heard you talking on the phone," she said. "Is anything wrong?"

"Neeley's at the hospital with Aggie. Tim's flying from Washington in the company plane and is due to land at the airport at eight-thirty. She wants us to meet him."

"I heard her say Friday that her daughter had a sore throat but it didn't sound so serious."

"Apparently it's more than just that. Neeley wants us to bring Tim there but not tell him why until we get him to the hospital."

"Maybe I'd better not go with you, then," Tracy suggested. "He's bound to have some baggage."

"There'll be plenty of room for all of us," he assured her. "I'd planned a romantic dinner at the nearest Pizza Hut but we can still grab a snack at the airport restaurant while we're waiting for Tim's plane."

III

It was nearly an hour's drive from the university city to the joint Greenville-Spartanburg airport. According to the flight schedule posted on the bulletin board, one commercial flight was scheduled to arrive in the next hour, a jet from Chicago on the way to Atlanta. The airport wasn't crowded and they found a comfortable booth in the restaurant with a fine view of the lobby. Lee ordered steaks and coffee and just after they arrived, the flight from Chicago was announced.

People began passing through the lobby almost immediately. Tracy was sitting facing the area, and having no eyes except for her, Lee paid little attention to the passengers.

"There's Mr. Porcher!" she exclaimed suddenly. "Or should I say Reverend Porcher?"

"Neeley said Alex flew to Chicago with Tim Friday but would be coming back tonight." Lee leaned out of the booth the better to see into the lobby. "I can see Alex but he's not alone."

"A heavy-set man is with him, and a woman."

"The man's Jake Schiller!" Lee exclaimed. "The woman looks familiar, too."

"I recognize her now," said Tracy. "She's one of the counselors who answers the telephone on the Logos Club broadcast."

"You're right! That's Magda Sanderson. She doubles as the head of the letter-opening room."

"From the looks of that dress and makeup, she doubles in something else," said Tracy cryptically.

Lee grinned. "Trust a woman to think of that but I believe she has a title—Assistant Treasurer, or something. That would have given her the right to attend the convention in Chicago."

"Isn't Schiller the faith healer who broadcasts from Atlanta Sunday mornings?" Tracy asked. "The one you told me about

"Glad to know you, Tracy," said the newspaperman. "Are you from the Charleston Ravenals? I've heard that, like the Lowells of Boston, they speak only to God."

Tracy laughed. "My great-grandfather was a maverick. He left Charleston a hundred years ago and moved Northwest to Lankashire. We're in textiles."

"I did a profile some time ago on Caleb Ravenal—only everybody in Lankashire County called him Cal—but he didn't tell me he had a beautiful daughter."

"I remember the piece you wrote very well," said Tracy.

"Maybe I can do a feature on Cal's daughter sometime," Jowers suggested.

"Wait a few weeks, Ray," said Lee. "Tracy transferred last fall to the School of Fine Arts and next week she's going to join the Gospel Troubadours as lead soprano."

"Hmm!" said Jowers. "If Lee's giving you that much of a musical share in the Club programs, Tracy, you must have a lot on the ball besides beauty. And Lord knows you've got plenty of that."

"What brings you out here tonight?" Lee asked.

"Neeley Douglas called me at home this afternoon. She said Tim preached in the National Cathedral this morning to the President and his family. She thought that would be enough reason for a picture of him getting off the jet tonight and a brief airport interview, even without Jake Schiller's power play in Chicago yesterday."

"That's our Neeley," said Lee. "Always in there pushing."

"I saw Alex Porcher get off the Atlanta plane a few minutes ago with Jake, and both of them were acting very buddy-buddy," said Jowers. "Are the lion and lamb going to lie down together, even though Tim kicked Schiller out years ago and Jake's been vowing publicly to get even?"

"Alex was attending the National Conference of Evangelical Broadcasters' meeting in Chicago over the weekend," Lee explained. "My guess is that he just happened to be on the same plane with Schiller and they started talking."

"With Schiller pumping Alex about the Gospel Broadcast Center's affairs, so he can use that information against Tim?"

the day we went to the hospital to see the Halliday woman?"

"Yes."

"He and Reverend Porcher certainly seem to be good friends. They've been talking there for several minutes."

"I'd give a lot to know what they're saying," said Lee and she looked at him in surprise.

"Why?"

From his pocket, Lee took the article he had torn out of the Atlanta paper and gave it to Tracy to read. When she finished, she looked up with an expression of perplexity on her face. "Why would Reverend Schiller make the motion he did at the Chicago convention?"

"It may have been simply a political move on Jake's part. For the past couple of years he's been trying to get himself elected president of the Evangelical Broadcasters' Association, but Tim has enough supporters to defeat him. Or again he may have only been trying to embarrass Tim. Actually, I doubt very much that Jake Schiller had any idea at the time that he could win on the motion to censure Tim in Chicago. By making it in the closing sessions though, when he knew Tim was already on the way to Washington, he could be sure that a lot of people who would have voted for Tim had already left, too. My guess is that all Jake really hoped for was to get newspaper coverage of an attack on Tim."

"How can Schiller and Reverend Porcher be so friendly, then, if you say Schiller is Tim's worst enemy?"

He couldn't fail to notice how easily the name came to her lips although only two days ago she had been stammering in obvious awe of Tim's presence, but he had a greater concern now.

"That's exactly what I'd like to know," he said.

"Were they friends before Reverend Schiller left the Center?"

"Not that I know of. As I remember it, Alex didn't come with us until several weeks after Jake Schiller left."

"Maybe they just happened to meet in Chicago and came home on the same plane."

"That could be true—and the same could be said of Magda Sanderson," Lee admitted. "But why would Schiller get off the plane with Alex—unless they had been discussing something they thought was important before the landing and needed to continue it in the lobby. Which means Magda Sanderson already knew what they had been talking about."

"All passengers on Flight 83 for Atlanta should be aboard," the voice of the airport announcer sounded over the loudspeakers. "Departure in five minutes from Gate Three."

In the lobby, Lee saw Alex Porcher and Magda Sanderson shake hands cordially with Schiller before he hurried from the lobby to reboard his flight for Atlanta. Meanwhile, Alex and the woman, talking together, moved toward the baggage-claim area and out of their line of vision.

"Reverend Porcher and the Sanderson woman are obviously on good terms," Tracy observed. "I'll bet that relationship goes even farther than any casual meeting in an airplane."

"Alex is a handsome fellow, and dolled up the way Magda Sanderson was, I wouldn't even have recognized her."

"What do you make of all of it?"

"I don't know but you can bet Jake Schiller will do anything he can to harm Tim. Last year, the IRS investigated Jake's church in Atlanta to see if the money he took in was really being used for nonprofit purposes. There was some talk then that Schiller had bought a lot of stock in his wife's maiden name, using money given to his Temple."

"Could he do that and get away with it?"

"Evangelists who preach on television get a lot of money through the mail," said Lee. "Much of it is in small amounts, too, usually tens and twenties in cash, and more than one crooked group has been found guilty of diverting some of it for purposes of their own."

"How could they do it?"

"It's practically impossible for the IRS to find out the truth, in a situation like that, if the people getting the money really want to hide it. The Gospel Center accountants keep accurate records because the senders are good candidates for future membership in the Logos Club. But a lone wolf like Jake Schiller could easily divert a lot of cash to his own pockets without reporting it either to the organization's trustees or to the IRS."

From overhead came the sudden thunder of a jet as the Atlanta plane took off.

"Are you going to tell Tim and Neeley about Magda Sanderson being with Reverend Porcher and Reverend Schiller?" Tracy asked.

Lee shook his head. "They could have accidentally taken the same plane out of Chicago; only about three flights from there a day stop here. Tim trusts everybody to be as honest as he is and, if he even suspected that Alex has been working with Jake Schiller to get control of the network, it would hurt Tim terribly. I'll just talk to Neeley and a few others of the old-timers around the Center and see what their reaction is."

"Neeley really runs the show, doesn't she?"

"Let's say she's sort of an executive vice president—with a finger on the pulse of everything that goes on. That way, she can take a lot of the burden from Tim's shoulders."

Tracy was silent and, when Lee glanced at her, he saw that she wasn't eating. Instead, a distant look was in her eyes, as if for a moment she wasn't aware of either him or her surroundings.

"A penny for your thoughts," he said.

The words brought her back to the present and for some reason she blushed deeply. "I'm sorry, Lee, I was thinking of something else."

Through an open window of the restaurant came the distant roar of a jet, and Lee glanced at his watch. "Eight-forty," he said. "That must be the Center jet bringing Tim home from Washington. Want to go outside and watch it land? Tim was an Air Force pilot before he went into the seminary. You'll see a real gung-ho landing."

A small group was waiting outside in the warm night air, among them a tall man with a camera and a strobe flash unit hanging from his neck. A roll of the inevitable newsman's copy paper stuck in the side pocket of his coat indicated his occupation. When he saw Lee and Tracy, he came over to where they were standing.

"Lee!" he said, shaking hands. "Glad to see you again."

"Likewise," said Lee cordially. "Tracy Ravenal, this is Ray Jowers from the Weston paper."

"I doubt that Jake could find anything against Tim," said Lee.

"You're right there," Jowers agreed. "In my book, Brother Tim is like Caesar's wife—above reproach. The same goes for Neeley—and Aggie too. That redheaded tyke is a doll."

"Did Neeley tell you Aggie's in the hospital?"

"Yes. Hope it isn't anything serious."

"Just a sore throat, we hope."

"So do I," said Jowers. "Tim worships that kid."

IV

The Learjet swept in moments later to a three-point landing and taxied to a stop some fifty feet from where the small group of people was standing. The landing ladder went down from inside the plane and Tim came out, carrying the usual minimum of luggage for a man who traveled far, fast and often—a valpack and a gaily wrapped package. Ray Jowers met him at the foot of the ladder and took a couple of pictures before they had a brief chat. Finally, Tim broke away from the reporter and came across the tarmac to the gate where Lee and Tracy were waiting.

"He looks tired," said Tracy.

"I guess he has a right to be," Lee agreed. "Friday night he was scheduled to speak at a dinner of the evangelical group. Saturday he was to hold a three-hour seminar before flying to Washington for the sermon this morning in the National Cathedral. That adds up to a very busy weekend."

Tim did look weary, Lee realized when the evangelist put down his bag to greet them.

"We're glad to have you back," said Lee. "You remember Tracy Ravenal, don't you?"

"Of course." Tim gave her his hand and his best smile. "When I last saw you on Friday before I took off for Chicago, Tracy, you were auditioning for Alice Turner's place in the Troubadours. I hope you got the job."

"She's exactly what we're looking for—and more," said Lee. "Wait until you hear her sing!"

"I'm looking forward to it," said Tim, as Lee picked up his bag and they moved into the terminal. "When will I have the pleasure, Miss Ravenal?"

"Lee will have to decide that," said Tracy. "Everything's happened so fast since Friday, I don't even know if I'm coming or going."

"That's the way we do things at the Center." Tim turned to Lee. "Are Neeley and Aggie okay? I was expecting them to meet me."

"Neeley called me on the mobile phone soon after I got back from Atlanta this afternoon. I wasn't supposed to tell you until we got to the hospital, but—"

"Then something *is* wrong?"

"It's Aggie. Neeley got hold of Art Michaels—"

"Isn't he a psychiatrist?"

"Technically, but he practices holistic medicine so any illness is within his province. Aggie will get the best possible treatment under Art's direction."

"Let's go, then. When did Aggie get sick?"

"Friday afternoon," said Lee, "after you left for Chicago. It looked like a simple sore throat—"

"I'd never have gone, if I'd known. Neeley should have told me."

"From what Neeley said, she didn't know until Aggie came home early from school," Lee explained.

"If anything happens to Aggie, I'll never forgive myself for not being here with her—and Neeley."

"How was Washington?" Lee asked.

"Perfect. The National Cathedral's a magnificent church; quite a change from Airmont, West Virginia. Word had apparently gotten around that the President was going to worship there today—"

"Or that Brother Tim Douglas was going to preach," said Lee. "With all due respect to the President, many people over the world are as familiar with your name as with his."

"I wouldn't vouch for that but he was very courteous," said Tim. "Invited me over to the White House afterward for Sunday dinner—just like you'd ask the preacher to go home with you in a small town or in the country."

"I hope you accepted," said Tracy.

"You bet I did!" Tim's face lit up in his familiar smile. "I'm sure the French chef at the White House was miffed, though. Guess what the President of the United States was having for dinner today?"

"Caviar. *Pâté de fois gras*. Stuff like that?" Lee asked.

"We had stuffed pork chops, turnip greens, boiled potatoes, and corn bread. It was just like what I used to eat in Mrs. Elder's boardinghouse when I came down here for a few months to get the radio station going and left Neeley and Aggie back in Airmont."

When Lee started to open the trunk of his car for the baggage, Tim said, "Just toss it in the back, Lee; there's plenty of room for three in the front. Tracy won't have to straddle the gear lever like with the first car Neeley and I owned. It was a second-hand Chevrolet we paid a hundred dollars down plus fifteen a month for, but even then the payments seemed to last forever. That was just before Aggie was born."

"You have only the one child?" Tracy asked as they crowded themselves into the front seat.

"One and only—unless we adopt another." Tim's tone was tinged with regret. "Neeley had a pretty hard labor and almost hemorrhaged to death afterward. I'd have lost her, if it hadn't been for a smart surgeon who happened to be in the emergency room at the time and did a hysterectomy in fifteen minutes. I made them take a quart of blood from me at one sitting, but passed out on the last half pint. When I came to, they told me both Neeley and the baby were okay and I'm telling you that was the best news I'd ever had, or hope to have—except maybe that Aggie's okay when we get to the hospital."

"Did the President have anything special to say?" Lee asked.

"He looks at the Club program occasionally. He's a 'born again' Christian, too, you know."

"I hope he didn't object to your videotaping the service at the Cathedral. It certainly won't hurt the image of the Logos Club to have you preaching to the President of the United States. We can run the tape during one of the Club programs."

"The President gave me permission to do just that and also show shots of him and his family. The White House photographer is going to send some prints taken there during the dinner, too. They'll look very good in our monthly newsletter to Club members."

"As soon as Tracy gets settled in, I want to put some photos and a brief bio about her in the letter," said Lee. "I've already made arrangements with Ray Jowers to do a feature on her as the newest member of the Troubadours."

"How does it feel to be on the verge of becoming a celebrity, Tracy?" Tim asked.

"I'm not."

"You will be. With your looks and the kind of songs Lee will choose for you, plus the voice he says you have, nothing can stop you. I must remind Neeley to set you up for an interview on the Club program soon."

"How did the seminar go?" Lee asked.

"Tiresome," said the evangelist. "A lot of evangelical TV programs are in financial difficulties and one or two are about to go bankrupt—all because most of them limit their programs to what Neeley calls 'Bible pounding.'"

"I suppose you heard of Jake Schiller's motion to censure," said Lee.

"Saw it in the Washington *Post*. It's just like Jake to take a shot at me when I wasn't there to defend myself, but Alex took up the cudgels in my behalf. He called me in Washington last night to tell me about it."

Tracy started to speak but was stopped by Lee's warning glance and Tim didn't notice.

"The trouble with a lot of the evangelists on TV and off," Tim continued, "is that they haven't learned yet to dress their sermons up with the kind of showmanship and rock music we've been using in the Club broadcasts for years. When I told them that, a few fairly frothed at the mouth and I could see that they would like to ride me out of town on a rail—the way Jake Schiller tried to do. But considering the remarkable success of the Logos Club, a lot of them are already beginning to see the light."

"Let's pray they don't catch up," said Lee.

"They won't," said Tim confidently. "With the team we've got—and now with Tracy added to it—we can't possibly fail."

After dropping off Tim and his baggage at the hospital, Lee came down the graveled walk to where he'd left Tracy in the car. In the sudden brilliance of the light when he opened the door to get in, she looked bemused and barely conscious of his presence.

"Anywhere you'd particularly like to go?" he asked but she seemed not to have heard.

"He shouldn't drive himself so hard," she said pensively. "He looks terribly tired."

"Tim's a dynamo," said Lee, then added, deliberately, "So is Neeley. That's why they make such an effective team."

She turned to look at him and in the bright beam of an approaching car he saw that her expression was troubled.

"Something wrong?" he asked.

"No. Why would you ask that?"

"You're like another person after you've been with Tim."

She frowned. "What do you mean?"

"Most of the time you're natural and easy to be with, like any college girl of your age except that you're more serious, intelligent and self-assured. But whenever you're near Tim, it's almost as if you were away on a different planet."

"He makes you think."

"About religion? That's what you might call his stock in trade."

"I didn't mean that—although I'd characterize him as charismatic."

"Aren't you avoiding confessing that you've become sort of infatuated with Tim?" he asked and was surprised at her instant reaction.

"Whatever gave you that idea?"

"You're not the first; young women go ga-ga over him all the time. What's more, they write him—and not always about the programs, either. Some of the letters are intensely personal; you could even call them love letters."

"I'd never do that," she said quickly—defensively, he thought. Then in a more even tone, she added, "What does he do with the letters?"

"Tim doesn't see them, except by accident. When the letter-opening crew happens to come upon one, they shoot it across to Neeley's office. I suppose she destroys them except for the few she showed me. Some of 'em can get pretty sloppy."

"The ones from girls who are infatuated with Tim?" Her tone had become angry again. "Is that what you're implying about me?"

"I didn't say that—"

"But you were thinking it! And I don't like the idea! After all, he *is* married—"

"Girls often fall in love—or think they are—with married men, especially celebrities like Tim Douglas."

"I think you'd better take me back to the dormitory," she said coldly. "I wasn't raised to have affairs with married men."

"Nobody said anything about your having an affair with Tim," he protested, as he pulled the car to a stop before Hubbard House. "If I said anything to hurt your feelings, I apologize—"

"Like you just said, there's nothing to apologize for." Before he could get out she'd opened the door and was running up the walk to the steps leading up to the door of her dormitory. "Good night!"

"Good night! But please don't—" The words were cut short by the slamming of the front door of the dormitory.

For a moment, Lee considered following her and trying to end their first quarrel before it could build up to a complete break, than gave up the idea. He couldn't help feeling depressed, however, as he drove to his apartment house.

He needed Tracy Ravenal badly to fill the empty place in the Center music program that would be left by Alice Turner's daily imminent departure in favor of motherhood. More than that, however, he was strongly attracted to Tracy as a woman, and until a few minutes ago he'd dared to think she felt much the same way. Now, he realized, his only block on the road to becoming really in love appeared to be her reaction to Tim Douglas' powerful appeal to young women. And that sort of thing, he knew from experience, was almost impossible to fight.

Forcibly, Lee put the thought from him in order to tackle another problem. How could Alex Porcher have fought so hard to defend Tim at the convention and yet be on obviously friendly terms with the Atlanta broadcaster just now in the airport? Lee pondered the question until he went to bed in his apartment but even when sleep claimed him, he couldn't find an answer—except that one of Alex's two performances had been staged for purposes of his own.

Chapter Six

Lee was fidgeting the next morning while preparations for the regular broadcast of the Logos Club went on apace. When the queue of visitors was ushered into the gallery, he saw that the end seat on the second row Tracy had occupied on Friday morning was still vacant. As he was passing across the right wing of the stage for a paper cup of coffee, Neeley came out of her office with the usual clipboard under her arm.

"Thanks for bringing Tim to the hospital from the airport last night, Lee," she said.

"Did they make a firm diagnosis in Aggie's case yet?"

"Nothing, except a tentative one of viral encephalitis. She did recognize Tim, though, and seemed some better when I went by the hospital this morning before coming to work." She glanced at the gallery. "By the way, where's Tracy?"

"Search me. She might not even be coming."

"You quarreled? Oh I'm sorry, Lee."

"It was only a slight misunderstanding, something I may be able to remedy."

Neeley gave him a probing look. "Was the quarrel over Tim and the tendency of young girls to become infatuated with him?"

Lee nodded. "Unfortunately, I used that very word and she didn't like it."

"Tracy's obviously a very high type of girl." Neeley's tone was serious now. "The kind who'd naturally be attracted to Tim's honesty, intelligence and charm—maybe even too much attracted at the start. You should have handled her more gently, Lee."

"I know that now. 'Infatuated' was certainly the wrong word."

"Well, cheer up. We're all going to be working together, so we can probably change it to just friendship."

"If she comes."

"Any girl in her right mind would," Neeley assured him. "I'll ask the hostess to keep the same seat open for her."

"Thanks."

"Why don't you take Tracy on a guided tour of the Center's facilities after the broadcast," Neeley added. "She's already seen the puppet show and might even find that she'd like to take part in some of the other projects. Once she realizes what an important part you play in the work of the Center, she'll come to know you better and hopefully your quarrel probably won't last very long."

From the set came Mike D'Agostino's call, "Five minutes!" and Lee moved across the stage to the piano. As he did so, the outside door opened and Tracy Ravenal hurried in to take her seat. He only had time to glance at her but when she smiled back, his heart leaped. Then the director's hand went down on the final count and Lee moved jubilantly into the opening declaration with which every program of the Logos Club began: "He's Alive!"

II

The first part of the Monday morning Logos Club program was uneventful. Lee and the Troubadours sang, then Alex introduced Tim. Before giving a brief description of the service in the National Cathedral in Washington, Tim asked the audience and those watching him to pray for the recovery of his daughter. He did not identify her illness, probably, Lee understood, because it had not yet been definitely settled.

The first guest was a reformed narcotics pusher. "Born

again" during one of Tim's yearly telethons, the pusher described in rather horrifying detail the life of a victim of "horse" or heroin addiction. The pusher was followed by the author of a new biblical novel, a retired professor of archaeology who had specialized in excavation of archaeological sites in the Holy Land. His talk was illustrated with color slides, projected on the screen at the rear of the set. That presentation completed the first sixty minutes of the program, taped separately because not all stations used the full ninety minutes.

During the short break before starting to tape the last thirty minutes, Lee went over to the gallery where Tracy was sitting in her usual corner seat.

"Glad you could make it," he told her.

"He was wonderful, wasn't he?" She didn't need to identify whom she meant. Her eyes were still on Tim, who was talking to Neeley in the wing at the right, behind the glass partition but visible from the gallery.

"The audience was certainly fascinated by Tim's description of dinner at the White House," Lee agreed. "Part of his success is due to his obvious sincerity. A lot of evangelists on TV get very histrionic in what is already a pretty charismatic business but Tim never does."

"Maybe that's why Reverend Schiller tried to censure him in Chicago."

"Fundamentalists in religion are always arguing about differences in theology. Each one usually has his own set of beliefs and denounces those who have different ideas, but in Jake's case I think it's something more than that."

"Like what?"

"I don't know yet but I hope to find out."

"The music was especially good this morning," she said, changing the subject.

"The only thing that's always completely religious about the Logos Club programs is the music," Lee agreed. "But if the Troubadours weren't all highly trained professionals—"

"Mainly because of you—"

"You're coming on faster than anyone we've ever brought into the group before."

"I almost didn't come in this morning," she confessed.

"When I left you last night, I'd decided to give the whole thing up."

"I owe you an apology for sticking my nose in your private affairs."

"It's all over, so let's forget it. I guess I did come down on you pretty hard."

"I deserved it. What changed your mind?"

"My father called from Lankashire; he always does on Sunday nights. When I told him I'd been offered a place with the Gospel Troubadours, he was so pleased and proud that I couldn't tell him I wasn't going to take it." She laughed. "Besides, he's giving me a Porsche."

"I'm glad—on both counts," he said. "If you'll wait a few minutes after the program is over, I'll take you on a guided tour of the Center. Now that you're part of it, I think you'll be interested in the breadth of the activities here."

"I'd like that."

"Two minutes!" Henry Waterford's voice sounded over the loudspeaker system from the control room. "Places, please."

"I'll meet you here on the set at the end of the broadcast," said Lee, as he moved to the piano where Jim Cates was already taking his seat on the bench.

At the end of the routine countdown, Lee and the Gospel Troubadours did a gospel-rock number. Alex came on then but stopped before a standing microphone instead of taking his usual chair. During the interval between the two sections of the program, he had been moving, as usual, through the rows of counselors, stopping for a bantering word with some who were regulars. As each of them tore one or more sheets from the notepads they'd been writing on when calls had come in, he glanced rapidly at the names and addresses printed there. Quickly separating a few, he had slipped them into the side pocket of his carefully tailored sports jacket.

One of the things that made Alex so valuable to Tim and the Center, Lee knew, was his phenomenal memory, enabling him to recognize instantly the name of any member of the Logos Club who called during a broadcast. Such requests received special attention over the air several times a week during the closing ten minutes of the first hour. In addition, those the

computer that kept the Center financial records revealed to
have been especially liberal contributors, received a personal
note dictated by one of the counselors but signed by Tim or
Alex.

At Mike D'Agostino's signal, Alex began to speak into the
microphone.

"Friends and fellow partners in Christ," he said, "you have
just heard Brother Tim tell you how it felt to preach to the
President and his family in the National Cathedral and have a
country-style dinner with them later at the White House. I'm
sure you understand that this event represents a real triumph
for Brother Tim, though he is much too modest to describe it
to you as that. Since yesterday was a special occasion, I asked
Tim to let me tell you some of the events that led up to that
day." He smiled. "I hope you won't mind if I substitute for the
film we had scheduled for this final portion of today's program," he added, to a spattering of applause from the audience.

"A little over six years ago, Brother Tim and his wife,
Neeley, came to Weston from West Virginia because he'd been
able to buy a defunct AM radio and UHF television station
here," Alex continued. "From it, he planned to broadcast the
message of our Lord and Savior's sacrifice on Calvary. Aided by
an electronic genius named Henry Waterford, who now directs
all broadcast activities of the Center, they managed to get the
station on the air, but only on radio at first.

"I'm sure many of you heard and were inspired by those
early radio programs but Brother Tim wasn't satisfied. You see,
he had a dream even then, a dream of reaching millions
through the rapidly growing miracle of religious television
broadcasting. Not knowing whether he was listened to by hundreds or by thousands, he began to talk on the radio about that
dream. Then one day, busy broadcasting the message of a living
Christ, Tim had an inspiration. Why not, he asked himself and
his unseen audience, let the people who heard him become
partners—stockholders, if you will—in the new venture in religious television.

"The rest is really history. In fact many of you in the studio
audience today have been stockholders from the very beginning, pledging your dollars to help Brother Tim bring his mes-

sage of hope and faith to the world and continuing to support his endeavors.

"*Logos* is a Greek word meaning literally The Word of God, so Tim and Neeley naturally chose it as the name for their first regular TV program. That was five years ago and today many thousands of other stockholders share in Brother Tim's dream. Knowing him as so many of you do, you also know that the dream is always growing, but to achieve that growth, we must have more invested capital. Only that can produce more dividends in the form of the messages of Christ's love for all being flung from the Center's broadcast tower almost every hour day and night.

"You, too, can become a stockholder in the Center and a partner in the Logos Club." Alex's voice vibrated with conviction. "Your check payable to the Gospel Broadcast Center mailed to us here at Weston, South Carolina, doesn't just make you a member of the Logos Club, the fastest-growing religious TV program on the air today. It will also start you as a subscriber to the monthly magazine listing all the programs provided here at the Center as well as stories about the people who make those programs possible. The magazine will bring you news about other activities in the network that carries our message to every part of the world—in the real voice of the participants where English is spoken or in other languages through dubbing. You'll receive many other rewards from membership in the Logos Club, I promise you, but none greater than the knowledge that you are a partner in making Tim and Neeley Douglas' dream come true."

As Alex stepped back, Tim took his place. "Thank you, Alex," he said. "And now to end today's program, Lee Steadman will lead us in the hymn that you will, I am sure, remember from your childhood, as I do; let us all sing together 'The Old Rugged Cross.'"

III

_____

While Alex and Tim were shaking hands and chatting with the departing studio audience, Lee met Tracy in front of the stage.

"Ready for the guided tour?" he asked.

"If you're sure you have the time."

"I do," he assured her. "While I think of it, we're going to have another rehearsal tonight for the concert in Atlanta. If you can spare about an hour and a half, I'd like you to stand beside Alice and sing the actual songs in harmony with the others."

"But I don't know the words yet. The first time I ever heard gospel-rock was last week when I came to the broadcast."

"We'll have the sheet music, so don't worry. During the Club broadcasts we always have the lyrics on the TelePrompTer but in concerts, we have to use sheets."

"Aren't you betting pretty heavily on a dark horse—meaning me?"

"I'm not worried. Evie Tornquist's success has proved that a pretty girl who sings gospel-rock can go a long way in this business."

Tracy gave him a sharp, appraising look. "Is that what it really is to you, a business?"

"The evangelical movement is big business any way you look at it." Lee opened the door to a larger room and Tracy saw about a dozen women working at individual desks. Several of them she recognized as having served as counselors during the broadcast; now they were all engaged in the same activity, opening mail. Nor was she surprised to see that Magda Sanderson, much more sedately dressed this morning than she'd been at the airport last night, seemed to be in charge.

As each envelope was ripped open with a letter opener, the check inside was smoothed out under a paperweight on the top of each desk. Money and bills were stored beside the checks. If the envelopes contained a note, the opener read it quickly, then placed it in one of several piles. The smallest pile of all was at one side.

"Not many people see this part of the operation," Lee told Tracy. "In fact, the only time money is mentioned on the Club broadcast is during the twice-a-year telethons, or, as Alex did this morning, capitalizing on Tim's White House invitation. Everybody works around the clock for twenty-four hours during the telethons but they generate a lot of new members for the Logos Club and the mail pickup always continues to be very high for several weeks afterward. The same is true after Tim's weekend evangelistic crusades like the one we're getting ready for in Asheville, a few weeks from now."

"Why do the letter openers separate just a few from the rest?"

"Those are for Tim or Alex to read." They were passing Magda Sanderson's desk, and Lee picked out a letter from the special file.

"May I show Miss Ravenal a sample?" he asked.

"Certainly." The supervisor was the soul of courtesy—and decorum.

"Dear Brother Tim," he read, "I listen to your broadcast every morning and just seeing and hearing you gives me the strength to go through the day. My husband is a good man but a heavy drinker and sometimes beats me because I refuse to sleep with him when he's drunk. If my husband was only like you, I would be happy in my marriage but every morning I wake up hating to face what the night may bring when he comes home from work drunk. I've tried to get him to watch you on television but he says evangelists are bloodsuckers preying on people's fears of Hell and the Devil.

"I know it's the Devil that makes my husband drink and beat me and I've tried to talk to him about throwing out the Evil One, but with no success. One day, I'm sure he will kill me in a drunken rage without knowing what he is doing. Then, perhaps the shock of finding me dead and cold in the bed will make him change his ways. If so, my death will not have been in vain.

"I'm enclosing a ten-dollar bill I saved from the food money to help your work in Jesus' name. Pray for me, please, dear

Brother Tim. Ask the Lord to answer my prayers by granting
that my death will make my husband into a new man.

> Yours in Christ,
> Delores Mirada"

"That's terrible!" Tracy cried.

"We get lots of letters like that one," Magda Sanderson
commented. "Only the most urgent ones are kept for Brother
Tim and Reverend Porcher."

"Will they answer her?" Tracy asked.

"Every letter gets at least a Xeroxed response," said the counselor. "Sometimes Brother Tim speaks directly to someone like
Delores Mirada on a later broadcast, referring her to a counselor near where she lives." Reaching into a wastebasket, she
pulled out an envelope with a foreign stamp. "But how can
you help someone in Recife, Brazil, except by a direct appeal
on television?"

"Even then, I don't imagine you can reach very many,"
Tracy commented.

"The Scriptures list only a few people Jesus helped by healing their bodies, but we know his words did bring comfort to
many souls and show them the way to eternal life. Brother
Tim's listeners write from all over the world to let him know
he has touched their hearts."

Tracy looked around at the long room and the piles of
money and checks on the desks. "Is it like this every day?"

"Five days a week. We have to put on extra people to open
the mail after a telethon."

"How much comes in?" she asked, but Magda Sanderson
shook her head. "I don't know."

As they moved away, Lee said in a lowered tone: "Last year
the budget was about fifty million dollars. If we had full use of
a satellite for broadcasting outside the country, Neeley thinks it
could rise to sixty-five million."

"No wonder you've got closed-circuit TV like a bank." Tracy
nodded toward one of the two small cameras that fanned the
room endlessly.

"Hal Baldwin, our business manager, had them put in a few
years ago, after the mail room was robbed."

"Didn't the letter openers mind?"

"They did at first but they soon got used to them. The monitor is in Hal Baldwin's office so he can alert the police at the first sign of trouble."

They had reached the end of the room and Lee opened the door leading to another, where banks of typewriters were competing with the roar of an offset printing press in the far corner.

"Part of the budget goes here to print the magazine that goes to all Logos Club members and the special material sent out all over the country and even abroad."

"What do you mean by special material?"

"From time to time, the Center buys a new mailing list—all TV evangelists do. Then they send out a special invitation to people to join the Club and pledge to pay a minimum amount each month."

"It's sort of breathtaking," Tracy admitted.

"Not very much like a Galilean walking beside the lake and talking to people he met," Lee agreed. "But you can see why it costs so much to operate something like the Gospel Broadcast Center."

"And all built around one man."

"The Christian religion is built around one man, but the evangelical movement has a lot more than one. As Billy Graham once said, competition for the 'evangelical dollar' is getting hotter all the time."

"Who are the leaders?"

Lee shrugged. "Depends on your point of reference. Using money taken in as a standard, I suppose Pat Robertson's '700 Club' on the Christian Broadcasting Network or perhaps Oral Roberts is probably the leader. Jim Bakker and his 'PTL' program are running almost neck and neck, with Billy Graham probably in third place."

"What about the number of real converts?"

"Unfortunately, there's no way to figure that number," he confessed. "Only a small percentage of those who respond to the invitation at the end of evangelical sermons eventually appear in the churches of the area and become members. As far as the 'Electric Church' is concerned, less than one in every hundred church members say they were converted by TV religious programs."

"Then why spend so much money—even part of a family's food allowance like Delores Mirada's—on these programs?"

"I've talked with Tim and Neeley about that. They think the main appeal of the Logos Club and other programs of the gospel network is to millions of people groping for help with personal problems. They don't find what they're looking for in their churches, or in popular psychology either, but thousands of letters and telephone calls asking for counseling prove that they do respond to programs like the Logos Club."

"Young people, too? I haven't seen many in the studio audiences."

"No, but the Club membership list is younger than is true of most TV evangelism programs. We think that's because Tim's preaching is low-key and, of course, there's the music. Actually, I'm not at all certain the main reason why this kind of evangelism appears to be successful isn't because it appeals to the fear of death that assails everyone as they grow older. When Tim tells them Jesus is waiting in the wings, so to speak, to save them, they grasp at what seems to be the only hope."

Tracy shivered. "Do you really believe that?"

"I don't know what I believe. That's why I enrolled in the Divinity School here at Weston after I graduated in music."

"Are you finding an answer there?"

Lee shook his head. "No—and I'm not too sure anyone else is either. The professors spend a lot of time arguing over matters of doctrine, or such things as how to get along with your board of trustees, deacons or whatever." He looked at his watch. "We'd better get going if you're to get any lunch before your afternoon class. Shall I pick you up at six forty-five tonight for the rehearsal?"

"I'll be ready," she said. "At the beginning of the year, I rented a practice room in the Music Department for the semester. If you can give me a list of what the Troubadours will be singing tonight, I'll try to run over some of the songs before dinner."

"Good." On a notepad Lee quickly scribbled the titles of a list of songs. "You'll find these among the records and the sheet music I gave you," he told her. "I'm glad you're interested enough to do that much extra."

Tracy Ravenal grimaced. "It's more like not wanting to make mistakes in the midst of one of your fine production numbers."

Chapter Seven

THE REHEARSAL WENT SMOOTHLY, WITH TRACY SINGING BESIDE Alice Turner. Several times, as Lee had instructed Alice, she remained silent. Each time Tracy's clear soprano kept the beat, the words going on as effectively as if she'd been doing it for a long time.

"You deserve an award for tonight," Lee told her as they were leaving the Center. "Name it."

"Singing always makes me hungry."

"I heard that," said Neeley Douglas, who had just come out the back door of the Center behind them. "And I'm sure I've got the answer to that yearning."

They stopped until she caught up with them.

"Tim and I were with Aggie at the hospital all afternoon," she said. "Thank you for your flowers, Tracy."

"Is there any change?" Tracy asked, but Neeley shook her head.

"The spinal-fluid pressure was higher this morning so they drew some off to relieve it. The fluid showed some increased protein, suggesting, according to Dr. Thorpe, the pediatric neurologist who's in charge, that the preliminary diagnosis of viral encephalitis is probably correct."

"Could we see her?" Lee asked.

"They've limited visitors to Tim and myself, since she's in isolation. All we can do now is pray; no known drug attacks the virus. Tim's at home working on the sermon for our Asheville crusade weekend after next," Neeley continued. "I've got a new young woman to be mesmerized by Tim's charm and personality."

"But he doesn't—"

"Turn it on to impress people? No. It's just part of his whole soul and being. That's what makes him the great man—and even more, the great evangelist—he is. Young women look at Tim and hear him teach love, forgiveness and everything that goes with them in the awareness of Jesus Christ. After that you can hardly blame them for asking themselves: How can I help believing in the power of such a man, when he's the living embodiment of everything Jesus meant, and still means? Besides, he's right there in front of them in person or on the television screen."

"I've seen that myself," Lee agreed.

"Tim is so confident that merely believing and depending upon Jesus will revolutionize the lives of others as it has his—and mine—that people can't help believing with him and loving with him. In the face of that serenity, it's easy for a woman who's looking for an ideal man as a mate—the natural role of womankind whether we admit it or not—to confuse Tim, the man, with Tim, the earthly embodiment of the Son of God. But like the three-dimensional pictures in an old stereopticon, they eventually look at the card and see that they've really been looking at two pictures merged to give the appearance of one."

"What happens then?"

"They wake up—like emerging from a hypnotic trance—and realize that the second Tim, the one on the TV screen, is unattainable by any other human." For a moment her voice sobered as she added, "It can be quite a shock; I know it was for me. I'm just thankful that I've got both of them for my own, but I still know I can never really own the second one entirely. He belongs to the whole world the same way Jesus did—and still does."

By the time Tim and Tracy returned from the tour of the house, Neeley and Lee had set the coffee table before the sofa facing the glass wall of the enormous living room looking out upon the lake. As Neeley was pouring coffee, a large speedboat appeared on the lake, its green and red running lights giving the appearance of an apparition as it raced across their field of

chocolate cake in the cakebox, and the coffee urn will be bubbling. If you don't have any other plans, why don't you stop by for a *Kaffeeklatsch?*"

Lee gave Tracy a questioning glance. When she nodded, he said, "We were on our way for waffles and coffee but your suggestion's a lot more interesting."

The home the Center provided for its president and executive director stood on a crag overlooking the lake, about equally distant from the campus of Weston University and the Center itself. A rambling structure of native stone built on several levels, it had been designed to merge with the landscape and create the illusion of being part of its surroundings.

"How beautiful!" Tracy exclaimed as they walked down a curving set of stone steps from the upper-level parking area to the entrance. "You even have a waterfall, don't you? I can hear it."

"Two of 'em," said Neeley. "There's a spring at the top of the crag, so the architect diverted the water to flow around either side of the house, making a waterfall at each level. You don't realize how lovely the sound of falling water can be until you hear it from inside the house and see it through the glass doors and windows."

"I can vouch for that," said Lee.

"Tim was pastor of a church in Lee's hometown of Airmont in northern West Virginia," Neeley continued. "It's less than a hundred miles from Fallingwater in southwestern Pennsylvania, where Frank Lloyd Wright built the most beautiful house you ever saw."

"I've been there," said Tracy.

"Then you know how really lovely it is," said Neeley. "Tim and I loved Fallingwater so much that, when the trustees of the Gospel Broadcast Foundation insisted we needed a home larger than the shack we'd been living in since we first started broadcasting, we asked the architect to include as much of the beauty of Fallingwater as he could. He even added a hidden sauna and pool on the ground level. Tim likes it but the spring water is always cold and the idea of parboiling myself with steam and then jumping naked into a pool of cold water gives me goose bumps."

They entered a vaulted living room extending across the entire width of the house, except for about twelve of its fifty feet at one end, which had been cut off to form a small, intimate study. There they could see Tim Douglas stretched out in a Lazy Boy rocker with a book in his lap.

"He always pretends to be thinking when he's in the study at night, but that rocker is better than a sleeping pill," said Neeley. "He's usually snoring before he gets his legs stretched out."

"Maybe we shouldn't—" Tracy started to protest but Neeley laughed. "I've got to wake him to get him to bed anyway. Then he'll want food, even if it's only milk and crackers."

Raising her voice, she added, "Darling! We've got company! Wake up!"

Tim Douglas swung the chair's foot support down and stood up, rubbing his eyes a little sheepishly. "I was reading some heavy stuff and must have dropped off," he said, coming across the room to greet his guests. "Welcome to our humble abode, Miss Ravenal."

"Please, it's Tracy."

"Of course. We're all working together in the service of the Lord, aren't we? Glad to have you aboard, Tracy. You too, Lee."

"I lured them here instead of some romantic hideaway with the promise of chocolate cake and coffee." Neeley was taking off her jacket. "Why don't you show Tracy the rest of the house, Tim, while Lee helps me in the kitchen?"

"Neeley and I are convinced that God led us here because it's an ideal spot for our own work," Lee heard Tim saying as he and Tracy disappeared down the stairway, carved from the original stone of the cliff, to the floor below, where the bedrooms and the sauna and pool were located.

II

"I'm afraid our coming in—even with the temptation of chocolate cake and coffee—was an imposition on Tim," said Lee as

he lifted a metal cakebox down from its place on top of the refrigerator and opened it. "That Chicago and Washington trip must have worn him out."

"Don't feel guilty about coming out tonight," said Neeley. "Nothing charges Tim's battery like talking to a beautiful young girl, and Tracy is all of that. She looks older than the average college freshman, though."

"She's twenty-three," said Lee. "Her first two years were spent near her home at a community college that has a fine music program. She wasn't sure she wanted to go into music, she tells me, so she spent a year in France and Switzerland before coming back to enroll at Weston."

"That accounts for her maturity compared to most undergraduates."

"If Tim hadn't asked me to audition her, I doubt that we'd ever have found as suitable a soprano for the Troubadours—at least not one we could afford to hire."

"She's as good as Alice Turner, isn't she?"

"Better. Her highest notes sound as if they'd been produced by a bell."

Neeley gave him a quick appraising look. "You like her very much, don't you, Lee?"

"More than any girl I've been with," he admitted. "She's got a good brain along with that lovely voice—"

"And body? Surely you haven't missed that."

"Not likely."

"Are your feelings toward her returned—to use a trite phrase?"

"I don't know," Lee admitted candidly. "We enjoy being together and we have the same tastes in most things—particularly music. But sometimes—" He stopped and didn't go on.

Neeley looked up from where she'd been cutting the cake and put a gentle hand on his arm. "Are those the times when she's near Tim?"

"Usually, but that's certainly not his fault."

"Don't be too disturbed, Lee; it's happened before—lots of times. I'm fortunate to be married to one of the most adoration-inspiring men the world has ever known in these times—perhaps second only to Jesus of Nazareth. Tracy isn't the first

vision, only to disappear, borne upon the invisible waters, like some wraith from another planet.

"That reminds me of Lake Lucerne," said Tracy Ravenal. "I spent six months in school there after I left the community college at Lankashire. I lived in a *pension* and after dinner we used to sit on a wide balcony that ran across the lakefront side of the building and watch the boats go by."

"Did you take the cable car to the top of Mount Pilatus overlooking Lucerne?" Tim Douglas asked.

"Oh yes. It was in spring and the edelweiss was in bloom."

"There's a fascinating biblical legend about that mountain accounting for the way it got its name," said Tim. "Did you happen to hear it while you were in Switzerland?"

"Not that I remember."

"According to the legend, after Christ was crucified, Pontius Pilate suffered an emotional breakdown over his guilt at having murdered the Son of God. He became moody and inclined to carry out even worse acts of brutality than before. One day a false prophet arose among the Samaritans north of Jerusalem, claiming to have found the sacred vessels of Moses in a cave at the top of Mount Samaria. He invited the people there for a celebration, and promised to produce the holy vessels, but it turned into a riot instead. When Pontius Pilate sent armed soldiers to stop the celebration and slaughtered many Samaritans, he was ordered to Rome by the Emperor to stand trial."

"For his part in the crucifixion?" Lee asked.

"Oddly enough, no," said Tim. "The crime he was tried for was that of acting too precipitantly in his capacity as procurator of the province by ordering the troops to kill the Samaritans and cause political unrest. According to the legend, which begins to take on a fanciful aspect now, Pilate was tried and sentenced to death, but when his body was thrown into the Tiber, evil spirits threw him back three times."

"As polluted as the Tiber was when we were there last year," Neeley observed, "I'm not a bit surprised."

"One version of the story," Tim continued, "says Pilate's body was then taken to Switzerland and Mount Pilatus to be thrown down and crushed upon the rocks at the edge of Lake Lucerne."

Tracy shuddered. "I remember looking down from the cable car as we were going up. The guide said it was seven thousand feet straight down and it certainly looked that deep."

"Many of those apocryphal legends that weren't included in the canon of the New Testament are fascinating—like the legend of Paul and Thecla many people think really happened," said Tim.

"I like the story better about Mary Magdalene fleeing to Gaul and the Rhone Valley," said Neeley.

"It's fascinating to study legends and how they grow," Tim commented as he scraped the last of the chocolate icing from the plate. "People who deny Christ claim His whole existence was only a legend, but those of us who know Him in our hearts can give that statement the lie."

Lee glanced at his watch. "It's almost eleven!" he exclaimed. "I've still got to make some notes for a class in homiletics tomorrow afternoon."

"And I should prepare for a test in music theory," Tracy added.

"I haven't heard you sing yet, Tracy," said Tim, "but Lee and Neeley tell me you have a beautiful voice. How about 'rendering a selection,' as we used to say back in the West Virginia mountains?"

"I don't have any music—"

Lee had a sudden inspiration. "During your audition you sang 'In the Garden.' I think I remember enough of the score to play it from memory."

"It's Aggie's favorite, too," said Neeley. "I'll tape it with her little recorder, so she can hear it at the hospital. She'll love you for it, Tracy."

"In that case, I suppose I can't refuse," said Tracy. "I'm hoping Aggie and I can become good friends."

Lee moved to the piano while Neeley went to her daughter's room and came back with a small Sony recorder. "Ready when you are," she said.

As Lee's fingers rippled across the keyboard in the introduction, Tracy crossed the room to stand beside the grand piano. And when he completed the opening, her clear, sweet soprano filled the room. At the beginning of the second stanza,

Lee detected a change in Tracy's voice. A softening and a yearning note told him she was no longer just singing the words of a beautiful song but was now pouring out her heart—unconsciously. When he glanced at Neeley, he saw that she, too, had noticed the change but Tim was staring out the window at the darkness, apparently oblivious to everything except the beauty of the music and the words.

Lee's hands drew away from the piano keys as the final notes echoed through the big room and there was a moment of silence. Almost it was as if those who had heard the voice of the lovely young girl were too struck by her sincerity even to react. Then both Neeley and Tim broke into applause, which Lee echoed as he left the piano.

"That was lovely," said Neeley. "I'll take the tape to the hospital with me in the morning so Aggie can listen. She'll love it —and you."

"It was more than lovely," Tim echoed. "Your voice is truly a gift from God, Tracy."

III

Tracy was silent as she and Lee drove back to her dormitory at the university. Realizing the source of her mood, Lee didn't break it with conversation. In front of the building, he got out of the car and went around to open the door for her.

"I've never heard you sing so beautifully," he said as they moved up the graveled walkway to the front door of the dormitory. "You were really singing to Tim, weren't you?"

She turned at his question and he saw that her eyes were bright with what could have been unshed tears. "How did you know that?" she asked, almost in a whisper.

"Because I love you."

"Don't, Lee!" She groped for his hand. "Please don't!"

"I'm afraid it's already beyond my control."

"But I can never—" She broke off, then added brokenly, "I just don't know!"

Her cry of anguish made him want to take her into his arms and comfort her, but he knew better than to make a move that could destroy the confidence and trust she already felt for him. It had not yet, he sensed, ripened into love—and might indeed never do so. But there was a chance that she might, in time, turn what she felt toward Tim into the only channel her conscience would ever let it really take, so long as Neeley was Tim's wife. And that was the unasking love for others a young rabbi from Galilee had given the world nearly two thousand years ago, a love that might force her to eschew marriage entirely—or even lead her to a convent.

Obeying a sudden impulse, he said, as he opened the outer door to Hubbard House for her, "I'm thinking of driving down to Atlanta for the concerts and making a leisurely trip back Sunday. Would you join me?"

"I'd love to," she said. "We can use my new Porsche. I haven't even had time to get used to driving it yet, so you can be the chauffeur."

"You're on," he told her. "Good night."

Chapter Eight

TRACY'S PROGRESS AS LEAD SOPRANO FOR THE GOSPEL TROUBA-dours quickly removed any reservations Lee might have had about her taking Alice Turner's place at the coming concerts in Atlanta over the weekend. On Thursday, as Lee was leaving the Center, he was stopped by the receptionist at the switchboard with the news that he was wanted on the long-distance tele-phone—from Atlanta. Wondering what could have happened this late to throw a hitch into the concerts, he was surprised when the operator added, "It's a Mr. Champion. Jeff Champion."

"Lee, old man! How are you?" Jeff Champion's voice had lost none of its booming cordiality in the years since Lee had seen him, following Jeff's leaving the School of Religion after the second year to join the Jake Schiller evangelistic team in Atlanta.

"Fine, Jeff," said Lee. "What's with you?"

"Same old seven and six. I was watching the Logos Club broadcast this morning. When you announced that the Gospel Troubadours are going to give two concerts in Atlanta this weekend, I decided to call and see whether we couldn't get to-gether while you're here."

"I'd love to, Jeff. How about Saturday afternoon?"

"I've got to be in Macon all day Saturday, making arrange-ments for a healing service Jake's going to hold there next week. When will you be going back to Weston?"

"Sunday morning after breakfast," said Lee. "The Troubadours will be traveling by bus but I'm going back by car, with my new soprano."

"Wonderful," said Jeff. "You and your girl friend can stay over and have dinner with me after Jake's Sunday-morning sermon and healing service. You'll have plenty of time to get back by dark and you'll hear a stem-winding sermon—something you don't get from Brother Tim—plus a healing show that will make your eyes bug out."

"I don't know—"

"What else have you got to do?"

"Nothing, really," Lee admitted.

"Then it's a date. Anybody can tell you where the Temple is, but come early so you can get a seat down front. I'd come to the motel and get you, but I'm always running from pillar to post before and during a Sunday-morning healing service, besides having to handle the music and do a solo myself. Afterward, I'll give you a dinner atop the Regency Hyatt House you'll never forget and we can chew the fat about old times for a while before you have to start back."

"It sounds exciting."

"Fine." Jeff Champion settled the question for him. "Got to run. I'll meet you in the lobby of the Temple after the service."

The chance to talk to Jeff, whom he'd always liked—in spite of the fact that Champion was something of a high roller and a scalawag—might give him an opportunity to discover something about the activities of Jake Schiller, Lee thought. More particularly, he might get a clue to the reason for Schiller's attack upon Tim and the Center at the Chicago convention.

II

"Do you mind if I change the program for the weekend a little?" Lee asked Tracy when he met her in front of the Center after the morning broadcast of the Logos Club was finished. The rest of the Troubadours, plus the enlarged combo, had already been loaded on the Center bus and headed south for Atlanta, roughly 125 miles away.

"Not at all, I love shunpiking."

"Unfortunately, we may not get to do much of that. Jeff Champion called yesterday—"

"The roommate of yours who quit the School of Religion and went to Atlanta?"

"You've got a good memory. Apparently, Jeff's working for Jake Schiller as soloist, music director and general arranger—the sort of thing he would be very good at since he minored in music."

"No better than you," she said as they got into her sleek white Porsche.

"We go at it in different ways, but the result's about the same."

"I doubt that. Your friend sounds like a con artist."

"Maybe not that bad. He saw the Logos Club program Thursday morning, when I made the announcement about the Atlanta concerts, and invited us to attend one of Jake Schiller's healing services."

"What sort of a favor will he be doing us with that?" Tracy asked doubtfully.

"I'm no more enthusiastic about it than you seem to be." Lee swung the Porsche out of University Boulevard paralleling the lakefront and into the busy traffic on the interstate. "It will give us a chance to see Jake in action, though, and maybe get some inkling as to why he's fighting Tim."

"We know that already. Schiller hates Tim because he fired him for stealing."

He looked at her, stretched out in the reclining seat beside him, with her red-gold hair spilled across the headrest and thought she was the most beautiful thing he'd ever seen. "If we're ever married—and you can consider this a proposal," he told her, "I'm never going to try to keep a secret from you."

"You were talking about Jeff Champion." Her tone assured him she had not been at all offended by the proposal—even though she had evaded giving him an answer.

"Jeff wants us to have Sunday dinner with him after the service at that sky-high restaurant atop the Regency Hyatt House. I accepted, pending your approval."

"That's more like it," she said with enthusiasm. "I love the view from there."

"I have to admit I've never been able to afford the place. Is it a deal? We should get back by seven or eight Sunday night."

"Make it twelve," she said. "There must be some place between here and Atlanta respectable enough for two members of the Gospel Troubadours to dine and dance."

III

The concerts at Georgia State were a rousing success, most of all for Tracy. She was called back the first night for a solo, and the second for two.

When the rest of the group left by bus for the return journey to Weston about ten o'clock Sunday morning, Tracy and Lee in the Porsche headed for Jake Schiller's Temple of Our Savior, at an address Lee had gotten from the telephone book.

For all its high-sounding name, the Temple proved to be an unimpressive structure, located in an equally unimpressive neighborhood of small homes and dingy-looking apartment houses near a large textile mill, a typical southern blue-collar neighborhood.

"This could be part of a South Carolina mill town," said Tracy when Lee parked the car next to the sanctuary, obviously a former tobacco warehouse.

"With the typical fundamentalist and conservative—to say nothing of racial—convictions those towns always have," Lee agreed. "Shall we see what it's like inside?"

"I suppose so," she said doubtfully. "At least they're using TV; a microwave antenna is sprouting from the roof."

"Probably aimed at that tall tower you can see a few miles away to the north," said Lee. "Religious TV broadcasting stations often save money by renting tower facilities from large commercial stations. With the height of that tower, Jake can probably be seen and heard halfway to Macon on the south and Charlotte on the north."

Considerable work had been done inside the structure to make the broad expanse of what had been a tobacco selling floor look like a church. A girl at a table in the lobby, formerly the office, was handing out literature on the activities of the Temple, featuring a picture of its pastor on the cover. Another brochure described the GRN, identified as the "Georgia Religious Network" with the nine stations currently carrying the Temple programs indicated on a small map. No usher greeted them, but inside, the former warehouse was already a third full of people. When they sought to take seats near the front, a svelte-looking blonde, who looked out of place in such relatively sleazy surroundings, touched Lee on the shoulder.

"The three front rows are reserved, sir, for the sick who come to be healed," she said.

"I'm sorry," said Lee. "Jeff Champion told us to come early and sit near the front."

"Are you friends of Je—Mr. Champion?"

"We were roommates in college at Weston, before he came to Atlanta."

The blonde looked at him more closely, then smiled. "You're Lee Steadman of the Gospel Troubadours, aren't you? I'm Eileen Stoddard, audience co-ordinator for the Temple."

"Miss Tracy Ravenal, Miss Stoddard," said Lee.

"How lovely you are, my dear." Eileen Stoddard shook hands with Tracy. "I saw you on a Logos Club broadcast last Thursday."

"Jeff saw that one, too," said Lee. "Do you watch all our programs?"

"Not all." The blonde smiled archly. "But we do have to keep track of our competitors, even if we're still a small operation. Do you know Reverend Schiller?"

"No," said Lee. "I came to the Christian Broadcast Center after he left Weston."

"I wish you could meet him," said Miss Stoddard. "Our Lord has endowed him with tremendous vitality. He's doing great work in the Kingdom and keeps us all inspired to do our best, but he's always completely exhausted after one of these healing services and goes home at once. Maybe another time."

"Does Reverend Schiller hold only healing services?" Tracy asked.

"Oh no," said Eileen Stoddard. "Only on Sunday mornings and occasionally on Wednesday evenings."

"Do you televise all of them?" Lee asked.

"Always. They're the most popular programs broadcast on the GRN. I'm sure we'll soon have to change the name of the network, though. We're already reaching into South Carolina and the Florida Panhandle." She smiled. "But I don't have to tell you two anything about religious TV. You're already headliners in the most prosperous show of its kind on the air."

"Have you been in religious television very long?" Tracy asked, then added quickly, "I'm not being personal. It's just that I haven't yet made up my mind whether I want a career in religious music."

"With that lovely voice and your beauty, you can write your own ticket, I'm sure. It's a growing field, too. After all, look what Evie Tornquist has been able to do—along with a lot of others."

"I'll have to think about it," said Tracy.

"There are other rewards than fame or money to this kind of work," the blonde assured her. "Knowing you're in the service of our Lord and will be with Him in His Kingdom are the greatest rewards of all."

"I'm sure of that," Lee agreed.

"I've been in religious TV and healing by faith ever since I was 'born again' and gave up a small-time stage career," said Eileen Stoddard with a wry smile. "I'd had some experience handling the crowds at healing services with the Kathryn Kuhlman organization so, when he started the Atlanta ministry, Reverend Schiller asked me to come with the Temple and GRN. Many of the sick who come to be healed aren't able to look after themselves, so it's my job to place them where they can reach the platform easily and even push the wheelchairs up to the platform at times."

She glanced over the front rows where the seats were beginning to fill up. "Will you excuse me? Unless I place what we call the 'wheelchair brigade' near the ramps to the stage, there's sometimes a jam when the healing service begins."

"Of course," said Lee. "Thank you for showing us around," he called to her retreating back as she teetered up the aisle on spike heels.

"What do you think of her?" he asked Tracy as they walked down to the platform so he could study the arrangement of the ramps that enabled wheelchairs and those too weak to climb steps to reach the healer.

"That hair shade is courtesy of Clairol," said Tracy cryptically. "And that religious fervor is as phony as—as a padded brassiere."

Lee gave her a startled look, then laughed, "Who are you, anyway? Miss Sherlock Holmes?"

"It doesn't take a detective to spot a female phony," she said. "Any woman can do it—by instinct."

"We'd better find seats," he said. "It's nearly ten-thirty and this place is going to be packed."

As they passed the end of the front row, Lee paused beside a fat woman whose grossly overweight body flowed over the edges of the chair she was occupying. "May I ask what your trouble is?" he inquired.

"Whiplash," she said. "A teen-ager high on drugs ran into the back of my car when I stopped for a traffic light. I was in the hospital for three months. The kid didn't have insurance, but a company I was lucky enough to have an accident policy with is still paying benefits."

"If you're healed this morning, would you be willing to give up the insurance payments?" Lee asked.

"Of course I would. What the hell are you hinting at, Buster? That I'm faking?"

"Not at all," Lee assured her hastily. "Not at all."

"Of course, I would have to be certain I'm well," the fat woman added on a pious note. "It would be blaspheming against our Lord not to admit that I was cured by the intervention of Reverend Schiller with Jesus in my behalf. Could I deny credit to my Lord, and Reverend Schiller, for freeing me from the pain that has wracked my body for ten years?"

"I suppose not," Lee admitted as he moved on to another sufferer who was sitting in a wheelchair.

Moments before, this man had been conversing amiably with

another but Lee's inquiry as to his spirits changed his attitude completely.

"I've been afflicted with multiple sclerosis by God in punishment for slaying a man in the heat of anger because he seduced my young wife," the crippled man admitted. "In her innocence she didn't realize what that archdeacon of Satan was doing."

"Have you been treated for your multiple sclerosis?" Lee asked. "I seem to remember that it undergoes spontaneous remissions."

"I've been to a neurologist in a veterans' hospital—three times, in fact," the victim admitted. "Through God's grace, I've been helped, too, though one arm is paralyzed. We who have MS know that we are forever afflicted unless, by repentance and placing our reliance on the broken body of our Lord, we are healed. Fortunately for the unfortunate, like myself, Brother Schiller is a servant of the Lord, a worthy vessel from which salvation has been poured out to many thousands. He will heal me, if he can. But if God decides to punish me even more for the enormity of my sin, I will accept it, knowing all power and all justice are in His hands."

The patient pulled a pack of cigarettes from his pocket. As it came out, a hundred-dollar bill fell into his lap.

"Oh! Oh!" he said, picking it up quickly with the hand he'd said was useless and cramming it back into his pocket. "Can't afford to lose that. Healers don't come through anymore like they did in the old days."

"Do you mean you were paid to come here tonight?" Lee asked.

"Ain't you two with the healing crew?" the sick man demanded suspiciously.

"No," Lee admitted, "but we're very much interested in Brother Schiller's work. Mind telling me what you meant by what you said just now—about healers?"

"Nothin', buddy." The man's voice was suddenly hostile. "Forget it!"

"But you—"

"I said 'forget it!' didn't I? I came here today looking for a miracle and that's all I've got to say."

Quite overcome by the eagerness of the penitents to be

healed and—he admitted freely—by his own doubts, Lee
started to join Tracy in the fourth row, where she was holding
his seat. The voice of Eileen Stoddard, however, stopped him
before he could escape.

"Brother Steadman," she called and now her tone was one of
authority. "I need help to get these people down to the front.
Won't you help me?"

Lee's first instinct—in the face of all these infirmities, plus
Tracy's presence—was to flee but he could not refuse Eileen
Stoddard's plea.

"Where do you want them?" he asked.

"I always instruct the ushers to reserve a row of seats at the
very front for those not in wheelchairs," she said in a busi-
nesslike tone, considerably different from the pious righteousness of her previous conversation. "Those in wheelchairs
go in front so they can more comfortably leave the chair and
seek Reverend Schiller's divinely inspired healing power."

Lee busied himself pushing wheelchairs down the aisles
through which the crowd was now moving into the auditorium
and arranging them in a line across the front of the stage at the
edge of the raised floor. Meanwhile, Eileen Stoddard was guiding those using canes and crutches—most of them surprisingly
agile in spite of their infirmities—into the front row of seats
back of the wheelchairs.

"Thank you, Brother Steadman," said the blonde when the
chairs were filled. "You've been a great help."

"It was a privilege," Lee managed to gasp.

"I've known many musical directors for evangelistic campaigns, but you're by far the most sincere." Her tone was very
warm, almost intimate. "Perhaps at another time we can learn
to know each other better, since we're both working in the service of our Lord."

Lee fled without answering and joined Tracy in the fourth
row.

"Thanks for holding the seat for me," he said.

"I enjoyed watching that blonde maneuver you into doing
her work for her," said Tracy, a little tartly. "She's a smooth
operator."

"I learned one thing." He ignored the note of criticism in

her voice. "Some of these people have been paid to come here today."

"Isn't that standard practice with faith healers?"

"I've heard it but never had the proof before. Watch that man in the wheelchair at the end of the line. Unless I miss my guess, he'll be among the first to go to the platform and be healed."

Tracy smiled, and reached over to squeeze his hand. "Forgive me for sounding like a fishwife. It's encouraging to know you're not quite the dope I was afraid you'd turn out to be where that blonde was concerned."

Promptly a few minutes before ten-thirty a choir of, Lee estimated, some fifty people robed in bright blue, filed into place on the platform behind the pulpit. At the stroke of the half hour, Jeff Champion, robed in black with a purple hood—which he had no right to wear, Lee knew, having left the School of Religion at Weston before receiving his divinity degree—stepped to the pulpit and intoned, in a voice carried by the loudspeaker system to every corner of the large warehouse:

> O come let us sing unto the Lord; let us make a joyful
>   noise to the rock of our salvation.
> Let us come before His presence with thanksgiving, and
>   make a joyful noise unto Him with psalms.
> For the Lord is a great God, and a great King above all
>   gods.
> In His hand are the deep places of the earth; the strength
>   of the hills is His also.
> The sea is His, and He made it; and His hands formed the
>   dry land.
> O come let us worship and bow down; let us kneel before
>   the Lord our maker.

The only musical instrument on the platform was a piano. When it struck the opening chord, Lee was startled to hear Jeff Champion, in a vibrant baritone, sing the opening stanza of "He's Alive!"

"Some friend!" said Tracy *sotto voce* beside him. "Stealing *your song.*"

"Unfortunately, I don't own the copyright, but you have to admit that he has a good voice."

An impassioned prayer, again delivered by Jeff Champion, asked that the saving, and particularly the healing power of Jesus Christ descend upon the assemblage and flow through the hands of its leader to the sick and afflicted gathered there to receive the boon of God's mercy through His Son. Afterward Jeff led the choir and the congregation, which now filled every seat, in a rousing old hymn with a strong evangelistic theme. When the final "Amen" had died away, Jeff Champion turned back to the pulpit from leading the choir and began to read from a chapter in the Book of Revelation. The first words were:

And I saw a great white throne and Him that sat on it, from whose face the earth and the heaven fled away; and there was found no place for them.

And I saw the dead, small and great, stand before God; and the books were opened, and another book was opened, which is the book of life, and the dead were judged out of those things which were written in the books, according to their works.

And the sea gave up the dead which were in it; and death and hell delivered up the dead which were in them, and they were judged every man according to their works.

And death and hell were cast into the lake of fire. This is the second death.

And whosoever was not found written in the book of life was cast into the lake of fire.

"This is going to be the old 'Lake of Fire' sermon," Lee whispered to Tracy as Jeff Champion closed the Bible. "It's an evangelical standby. I used to hear Hard-Shell Baptists preach it back in West Virginia."

"And now it is my honor," Champion's voice boomed from the loudspeakers, "to present a true prince in the Kingdom of Christ here on earth, the founder and guiding spirit of the Temple of Our Savior."

Jake Schiller was a commanding figure. Apparently in his late fifties, he was blackhaired—worn long—and handsome. Well over six feet, black-robed with a purple hood and fringed white stole, he towered even over Jeff Champion, who promptly retired to a seat in front of the choir. A stir of interest went over the audience as the healer strode to the pulpit, an open Bible in his hand.

The sermon that followed was, for Tracy and Lee, mercifully brief, but the audience quite obviously loved it. Microphone in hand, Schiller raged back and forth across the platform. In one breath, he roared damnation to those who did not throw themselves upon the mercy of Jesus Christ for their sins to be washed in His blood shed on Calvary, lest they be cast into the lake of fire. In the next, he pictured the City of Gold in heaven where all must one day appear before the jeweled throne of God, painting in glowing terms the welcome to be received by those washed clean of their sins by the shed blood of God's Own Son as a sacrifice for their sins.

Good deeds, even charity and love for one another, however admirable, would not help, he warned. Only the sacrifice of Jesus on the Cross, freely acknowledged with their sins before all, could bring healing in this earthly existence or eternal life in heaven. Its glories he painted in glowing terms with readings from the Book of Revelation in the Bible he held in his hand, wielding it like a director's baton to make his points.

The sermon finished, Schiller did not, to Lee's surprise, ask for converts to come forward. Instead, Jeff Champion led the choir in a rousing hymn while the collection baskets were passed and the preacher, alternately praying and quoting Scripture, exhorted the congregation to give until it hurt so his work could continue and expand. After the collection, there was a brief pause, while the pulpit was removed to a corner of the platform to give greater room for the healing session. When these preparations were finished, the evangelist stepped forward to the edge of the platform and held up his hands.

"Let us all pray in silence for the healing power of our Lord Jesus Christ to flow to the sick and afflicted through my hands in true miracles this day," he said solemnly.

The audience bowed their heads and remained silent for fully a minute before Schiller announced a resounding "Amen" and stepped back to a position just in front of the choir, leaving a wide space of the platform before him.

"In order that none may doubt the truth of whatever healing power our Lord and Savior will grant to me today," the evangelist announced, "hear these words from the New Testament. They are my commission to heal in the name of Jesus of Nazareth:

"*Then he called his twelve disciples together and gave them power and authority over all devils, and to cure diseases. And he sent them to preach the kingdom of God and to heal the sick. And he said unto them, 'Take nothing for your journey, neither staves, nor script, neither bread, neither money, neither have two coats apiece. And whatsoever house you enter into, there abide and thence depart. And whosoever will not receive you, when ye go out of that city, shake off the very dust from your feet for a testimony against them.'*

"*And they departed and went through the towns preaching the gospel and healing everywhere.*"

Jeff Champion had moved to a position about six feet to the left of the healer. Several well-muscled young men in white suits now took their places strategically located on the platform. Two stood at the foot of the right-hand ramp where they could help those coming forward to be healed, and two others just behind the healer. Their purpose was quickly revealed when the first petitioner, the fat woman with the "whiplash," came before Schiller. Promptly at his touch, she uttered a shrill cry and sagged to the floor, presumably unconscious but not before the two young men behind the healer could catch her and ease her down.

"Leave her alone," Schiller ordered the two assistants. "Don't you see that she has been slain in the Spirit? When she arises, she will be healed."

The wheelchair patient Lee had talked to before the service was the next to come. His chair was pushed by Eileen Stoddard, who turned it over to Jeff Champion at the edge of the platform and went back for another waiting hopeful. When

the chair reached the center stage where the healer was standing, with TV cameras centered upon him from three angles,
the man began to cry, the tears running down his face.

"I have multiple sclerosis," he sobbed. "I have lost use of
one arm and both legs. Ask our Lord to heal me so I may walk
again even if I may not be cured."

Eyes closed, the healer placed his hands on the man's head
and began to pray: "O Christ, you have heard the plea of this
sinner who asks only strength to his muscles. Bring him a cure,
Lord, a cure from the disease that threatens his life."

"I repent!" the sick man sobbed. "Lord, forgive me for I
have sinned."

"Hear him, O Lord! Pour out thy grace in new strength to
his muscles that he might walk again," Schiller exhorted.

"I can feel it!" the patient cried suddenly. "Strength is coming into my arms."

"Move them," Schiller urged, and the alleged victim of a disease known everywhere to have a hopeless prognosis began to
move first his arms and then his legs. Kicking out from the
wheelchair in what seemed to be a sudden surge of strength, he
even stood upon the legs that he had said were paralyzed.

"Take your chair with you as you go," Jeff Champion urged
while the healer continued to pray in a monotone, his eyes
closed and seemingly oblivious to the clamor of the audience
from whom came shouts of "Praise the Lord!" "Hosanna!"
"Hallelujah!" "Blessed Jesus!" and other sounds.

Watching from the fourth row while the choir chanted one
invitational hymn after another in low voices, Lee could almost
believe he was seeing a true series of miracles, particularly when
the healed penitent leaped from his wheelchair and, pushing it
before him, moved across the stage and down the ramp on the
opposite side to the floor of the auditorium.

Tracy, too, he realized, was caught up by the air of excitement pervading the auditorium, when her small hand crept
into his.

Lee wasn't surprised when the bright flare of a strobe flash
revealed the presence of a still photographer recording on color
film the miracles being performed on the stage. But he couldn't
forget how well the man pushing the wheelchair had been able

to use the arm he claimed was paralyzed when the pack of cigarettes and the hundred-dollar bill had fallen out of his pocket before the service began.

A line of people—some dragging one foot and with their mouths on the opposite side twisted by strokes—moved with difficulty as they shuffled along and were helped up the ramp. About a yard away from the healer, Jeff Champion quickly questioned each of them as they moved forward for the laying on of hands and the prayer which, eyes almost closed in what appeared to be a trance, Schiller murmured in a continuous monotone.

One after another, obviously in the grip of an almost ecstatic state of hope, they came sobbing and praying until the hands of the healer touched them. A few fell in a faint, to be caught by the two young men and laid out in a row at the back of the stage. Nobody paid any attention to those "slain in the Spirit," and after a few minutes they usually scrambled to their feet and, looking a little sheepish, made their way down the left-hand ramp and found their seats.

A few underwent a real change when crooked bodies were straightened almost to normal as they stumbled across the stage after Schiller's ministrations. Some, barely able to walk up the ramp, leaped in joy as they left the platform, their bodies fired with the surge of emotional energy. Others, however, pushed along by Jeff Champion's urging voice and not always gently pressing hand, were unchanged and the knowledge that hope had once again failed them was written on pain-racked faces as they left the platform.

Lee saw Jeff seize a boy waiting in the line and thrust him forward, the sensitive microphone attached to Jeff's robe picking up his voice when he asked, "What's your trouble, son?"

"Left ear. Can't hear."

"Move forward," Champion ordered, clapping a hand over the boy's right ear, apparently to shut out any hearing from it. Lee could see, however, that what Champion actually did was cup his hand, letting it act almost as an ear trumpet to the boy's good ear.

"You can hear!" Jeff instructed the boy when the healer's hand touched his head.

"I can hear," the boy answered almost by rote.

"Praise God!"

"Praise God!" the boy repeated.

"I'm healed!"

"I'm healed!" the boy echoed.

"Go and sin no more," Champion counseled the boy as he pushed him forward so another could take his place, while a ripple of applause came from the now thoroughly entranced audience.

"Neat!" Lee said aside to Tracy. "Did you see how Jeff made that hand over the boy's good ear act as an ear trumpet? There's a guy who has a healing service on TV every Sunday morning, I've seen him do just that a hundred times."

The aisles leading to the stage were jammed now with those seeking to be healed while, on the platform, Jeff Champion and the men helping him were hard put to maintain the line across to the center, where Jake Schiller stood. Beyond him the other two were busy catching those, usually women and often fat, who were "slain in the Spirit" at the healing touch.

"It's like a one-ring circus," Tracy whispered to Lee and received an angry look from the woman sitting next to her.

"Brother Schiller is performing miracles!" she snapped. "How dare you call it a circus?"

Chapter Nine

At exactly five minutes to twelve, Jake Schiller turned abruptly and strode into the wings, disappearing from the platform even though a half dozen supplicants were still waiting there. These were quickly urged from the platform by Jeff Champion and his assistants. Meanwhile, Eileen Stoddard was moving from one to another of those "slain in the Spirit" who had not yet recovered consciousness.

Breaking ampules of what appeared to be ammonia under their nostrils to awaken them, she urged them to their feet so they could be led down the ramp from the platform. Many, Lee noted, were still as crippled as when they had come up the other ramp to be healed. Meanwhile, Jeff Champion was leading the choir and the audience in a hymn. That finished, he delivered the benediction, and people started moving out of the now overly warm warehouse.

Taking Tracy's hand to protect her in the crowd, Lee shepherded her to the former office. "Jeff said for us to meet him here," he told her. "Are you okay?"

"Just disgusted! How could anybody call that religion?"

"A lot of people fall for it—probably because they want to. After all, if you've been sick or crippled for a long time, I suppose you can't be blamed for grabbing at straws."

Jeff Champion joined them about fifteen minutes later. He was mopping his brow with a handkerchief, and his shirt collar was limp.

"Give me a minute to wash my face and straighten up a little," he said after Lee introduced him to Tracy. "I was in shirt sleeves under that robe but the TV lights on the platform made it as hot as Hades."

"It was bad enough where we were," said Lee. "Suppose we wait for you in the parking lot where we can turn on the car air conditioner. It's a Porsche."

"Good! I'm driving a Jaguar. You can follow me to the Regency Hyatt House."

At the hotel, they were whisked to the rooftop restaurant in the outside elevator overlooking the central well of the hotel. A deferential head waiter greeted Jeff Champion by name and ushered them to a reserved table near the glass wall from which a half-circle panorama of downtown Atlanta lay before their eyes.

"Quite a show this morning, wasn't it?" said Champion when the waiter had taken their orders.

"I never saw anything like it," Tracy admitted. "Are the services like that all the time?"

"The healing sessions are. By the way, Eileen warned me that she thought you spotted some of the shills, Lee."

"Shills?" Tracy asked.

"It's an old carnival term," Jeff explained. "The barker in a skin game lets somebody in the crowd win, to bring in the suckers."

"Oh!" she said, obviously startled by his frankness. "And you make no bones about admitting it?"

"Everybody in the field does it." Champion shrugged. "Why should we be different?"

"That fellow with multiple sclerosis who was second on the platform," said Lee. "A hundred-dollar bill fell out of his shirt pocket while I was talking to him."

"His price went up this time; we used to get him for seventy-five," said Jeff. "But when people see him pushing that wheelchair down the ramp after Jake gives him the healing touch, he's worth every nickel of it."

"Does he really have multiple sclerosis?" Lee asked.

"Oh yes. Leo has had it for years; some mornings he can't even walk. Whenever we use him, he takes a shot of cortico-

Jeff Champion chuckled. "With Caleb Ravenal for a father and the family millions in prosperous textile mills, you've got a perfect right to be anything you please—besides being beautiful enough to have your own way wherever you are."

"The brochure we were given when we came in said the GRN is growing steadily," Lee changed the subject. "Is that just propaganda?"

"Not quite, but almost," Jeff Champion admitted. "When Jake first came to Atlanta, he had to start low and small. The warehouse was the only building big enough to hold the kind of congregations he wanted to draw but the locale is strictly lower-middle and blue-collar. He's had to gear his sermons to the intelligence and cultural levels of the congregation and that's quite different from what you'll hear preached in Druid Hills."

"You can say that again," Tracy interrupted.

"Of course, we would much rather draw a broader-based clientele," Jeff Champion admitted, "something nearer the retired professional and upper-middle-class group that make up the bulk of your Logos Club membership. I can tell you one thing, though: Jake would do a far more thorough job of milking that mailing list of yours than the Broadcast Center organization has been doing."

"Fortunately, I'm not concerned about that end of it," said Lee. "It's all I can do to keep up with my studies while handling programming and directing the Gospel Troubadours."

"I heard you both singing on the Club program when I watched last Thursday," said Jeff Champion. "Have you and Miss Ravenal considered going in for duets? You're both very, very good individually, and as a team you'd be sensational."

Lee glanced at Tracy. "Tracy and I have not discussed it but I like the idea."

"Duos and trios do very well in the gospel-rock field," said Jeff. "Even conservative TV programs like Robert Schuller's 'Hour of Power' use them occasionally."

"It's something to think about but that's up to Tracy," said Lee. "Maybe we'll try one in a week or two, though—just for size."

steroid ahead of time to give him the strength he needs to go through his act."

"The fat woman with the whiplash who went first," said Lee. "Is she a shill, too?"

"One of the best! The sight of Phoebe being slain in the Spirit is enough to bring the marks down the aisle in droves. At first it was pretty hard on the catchers; you couldn't help seeing them standing behind Jake to ease the women who faint to the floor. Phoebe soon learned how to fall, though. Maybe you noticed that she sort of oozes down into a puddle."

Tracy couldn't help laughing, then sobered. "All of this is really like a theatrical performance to you, isn't it?"

Even Jeff Champion was momentarily taken aback by the note of contempt in her voice, but recovered quickly. "Showmanship is part of it, yes, but that isn't the whole thing by any means."

"There's money, too, I'm sure."

"Nor that either. Religious faith is one of the strongest of human emotions, even as strong as the sexual drive, and God knows that's universal. Maybe we don't really perform miracles; even Jake doesn't claim to heal anyone personally. But if he can stimulate a deep enough religious faith in a sick person, there's a good chance that his illness will be helped, if not cured."

"How can you be sure of that?" Tracy asked.

"About 80 per cent of human ills are psychosomatic in origin or strongly influenced by emotions, Miss Ravenal. By easing emotional tension with religious conviction, you're certain to help about three out of every four people who come to healers seeking a cure. It's as simple as that." He smiled. "Satisfied that I'm not a complete fake?"

"I guess so," she admitted. "But I still don't like your methods."

"I don't particularly like them myself, but they work. And after all, our shills aren't much different from the church people who, knowing others will follow, stand ready to come forward first when Billy Graham gives the invitation."

"I didn't know that either," Tracy admitted wryly. "I suppose you think I'm unbelievably naïve."

"It's okay with me," said Tracy. "You're the boss where the Troubadours are concerned."

Lee looked at his watch and was surprised to see that it was almost three o'clock. "We'd better be going," he said. "It's a long drive back to Weston."

"I'd like to return to the School of Religion someday and get my degree in theology," Jeff confessed, "but I'm much too busy promoting Jake Schiller's GRN right now to tackle anything else. Besides," he said with a satisfied smile, "how many young preachers can afford to drive a Jaguar?"

"Not me," said Lee. "The Porsche belongs to Tracy."

"Thank you for a very interesting morning and a lovely Sunday dinner," Tracy told Champion graciously as their cars were being brought from the hotel parking lot. "I never thought, when I transferred to Weston, that I'd get into anything like this gospel-music field, but it *is* exciting."

"Look into the possibilities of becoming a team," Jeff Champion urged them. "I've an instinct for things like this and two clean-cut, obviously sincere young people like you could easily become the stars of the gospel-rock circuit. You might even outdraw Pat and Debby."

II

Once out of Atlanta, Lee set the cruise control on the Porsche to the legal fifty-five miles per hour for the hundred-odd miles back to Weston. Tracy promptly went to sleep with her head on Lee's shoulder and, putting his arm around her, he easily guided the car along the four-lane highway. She woke up, hungry, about fifty miles from Weston and they stopped at a Howard Johnson's for giant sundaes before continuing on home.

"Want to go in?" Lee asked when they reached Hubbard House, "Or can you handle some waffles at Mabel's?"

"No more food," she said. "I'm going upstairs, crawl into

bed, and sleep till it's time to go to the Center in the morning. By the way, what are we singing?"

"I don't have the least idea. Want to try one of those duets Jeff Champion recommended sometime this week?"

"If you do. Good night, Lee." Then she sat up straight. "How are you going to get home?"

"After this weekend and all the food I've put away, I'm going to run. See you at the Center tomorrow morning."

"Tomorrow morning," she said and reached up on tiptoes to kiss him with a feather-light touch of her lips that threatened momentarily to become something more—until she gently pushed him away. "Not just yet, Lee. Some other time, maybe."

"Some other time, *positively*," he told her. "Okay?"

"Okay—maybe," she called back when she was halfway up the walk to the front door of her dormitory.

Lee jogged the mile to his apartment, and an extra half mile along the lakefront, without even feeling his feet touch the ground. He was toweling himself after a shower when the telephone rang. Wrapping the towel around himself, he went to answer it.

"Lee?" It was Neeley. "I called to ask how the concerts went."

"Perfect," he said. "They kept calling Tracy back for encores. We drove her new Porsche down to Atlanta and back."

"I know. The rest of the Troubadours came in on the bus shortly after noon. I saw them when I was coming home from the hospital."

"How is Aggie? I've been worrying about her ever since I left."

"I'm afraid it's serious, Lee." Neeley's voice was sober. "They did a spinal puncture again today and the pressure was quite high. Dr. Michaels says that indicates a severe virus inflammation of the brain."

"How is Tim taking it?"

"He's confident that God will not let anything happen to her, but I'm afraid my faith isn't as strong as his."

"We'll all pray for her," said Lee. "Can I see you in your office for a few minutes tomorrow after the broadcast?"

"Certainly. Anything wrong?"

"I'm not sure. Tracy and I went to a healing service this morning in Jake Schiller's Temple. Do you remember Jeff Champion?"

"Vaguely. Wasn't he in the seminary with you for a year or two but quit to join Jake in Atlanta?"

"Yes. He's Jake's *factum factotum* now. Tracy and I had dinner with him afterward and I need to talk to someone about the things we saw and heard."

"I'll be the sounding board, darling; you can bounce your troubles off me," Neeley assured him. "I'm used to it after all these wonderful years with Tim. Good night."

"Good night. I won't forget to pray for Aggie."

III

The Monday broadcast was uneventful. Distraught by Aggie's failure to respond, in spite of his prayers and the invitation he'd issued over the air for listeners to pray with him for her recovery, Tim was not his normally ebullient self. Fortunately, the guests were two movie stars who, although fading somewhat in their celluloid careers, were doing well in TV series and could carry the program, with help from Alex. The Troubadours performed perfectly, as usual, and Tracy's solo version of a traditional hymn, "Faith of Our Fathers," plus Lee's rendition of a popular gospel-rock tune as a solo, evoked thunderous applause from the studio audience.

"How about us trying a duet of 'I Come to the Garden Alone'?" Lee asked Tracy while Tim and Alex were speeding the studio audience on its way. "It has plenty of opportunity for harmony."

"All right," she said. "Do you want to rehearse now? I can spare a half hour."

It took them less than a half hour to work out minor questions of harmony. The final version, achieved in no more than twenty minutes of rehearsal, was perfect.

"That's it," said Lee. "I'd go with you back to the university, but I've got to talk to Neeley about yesterday."

"Do you think Schiller is trying to sabotage Tim's work?" she asked. "After all, he did bring those charges in Chicago."

"Neeley knows Jake better than I do. I want to bring her up to date on our weekend and hear what she thinks. If our duet turns out okay tomorrow, I'd like to talk to her about recording it as a demonstration record we can show to some of the recording companies, along with a few of your solos."

"It's not fair to shortchange yourself," she protested.

"Just knowing I was instrumental in your getting a chance at the career you deserve in gospel music will be enough of a reward for me," he assured her. "See you tomorrow morning."

In her office Neeley listened carefully while Lee gave a detailed account of their experience with Jeff Champion and the dramatic healing service he and Tracy had witnessed.

"Jake was always good at that sort of thing," Neeley said when the account was finished. "He wanted Tim to go into it but, with so much charlatanism accepted as part of the healing field, Tim wasn't willing to go along. It was one of the reasons why he broke with Jake, besides the money. If Tim had been convinced that Jake was really sincere in furthering the Kingdom of Jesus Christ on earth, he'd have been willing to forgive him for stealing the money."

"That took a lot of forgiving."

"I'm the most fortunate of women to be married to a man who, as much as any mere human can, personifies most of the qualities Jesus of Nazareth manifested while He was on earth, Lee. It's a hard standard to live up to, when you're a mere human like me, though. Sometimes the burden of protecting him from the 'slings and arrows of outrageous fortune'—as Shakespeare termed it—gets pretty heavy. Right now, too, I'm so worried about Aggie that I'm not quite up to doing my share so I'm going to have to depend on you and others—"

"What can I do?" Lee asked.

"Watch and wait. I'm sure Jake is scheming no good for Tim and the Center, but I don't know what Jake's next move will be, after the Chicago ploy. He couldn't have hoped to bring it off but what worries me is how close he came to doing it. Tim's refusal to subscribe to the hard-line fundamentalist doctrine preached by Jake and most other leaders in the evangelical movement on television is Tim's Achilles' heel. You and I must see that he doesn't get wounded there."

IV

Wednesday morning the week suddenly stopped being uneventful. The gallery was already filled when a hostess ushered in a middle-aged man who was operating a motorized wheelchair. He was accompanied by a slightly younger-looking woman and his legs were stretched out before him on the wheelchair supports, making it a little difficult for him to maneuver the vehicle into a small area set aside for that purpose at the end of the gallery.

The Club program that morning contained nothing unusual, but just as the Troubadours were finishing a song, Lee was startled to hear a loud voice shout: "Brother Tim! I challenge you to heal me in person as you claim to have healed so many thousands over the air."

The speaker, Lee saw when he turned quickly from directing the chorus, was the man in the wheelchair. Before Mike D'Agostino, who was signaling the audience for applause, realized what was happening, the motorized chair moved rapidly up the ramp by which Tim and Alex descended from the stage at the end of each broadcast to speed the guests on their way.

Center stage, Tim had apparently not noticed the wheelchair coming up the ramp until the occupant shouted the challenge. Startled, Mike D'Agostino and Lee both tried to seize the vehicle as it moved past them, and Tim was even forced to jump aside to keep from being bowled over by it. He waved them back, however, and when the chair came to a halt, he reached down to take the hand of the man who had issued the challenge to be healed.

Glancing at the large monitor over the rear projection screen, Lee saw the dramatic picture that was appearing that very moment by satellite transmission upon television screens all over the world, as well as being recorded on videotape—the agitated face of the man in the chair and Tim Douglas reaching down to take his hand.

"What troubles you, my brother?" Tim's voice was as soft as if he were speaking to a child.

"My legs! The arteries are clogged! The doctors say they'll have to amputate!"

Reaching down, the impetuous visitor pulled up the cuffs of his trousers, revealing that his feet and lower legs were bare. Moreover, their color was the whitish pallor of death itself, almost as if they had already been severed from his somewhat stocky torso.

"You claim to have healed thousands! I've heard you read letters from them over the air," the crippled man challenged Tim. "Now heal me before my legs are gone and it's too late!"

The silence in the studio was electric, broken only by the faint whir of the cameras centered upon the dramatic scene at the center of the set, plus the soft click of the Nikon camera wielded by Mike D'Agostino. Mike doubled as public-relations director for the Center, and the still camera always hung from a strap around his neck, ready to record on sharp color film any unusual event that might happen during a broadcast.

"I can promise you nothing, my brother, for I'm only an instrument in the hands of our Lord Jesus." Tim's voice had taken on a new timbre. "Yet, if you believe in Him—"

"My faith is not strong enough to open the arteries of my legs and let the blood flow through." The crippled man was sobbing. "If you ask Jesus to heal me, Brother Tim, I know He will. Only lay your hands upon my body and pray."

"I will do what I can." Kneeling beside the extended leg supports of the wheelchair, Tim touched the pallid skin of the sick man's ankles with hands that were infinitely gentle. "Think of your feet becoming warm while we all pray for you to be healed of your infirmity," he suggested.

As the studio audience and the crew—except the cameramen, whose eyes were fixed on the small viewing screens at the back of their instruments—bowed their heads, Tim began to pray,

softly at first, then in a tone of steadily increasing confidence as
he continued:

"Lord Jesus, I am but your servant. Yet, if it be your will,
pour out your holy compassion upon this man that he may be
healed of his infirmity through your Grace. Give to me and to
him the strength of faith needed to make him whole—"

"My feet! They're getting warm!" A cry of hope, of rising
faith came from the man in the chair. "I think I can feel the
blood flowing through already!"

Lee's eyes were drawn to the large monitor screen, where the
color of the sick man's skin was being faithfully recorded by
Camera One. The powerful lens had been moved in until it
was hardly a foot from the pallid legs, filming a close-up so
large that it filled the monitor screen. Nor could anyone watching doubt the change of tint. A faint pink color was indeed
coming into the skin that, moments before, had been marble
pale from a sharply restrained blood supply. While he watched,
Lee saw the color brighten steadily until the skin reached almost its normal hue.

"A miracle!" screamed a woman from the gallery. "We're
seeing a miracle!"

Others took up the cry, and pandemonium gripped the studio as Tim still knelt beside the wheelchair, his lips moving in
prayer. His face was uplifted now, and suffusing it was a glory
which, Lee thought, must certainly be recorded by the cameras.
Yet he could not take his eyes from the dramatic scene being
enacted before him.

"Oh thank God! Thank you, Brother Tim, and thanks be to
Jesus!"

The man who had been healed pressed the switch control-
ling the supports that had held his legs in a horizontal position,
lowering them almost to the vertical. With Tim's assistance, he
touched first one foot to the floor, then the other. Standing ir-
resolutely for a moment, he hesitated before taking the first
steps, obviously still unable to believe the miracle taking place
in his own body. Then, as confidence returned, he took a few
faltering steps, his stride growing firmer and more sure of itself
with each moment. Followed by the cameras, and reaching out
with one hand to push his chair, the sick man moved across the

stage on ever stronger feet, their skin now pink and almost normal in appearance.

"Thank God! Oh thank God!" The woman who had come into the studio with him sobbed. "He hasn't been able to walk for more than a year!"

Tim embraced the man and helped him back into his wheelchair. As the vehicle moved down the ramp to the floor below, the evangelist stood in the center of the stage, his arms uplifted and tears streaming from his eyes as he cried, "Thank you, Jesus! Thank you for this miracle!"

Lee knew he would never forget that picture of Tim in his moment of greatest ecstasy, while Camera Two dollied in for a close-up of his face. And watching, some instinct told Lee how to bring this moving scene to its most dramatic close.

" 'Praise You Just the Same,' third stanza," he instructed Jim Cates and the chorus.

As the pianist struck the first chord, Lee himself took the opening notes of the stanza: "*And when I think of you upon that tree.*" The Troubadours chimed in on the second line and, together, the group sang the final verse:

> *I know that what you did, you did for me,*
> *And so until my days on earth are finally through,*
> *Wherever I am led I'll follow you.*
> *Jesus, my Jesus,*
> *If I suffer pain,*
> *Help me that I don't complain*
> *But thank you, Lord, and praise you just the same.*
> *I want to thank you Lord and praise you just the same.*
> *Praise Your Holy Name!*
> *Praise Your Holy Name!*
> *Praise Your Holy Name!**

As the last note drifted away, Henry Waterford in the control room switched to the station symbol and that of the network, while Tim fell back upon the sofa, exhausted.

Jerking off his headset with the small microphone attached, Mike D'Agostino handed it to Lee. "The last half hour is the tape of Tim's sermon from the National Cathedral," he said hurriedly. "Take care of it and the closing song, while I get some background on that guy in the wheelchair before he can get away. I'll develop this film, too, and if we can get some color plates made up in time for the newspapers, we might manage to make the last afternoon editions."

At the end of the first hour of broadcast, Tracy Ravenal came down from the step on which she had been standing with the rest of the Troubadours, her eyes shining with excitement.

"Wasn't he wonderful?" she cried.

Lee didn't need to ask who she meant. Her eyes were on Tim, who was now getting up from the sofa where he had fallen, exhausted, when the patient in the wheelchair left the stage. From the control room, Henry Waterford cued in the videotape of the sermon Tim had given at the National Cathedral in Washington, edited to fit exactly the final thirty minutes of the ninety-minute program.

On the large rear projection screen, the picture of the Cathedral appeared as the minister was introducing Tim Douglas from the pulpit. Accustomed to seeing Tim on the regular Club programs in a business suit or in slacks and sport shirt, with or without a jacket, the picture of him in a black robe startled Lee.

A murmur of amazement ran through the still-excited gallery, too, because Tim appeared to be much taller there than he did on the stage. His voice also took on a new quality when he spoke from the lofty pulpit of the Cathedral.

Tim's first words seized the attention of the visitors and even the idle camera crews sitting on the steps at the edge of the stage waiting to be cued by Lee for the closing announcements and the final musical number. His text was from the beautiful thirteenth chapter of Paul's First Epistle to the Corinthians.

Lee had never heard Tim sound more convincing, as he expounded the love of Christ for those who followed Him as an example of how those same followers should love each other. Listening, he found himself fantasizing that he was actually hearing Paul himself in a church somewhere on a Grecian isle, almost two thousand years ago. Caught up with the beauty of the sermon, Lee was startled when Henry Waterford's voice in the headset he'd automatically put on when Mike D'Agostino handed it to him, brought his attention back to the present.

"Get the Troubadours ready for the final number, Lee," said Waterford. "Tim has only about three more minutes."

The camera crews also wore telephone headsets and, hearing Waterford's instructions, were scrambling to their feet. At a signal from Lee, the singing group, who had been sitting on the steps where they stood during their musical numbers in the regular program, began to arrange themselves there once again, the girls straightening up their dresses and the boys shaking the wrinkles out of trousers and jackets.

Removing the headset, since he would be on camera during the final number, Lee placed it on the piano and took his customary place behind Jim Cates. On the screen, Tim was speaking the final words of his sermon and, when he bowed his head for the closing prayer, Lee nodded to Jim Cates to be ready. As the prayer ended, the pianist struck the first note of the song, and the rhythm guitars boomed out, with the Troubadours sounding as one the opening words of: "Now Is the Time."

The chorus sang the final line, and as the music died away, Camera Three centered on Alex Porcher, who had stepped from the wings onto the stage. His face appeared on the monitor screen as he closed the program with a brief prayer, then was replaced by the station emblem.

"Henry says Tim wants you and the rest of the executive staff in his office right away, Lee," the girl in jeans and T-shirt who had been operating Camera One said as Alex stepped down the ramp, up which the man who had been healed had sent his wheelchair upon the stage, and began to shake hands with the departing visitors.

"What's up?"

"I don't know. That's all he said."

Tracy was leaving the stage for the dressing rooms with the other girls to change into street wear. Her eyes were still aglow with the light that had been in them when she had spoken to Lee after the healing.

"I was going to the university with you," Lee told her, "but Tim has ordered a staff meeting immediately in his office."

"To discuss the healing?"

"I don't know."

"If you learn anything about it, call me tonight, please," she said eagerly. "I've never seen a miracle before, and I can still hardly believe I saw it."

"You saw it and so did I, but don't ask me how it happened."

"I know how it happened! It was Jesus, Lee! Jesus in the person of Tim himself! What other explanation could there be?"

She was gone, hurrying after the others, leaving Lee with the memory of how her face had been transfigured with conviction —plus another emotion he didn't even want to admit he had seen.

Chapter Ten

WHEN TIM DOUGLAS CAME INTO THE CHAPEL WHERE THE DAILY prayer service was held for all the staff who could attend, the energy that had seemingly been drained out of him at the end of the healing session had now been restored. His face was eager, his manner determined as he addressed the dozen or more people who made up what was known as the executive staff.

"After this morning, I'm considering putting healing sessions into the Club programs," he announced. "Since we've always worked together, I want your advice on how it can best be done."

"Not before the cameras, as it was just now." Neeley was the only one who dared to offer an immediate objection.

"Why not?" Tim asked.

"Imagine what it would have looked like on a million TV screens if nothing had happened after that man—I still don't know his name."

"It's Newton, Oliver Newton," said Tim impatiently. "Mike caught him before he could leave the studio and got a background story. He's typing it up now while prints are being made from the still shots he took in the studio for the newspapers."

"Newton, then," said Neeley. "I shudder to think of the marble-pale skin on his legs staying that way with the cameras right on it in close-ups."

"But it didn't stay! Jesus healed him! I felt the power flowing through my hands."

"Can you always be sure it will happen that way, though?" Neeley insisted. "No healer I know of even pretends to heal everyone. In a crowd people notice only the ones who appear to be healed, but with the camera on the disease itself—"

"Neeley's right, Tim." Henry Waterford came to her support. "I was watching the monitors in the control room and the color changes in that man's skin, as the blood started flowing through his arteries, was the most amazing thing I ever saw."

"Miracles are always amazing," said Tim, impatiently. "If they weren't, they wouldn't be miracles."

"Granted that you could always succeed, Tim—and only Jesus ever did that in the history of the world," said Alex Porcher. "When people with infirmities see the tape of today's broadcast on their television sets—and a lot of them have already seen it live—you're going to be inundated with requests. Who's going to choose the subjects?"

"You can't risk turning the Logos Club, the crowning accomplishment of your life so far, into a medicine show, Tim," Henry Waterford added.

"Don't make a decision like this on impulse," Neeley pleaded with her husband. "What happened today was a real miracle; we all saw it so we know that. Trying to repeat that miracle on demand could turn something fine like the Logos Club into a shambles. You heal thousands every year over the air; let's keep it that way."

"But the gift!" Tim protested. "I can't throw away a gift of healing that comes only from God, just because I might not succeed every time."

Lee spoke for the first time. "Last Sunday I watched a healing service in Atlanta, Tim—at Jake Schiller's Temple—and, believe me, it was a farce. If you go into faith healing on a large scale, you're likely to be tarred with the same brush—"

"I think you'd better explain what you mean, Lee," Tim's voice was suddenly stern.

Lee gave a quick synopsis of what he and Tracy had seen in Atlanta, sparing no detail. When he finished, there was silence in the room, until Alex said: "What Lee's been describing is a typical faith-healing service, Tim. I was with an organization like that once and I know all the tricks."

"But I'd never use them," Tim protested. "You all know that."

"We do, but the public doesn't," said Neeley. "And that means they would put you on the same level as the faith healers who make up the lowest form of television evangelism."

Lee had a sudden inspiration. "Granted that the Lord has given you a healing power, Tim," he said, "your first duty is to use it to help Aggie."

"Lee's right." Neeley picked up the idea quickly. "If your healing touch can cure Aggie, nobody could possibly need any more proof that you possess it. Then we'll plan how you can use it best."

"Thank you for the suggestion, Lee," said Tim. "How could I have failed to think of my own child? I'll go to Aggie immediately. Pray all of you, please, that I may bring healing power to her as I just did to Oliver Newton."

"Meanwhile," said Henry Waterford, "the record of the miracle you just performed is on videotape, and Mike also photographed it. We can send the tapes by cable to the commercial networks along with Mike's story and the pictures to the newspapers at the same time. When the news breaks on the national TV programs this evening, and tomorrow morning in the newspapers, the world will know Christ worked a miracle here today."

II

"It looks like Brother Tim is trying to put the doctors out of business, Reverend," Mabel greeted Lee when he came into the small restaurant for breakfast the next morning, the newspaper he'd just taken from the vending rack outside still unopened.

"Did we make the headlines?"

"Front page, second section. With pictures you wouldn't believe."

"I would; I saw it happen," he said as she put a steaming cup of coffee on the countertop before him. "Give me the usual, please. I want to read the story."

The headline spread across the top of the page said: "BROTHER TIM DOUGLAS PERFORMS MIRACLE— ON CAMERA." Beneath it was the subtitle: "TV Evangelist Saves Man from Double Amputation."

The story itself wasn't very long. First came a brief background on Oliver Newton, telling of the gradual crippling of his legs as the arteries were slowly closed by the disease process. Then his desperate decision to challenge Tim Douglas during one of the Logos Club broadcasts was described and the subsequent series of miraculous events.

The story had been telephoned in by Mike D'Agostino immediately after the healing had occurred, but what made it so spectacular were the still pictures Mike had taken. The shots in color had printed up beautifully in the newspaper, showing the startling contrast between the pallor of Newton's skin before the miracle and the pink color of returning circulation as it was occurring.

"Don't be surprised if I show up at the Center one morning with the finest crop of varicose veins you ever saw," said Mabel, as she put a large platter of eggs, sausage, toast and jam down before Lee. "How's your love life, by the way?"

"Not so good. I've got strong competition."

"I'll have to take that young lady aside and give her a briefing on what she'll lose if she doesn't grab you."

Lee had almost finished eating breakfast and was reading the story on Oliver Newton a second time when the pay telephone on the wall of the restaurant rang and Mabel answered it. "Sure, Dr. Michaels," Lee heard her say. "He's right here. I'll get him."

"For you, Reverend," she called to Lee. "Your friend, Dr. Michaels."

"Thought I might find you there when nobody answered at your apartment, Lee," said Art. "Sounds like you had a lot of excitement at the Logos Club yesterday."

"It was while it lasted. How's Aggie Douglas?"

"I just stopped by her room before starting rounds. The picture's not good, Lee. She's in a pretty deep coma now."

"Have you made the diagnosis?"

"I'm not in charge of her, but I talked to Jed Thorpe, the pediatric neurologist who is. He's pretty sure it's viral encephalitis and, with those things, about all you can do is give supportive treatment and wait for the outcome. What I called about was to ask whether you could come by my laboratory this afternoon around five. It's in the psychiatry wing of the hospital."

"Sure. What have you got to show me?"

"I might just perform a miracle, so keep it quiet. See you at five."

III

Lee caught Tracy Ravenal as she was leaving the Center that morning after the daily broadcast of the Logos Club.

"How would you like to go on a picnic with me Sunday?" he asked.

"I'd love it. Where will we go?"

"Tim has an outboard with a half cabin, in case of rain. He lets me have it when I want it and we could take a run down to the dam on the lake about five miles south of here. If the sun's shining, the water will be much warmer there than it is up here nearer the source, so we might get in a swim or do some water-skiing. Be sure to bring a bathing suit; you can change in the head."

"What about food?"

"No problem. I'll take my plastic cooler over to Mabel Saturday night; she puts up the best picnic lunches you ever ate. Shall I pick you up at the dormitory around nine o'clock? We can have breakfast at the restaurant and get the lunch before we go down to the dock where the boat is moored."

"Do you always think of everything?"

"Everything I can—especially where you're concerned. All you'll have to do Sunday is be ready about nine."

When Lee finished making up the order for sheet music for next month's programs, he took it down the hall to the large office where Hal Graham managed the burgeoning financial affairs of the Broadcast Center. Hal was short and pudgy, where Lee was tall and athletic, but the two had become fast friends soon after Lee joined the Center staff. Hal gave the requisition only a glance, then stamped his approval on it so it could be passed on to the purchasing agent.

"I was about to have a cup of coffee," he said. "Care to join me?"

"I'd like one."

Hal punched a button on his desk and shortly a secretary appeared with a coffee flask and, anticipating Lee's presence, two cups.

"I need this to wake me up for my first class after lunch." Lee took a drink of the steaming brew. "We had packed houses both nights for the Atlanta concerts, by the way."

"That was a foregone conclusion," said the business manager. "I heard you mention Jake Schiller's healing service at the staff conference yesterday. What was it like?"

"A carnival sideshow, but the audience loved it. Why do you ask?"

"I'm convinced that Jake's cranking up a campaign against Tim and the Center."

"The attack he made on Tim in Chicago at the Evangelical Broadcasters' meeting proves that, doesn't it?"

"It does to me," said Graham, "but I hesitate to speak to Tim and Neeley about it when they're so worried about their daughter. Do you know how she's doing?"

"The outlook still isn't good," said Lee. "Dr. Michaels has been watching her and told me this morning that she's in a coma." He hesitated a moment, then added, "But how could Jake possibly damage Tim and the Center?"

"I've been asking myself the same question," Hal Graham admitted. "I haven't found the answer either but I can see several ways it might happen. Aren't you about to finish your third year at Weston in the School of Religion?"

"Yes."

"What do you think of evangelical theology, the kind Schiller preaches?"

"Frankly, I don't understand it," Lee admitted, "no more

than I can understand how he was able to attack Tim in Chicago and get so many votes."

"I think I do," said Graham. "You see, Tim's not like Pat
Robertson, Jerry Falwell, Jim Bakker and a lot of the other TV
preachers. Even though Tim preaches what some people call
the 'old-time religion,' he doesn't use the Devil, the Second
Coming and a lot of other shibboleths to scare people into
becoming what they call 'born again.'"

"I know that," Lee agreed. "If Tim was a 'hell, fire and damnation—world ends tomorrow' preacher, he would never have
been invited to preach for the President and his family in the
National Cathedral."

"Or in the crusade he's been invited by the Asheville Ministerial Association to stage there weekend after next," Graham
agreed.

"Why would other TV evangelists fight him when they're all
in the same business—saving souls?"

"Because Tim bridges the gap between the kind of religion
you and I were raised up in and the kind people like Jake
Schiller preaches," said Graham. "I may be wrong, but I think
the main reason why the other evangelicals hate Tim is because
they sense that, if what might be called conventional ministers
used a little more of the techniques Tim has brought to a peak
in the Logos Club, they might start changing their approach
and eventually overcome the drift away from religion that ex-
ists today."

"And stop the loss of members by the established churches
all over the world." Lee looked at his watch. "I'd better be
going, my class meets at two."

"Just one more thing," said Hal Graham. "Something odd
has been happening for several months now. Money from the
mail collections has been disappearing and neither Neeley nor I
can account for it."

"I imagine the letter openers have been tempted more than
once to slip a bill into their pockets."

"That we could expect, even with the television closed-circuit monitors. But last week five hundred dollars disappeared in
one lump."

"Did you say 'five hundred'?" Lee asked, startled.

"Yes. Why?"

Lee hesitated momentarily, then decided to tell Hal Graham the story about Desire Halliday, which had been troubling him ever since he and Tracy had agreed not to mention it to anyone. When he finished the account, the business manager's expression was troubled.

"Who do you suppose hired the woman to fake a suicide?" he asked.

"Someone who realized it would be bad publicity for the Center when they revealed it but then decided against doing anything about publicizing it when he learned that the hoax had been discovered. Are you going to follow it up?"

Graham shook his head. "We lost nothing from the incident and five hundred isn't going to endanger our budget. My guess is that there's a connection between the incident and the money that's been disappearing, though."

"I agree," said Lee. "But finding the truth is another matter."

"One thing I do know, Lee: You're the best person to ferret out the answer to this mystery."

"Why me?"

"Everybody in the Center trusts you. Besides, with rehearsals at all hours to fit the college classes of the Troubadours, nobody would question your being here at any time of the day or night. If anything underhanded really is going on, you'd have a better chance of discovering the truth than anyone who works on a regular nine-to-five schedule."

"I don't much like the idea of spying."

"Neither do I, but you know how Tim is—he trusts everyone. Neeley's much more practical, but right now she's too worried about Aggie to concern herself about anything else."

Lee hesitated, then decided to tell Graham about what he and Tracy had seen at the airport the night they'd met Tim's plane on his return from Washington.

"I can explain Magda Sanderson's presence on the plane," said Graham when he finished the account. "A seminar on the handling of mail donations was part of the Chicago conference program. The Center paid her expenses."

"I'm glad that's settled."

"She's seen socially with Alex, too, at times," Graham continued.

"I guess I was oversuspicious because Jake Schiller was with them," Lee admitted wryly.

"The airport encounter could have been just a friendly good-by," Hal Graham agreed. "But we'll keep our eyes open just the same and I'll run a computer check on the mail donations. If somebody's really dipping into the till, I want to know about it."

Alex Porcher's office was just across the corridor from Hal Graham's. The door was open and Alex was working at his desk, but at the sound of the business manager's door closing, the evangelist looked up.

"Got time for me to talk to you about something, Lee?" he called.

"If it doesn't take too long. My afternoon class is at two."

"I won't keep you," said the handsome, black-haired evangelist. "Incidentally, congratulations on finding such an excellent replacement for Alice Turner. This morning was the first time I'd heard Miss Ravenal sing. Her voice is as lovely as she is."

"No doubt about that, but she still got the job purely on merit, not because of her father."

"I'm sure of that, knowing you. Cal Ravenal hasn't been active on the Board of Trustees for some time, although he still pulls a lot of weight in the northwestern corner of the state."

"I've never met him," Lee admitted.

A pile of letters, opened by the crew who removed donations, lay on Alex's desk beside the dictating machine, into which he had presumably been dictating answers.

"Since we broadcast Tim's sermon in the National Cathedral, we've been getting a lot of mail wanting more of them on the air," said Alex. "A lot of stations on the network have been asking for them, too. They're always having trouble filling their programs without having to rerun ancient stuff like 'Leave It to Beaver.'"

"The sermon was very good. I can see why the stations and viewers would want more."

"Tim and I don't quite see eye to eye when it comes to theology," Alex admitted. "I guess my fundamentalist upbringing and early experience account for my views being less liberal than his. Anyway, he wants to tape more weekend crusades, starting with the one at Asheville a week from tomorrow. The Center can supply them to stations as individual programs, the way Billy Graham, Oral Roberts and some others do."

"Will that mean taking a camera crew to each crusade?"

"Probably not at first. We'll schedule them in cities where we already have gospel network stations that can televise with local crews. We can't rely on local choirs to furnish the kind of music that should go with Tim's sermons, though, and that means taking the Troubadours. Do you think you can manage it?"

"If the crusades are only scheduled for weekends like the one in Asheville, I probably can, but there'll be additional expense."

"We can charge that to the crusade expenses before we split with the local ministerial groups. One reason why they're anxious to bring Tim to their cities is because we give them a much better split than most traveling evangelists do. Of course, we make up the loss by adding the names of all who come forward and accept the invitation at the end of the sermons to our mailing list."

"Sounds like a mutual backscratching," said Lee, and Alex laughed.

"You could call it that. We just learned that one of the trustees has a large company jet he's thinking of trading on a new one. If Tim can persuade him to donate it to the Center as a tax deduction instead, we'll have a plane that can handle the entire group for the crusades. And that, of course, would widen considerably our fields of action."

"Would the Troubadours go in the plane then instead of taking the Center bus?"

"That's the general idea," said Alex. "What I really called you in for was to ask you to help me out with preparations for the Asheville crusade."

"I'll do anything I can."

"I'm going to Asheville right after the broadcast Friday to make some last-minute arrangements. Something has come up, though, that may make it necessary for me to fly from Asheville to Atlanta on Saturday morning, missing the luncheon we'd scheduled for the ministers participating in the crusade. It's pretty important to keep them happy, so I was wondering whether you could go with me and handle the luncheon?"

"I have a date for Sunday."

"That's no problem. You'll be finished with the luncheon in plenty of time to catch the five-o'clock plane back to Weston Saturday afternoon."

"I should be able to make it then."

"Good," said the evangelist. "Since you'll be finishing your seminary course in another year, it will be a good opportunity for you to learn some of the techniques of modern-day evangelism. They're quite different from the Billy Sunday variety I was brought up on."

"I went to a few tent revivals in West Virginia so I know something about those," said Lee. "One thing they didn't lack was showmanship."

"It's just as important today as it was then. I'll order our plane tickets and make motel reservations. We'll stay at the Rock Creek Inn. The plane leaves at one."

"I'll meet you at the airport," Lee promised as he prepared to leave the office. "Since we'll be coming back at different times, we'd better take two cars."

"We'll have to." Alex glanced down at the program schedule for the next day lying on his desk blotter. "I see that you and Miss Ravenal are going to sing a duet tomorrow."

"'I Come to the Garden Alone.' We'd never discussed our doing duets until Jeff Champion suggested it last Sunday in Atlanta."

"Champion? I don't seem to remember the name."

"He was in my class at the School of Religion a couple of years ago but dropped out to work in Atlanta with an evangelist named Schiller."

"The one who made the motion in Chicago to censure Tim?" Alex's tone was studiedly casual.

"Yes. He has a healing ministry in Atlanta."

"Oh yes. Big handsome fellow, isn't he? We had a debating tilt when I defended Tim. I'll look forward to hearing your duet tomorrow."

As Lee drove out of the Center parking lot, however, he couldn't help wondering why Alex had lied about knowing Jake Schiller when, judging by their behavior in the airport at Weston the night he and Tracy went to meet Tim, they were very well acquainted indeed.

IV

Lee saw Tracy Ravenal crossing the campus as he was leaving his final class that afternoon. She looked especially beautiful in the late-May afternoon sunlight.

"All ready for our first duet tomorrow morning?" he asked.

"If you are."

"The way our rehearsal went yesterday, we'll both be in fine form," he assured her. "In fact, if Jeff Champion is any good as a prophet, we may be on the threshold of a new career as recording artists."

She hesitated momentarily before answering but he understood the reason and her next words were proof. "That wouldn't mean we would have to stop being on the Logos Club programs, would it?"

"Not a chance. I've got another year in the School of Religion and you still have a year at Weston. Besides, we couldn't let Tim and Neeley down after what they mean to both of us."

"How about Aggie?" Tracy asked. "Is there any change?"

"Art Michaels says not. She's still in a coma."

"I just asked about her at the hospital and they have her listed as critical. I suppose that means a change for the worse."

"Art says these cases of encephalitis just have to run their course to recovery or—" He changed the subject. "Alex wants me to help canvass Asheville next Friday and Saturday evening and make sure everything is set up for the crusade there."

"Doesn't that mean you'll have to call off our picnic on Sunday?"

"I wouldn't have said I'd go if it did. Alex has to fly down to Atlanta Saturday morning on business, so I'll handle the luncheon for some of the sponsoring ministers, but I'll be back on the four-o'clock plane Saturday afternoon. It's a long time since I've taken even a day off and I'm certainly not going to give up our outing on Sunday."

Chapter Eleven

ART MICHAELS MET LEE AT THE DOOR OF HIS LABORATORY ON THE fourth floor of the psychiatric building and conducted him to a room whose walls were covered with the recording dials of a multitude of instruments.

"This is the biofeedback laboratory," the psychiatrist explained as he crossed the room to where an elderly man was sitting on a table with his feet stretched out before him. They were pale, like Oliver Newton's had been, Lee saw, and the skin had a bluish tint that didn't look at all healthy, even to his medically untrained vision.

"This is Rabbi Israel Metzger, Lee Steadman," said Michaels.

Lee shook hands with the rabbi, a jovial-looking man with a neatly trimmed gray beard. "Too bad Mr. Steadman isn't a Jew," said Metzger. "When I was in the hospital, my roommate was a Methodist, so I had to watch Tim Douglas' Club programs on TV every day. You'd make a fine cantor, Mr. Steadman."

"Thank you. I have a record of the 'Kol Nidre.' It's one of the most moving pieces of music I've ever listened to."

"We Jews are masters of the lament; you should hear the cries from my congregation at budget-raising time," Rabbi Metzger said with a chuckle. "The Psalmist tells us to *'serve the Lord with gladness: Come into His presence with singing,'* so you and your Troubadours are obeying him very well."

"With your philosophy, I'm sure Tim Douglas would love to

have you as a guest on the Logos Club program someday, sir," said Lee.

"I would enjoy that, especially your singing."

"Rabbi Metzger came to me six months ago with a severe case of intermittent claudication," said Michaels. "For your information, Lee, that's a condition where the arteries of the legs are so narrowed by sclerosis and spasm that the sufferer cannot walk much more than a few steps without severe pain."

"Couldn't even make it from my bed to the bathroom without stopping to rest several times," the patient added.

The psychiatrist reached for a switch, and the shades on the two windows were quickly lowered. When he pressed another switch, a motion-picture projector began to whir softly and a film, in color, appeared on a small screen in the corner. The scene was a patio inside a garden into which a man walked slowly, as if putting each foot before the other was an effort. Every half-dozen steps, he was forced to stop and sit for a moment on one of the benches. Lee had no trouble recognizing the principal actor in the film. It was Rabbi Metzger, and his normally cheerful features were twisted with agony each time he was forced to stop to rest after taking a few steps.

"I took this film in the rabbi's garden the day after he first came to see me," Art Michaels explained. "The next one I'm going to show you was taken after two months of treatment, at first every day in the hospital and now three times a week as an outpatient."

The scene was the same as in the first film, but this time, when Metzger came on screen, he was jogging along with no sign of the pain that had been there before.

"That's a miracle!" Lee exclaimed.

"Of a sort," Art agreed, as he switched off the projector and raised the blackout shades. "We see them here almost every day in the holistic-medicine section. Actually, I played only a very small part in that particular miracle, though. Most of it was accomplished by the rabbi himself."

"But how?"

"I'm about to show you." Art Michaels was busy applying small plastic sensors along both of the patient's legs, connecting them to wires that ran to a rather complicated bank of dials and other recorders on a panel against the wall.

"These sensors will measure blood flow in the legs as well as oxygen tension in the blood passing through the vessels," he explained, as he finished attaching the small connections. "You can see that the basal figures they are recording have already begun to appear on the bank of dials on the wall. They'll increase as soon as the patient starts thinking of something hot."

"I could probably get the same effect by reading Dante's *Inferno*," said Rabbi Metzger, "but I'll imagine I'm back home in Illinois on a cold winter day with my feet on the raised hearth, toasting my toes."

"Raising the temperature of an extremity means the blood flow through it is being increased," Art explained.

"How are you going to apply the heat?" Lee asked.

"I'm not; the patient is already doing it. In the process, he will dilate the arteries going to his legs—"

"And actually raise the temperature of the limb?" Lee asked incredulously. "That's impossible!"

"Take a look at the temperature record; it shows very minute changes."

A change was indeed already being recorded, Lee saw when he studied the indicator Art Michaels pointed out to him. Not only was the surface temperature of Rabbi Metzger's blood-depleted legs rising, as recorded on the sensitive biofeedback instrument, it was also visible in the gradual pinkening of the skin, which just a few minutes before had been almost as pale as marble from blood lack.

"Take a look at the blood-flow indicator and the oxygen-tension measurements." Art Michaels indicated two other recorders. "A good subject like the rabbi here can raise the temperature in an extremity by as much as ten degrees Fahrenheit."

"Are you telling me he's actually increasing the blood flow to his legs as well as the amount of oxygen going to them merely by thinking warm thoughts?"

"Hot thoughts, Mr. Steadman," said Metzger. "My feet are beginning to feel like they're burning."

Lee shook his head slowly. "I'd never have believed it—"

"Unless you saw it happen with your own eyes," said Art

Michaels. "When I read about the way your boss healed a man whose circulation in his feet and legs was so poor that he was threatened with amputation—as Rabbi Metzger was before I first saw him—I asked the rabbi to come by this afternoon so we could stage this little experiment for you."

"Are you saying what Tim did was a fake?"

"Not at all. I'm just showing you how it could have happened, given two preconditions."

"What are those?"

"First, the man had to believe in Tim Douglas' healing power strongly enough to help increase the blood flow; and second, your employer apparently knows quite a bit about biofeedback or at least has some instinctive knowledge about it. The newspaper accounts I read of the so-called miracle said Douglas asked the patient to think about his feet becoming warm—and they were, just like you're seeing Rabbi Metzger's feet and legs do right now."

"I'm a little shook up by the whole thing," Lee admitted.

"So was I, Mr. Steadman," said Metzger as Art began to disconnect him from the recorders. "But after the good doctor here explained the body processes involved—"

"Then there really is an explanation?"

"Of a sort, though a lot of gaps still remain that we haven't quite filled in," Art Michaels admitted. "What you have just seen involves something called the limbic system inside the brain. That's not a very well-defined anatomic entity either, so it's simpler to compare it to a telephone switchboard. Emotional nervous energy, such as Rabbi Metzger has been generating by imagining he was sitting before a fire, is channeled from the cortex of the brain to the limbic system and thence down to the hypothalamus."

"You're losing me," Lee warned.

"Largely because I'm trying to explain something that we really don't clearly understand," the psychiatrist admitted. "Lower animals have a primitive sort of brain called the hypothalamus that operates by reflex largely through what we call the autonomic nervous system. This is the system that causes rapid changes, particularly in the muscles and the circulation, preparing the animal for fight or flight in a situation involving danger."

"I'm fairly familiar with the stress reaction," said Lee. "I studied it in a physiology course I took here at Weston while I was an undergraduate."

"Then you can understand what we do a little more easily," said Michaels. "Actually, the purpose of biofeedback training is to teach the patient how to channel his emotional energy through the limbic system to the more primitive part of the brain. Here the explanation becomes much more difficult, though. You see, when an animal—or a person—sets in motion the stress reaction, he's preparing the whole body either to run away or to stand and fight. Let me remind you again that the whole body is involved."

"It must be somewhat like the way I feel when Mike D'Agostino starts the countdown for the opening of a Club broadcast and I get ready to sing out, 'He's Alive!' "

"That's an apt description," Michaels conceded. "In feedback, however, we can watch the changes in various parts of the body taking place by means of instruments that register and record temperature, blood flow, oxygen tension and other parameters very, very minutely. The changes themselves can be understood in accordance with the old stress-reaction theory you studied in college, and undoubtedly biofeedback can explain a lot of so-called miracles that faith healers appear to achieve. The real miracle, however, lies in the ability of the patient to change the condition of his own tissues quickly, and often unconsciously, purely by channeling properly the energy generated emotionally in his cerebral cortex. Moreover, learning to achieve voluntary change in the autonomic control of small artery size and consequently the amount of blood flowing through give a victim of, say, migraine or even the cold fingers of Raynaud's disease a method of curing himself."

"I still call it a miracle," said Lee.

"So do I, Mr. Steadman." Separated from the terminals of the biofeedback indicators, Rabbi Metzger had gotten off the table and was putting on his shoes and socks, his feet still pink. "Our medical friend here is a miracle worker, even if he doesn't go to synagogue or church."

"You were jogging in the film, sir," said Lee. "How much of it can you do now?"

"Not very far and even then I have to imagine I'm running over warm earth," Metzger admitted. "But compared to what it was like before—" He didn't finish the sentence; there was no need after what Lee had seen recorded on the dials and other indicators in the room.

"Can I ask you one thing more?" Lee inquired.

"Certainly."

"The Old Testament describes miracles, too. Do you think they can be explained away like the healing of the man on the TV program the other morning?"

"Miracles are in the eye of the beholder, my son," said Rabbi Metzger. "When Elijah prayed on top of Mount Carmel for God to send fire and ignite the wood on his altar, after the priests of Baal had failed, the fire from heaven could indeed have been sent by God. It could also have been a strike by lightning, however, since hills are known to attract it. But why ask, when everything that happens is through the will of God? The only difference between Jew and Christian is that you believe a Prophet of Nazareth, who was crucified on Golgotha outside Jerusalem, was the Son of God and a sacrifice for the sins of mankind. We Jews believe Jesus of Nazareth was a holy man who defied the mores of his time and, like many before and since, lost his life, but that doesn't change the fact that we worship the same God."

Art Michaels left the laboratory with Lee. "What's your reaction to my little demonstration?" Michaels asked. "I hope it doesn't shake your faith."

"A little perhaps," Lee admitted. "But you did describe the medical explanation for what happened, even if I don't understand all of it."

"Doctors don't understand everything that happens either. It's all a part of what is coming to be known as holistic medicine."

"Could you tell me again if this is a new science?"

"A very old one; you'll find it described in the *Aphorisms of Hippocrates*, written long before the Christian era. Holistic medicine—the name we give it today—merely recognizes that a patient's mental state is reflected with almost physiological exactness by his physical state. Oliver Newton was a prime example of that when Tim Douglas achieved his miracle. You just saw what it has done for Rabbi Metzger."

"Doesn't holistic medicine explain faith healing?"

"And miracles," said the psychiatrist. "You've heard of the grotto at Lourdes in France where millions go to be healed, haven't you?"

"I read an article about it, but the writer didn't explain what happens there."

"Neither has anybody else—entirely. The French Government has maintained a clinic at Lourdes for many years, studying the so-called miracle cures. Most of them they can explain the same way I just explained Oliver Newton's 'miracle' to you, but by the last count I saw, in seventy-five cases they weren't able to explain what happened by any known medical principle."

"How long have you been treating Rabbi Metzger?"

"About six months."

"Were the results in the beginning as dramatic as what I saw just now?"

"Far from it. It takes awhile to teach the patient how to use biofeedback techniques to treat his own symptoms."

"Then how could it explain what happened yesterday with Oliver Newton?"

"I asked myself the same question and I think I have a possible answer. Newton obviously went to the broadcast with the intention of practically daring Tim Douglas to heal him."

"The exact word he used was 'challenge.' He sent his wheelchair up the ramp to the set so fast he almost knocked Tim down."

"Did Newton appear to be excited?"

"Very much indeed. Would that make a difference?"

"Excitement, plus the hope that would lead him to make such a dramatic move, no doubt poured a lot of adrenalin into Newton's system, speeding up his heartbeat and raising the blood pressure considerably."

"Which would send more blood to his legs and feet. I remember that much from college physiology."

"The emotional energy of the excitement, plus the religious fervor of appealing to Christ, could all have been channeled by the limbic area of his brain into his autonomic nervous system," said Michaels. "From there, it would have gone to the smooth muscles in the walls of his arteries, dilating them and energizing considerably the voluntary muscles of his feet and legs."

"Even causing the color changes that showed up so beautifully in the still pictures?"

"It could very well have happened that way."

"What's going to happen when that emotional energy starts to subside?"

"Unless Oliver Newton's arteries continue to carry an increased supply of blood and the elevation in the rate of flow continues long enough to improve the circulation, as it did for a brief period yesterday, Newton may still wind up losing both legs."

"If some enterprising newspaper reporter decided to do a follow-up story on Newton, Tim would be discredited, to say nothing of the blow to his own faith."

"Is that so important to you?" Michaels asked.

"It is to Tim and the thousands of people he turns to faith in Christ. That makes it important to me."

"The more I see of Tim Douglas, the more I'm inclined to believe he's the real article instead of just another of these fundamentalist religious quacks I see spouting on the TV screen."

"Don't tell me *you* look at the 'Electric Church'?" said Lee with a smile.

"Some are very good. Robert Schuller's 'Hour of Power,' for example, is one of the best. Right now, though, I'm more concerned about a man whose legs might be saved with biofeedback training, judging by the way his body reacted yesterday on TV. It'll be bad enough for him to lose them, but Tim Douglas has a lot to lose, too, if Oliver Newton's condition right now is what I think it is. So why don't you get busy and find out?"

"Will you take Newton as a patient if I learn that he still needs the help you can give him?"

"Of course. Why do you think I staged this little demonstration in the first place?"

Chapter Twelve

THE STORY LEE HAD CLIPPED FROM THE MORNING PAPER GAVE him Oliver Newton's address, a small house in an older section of town. Flower beds ringed the house with a riot of spring colors, and the front door was open, though the screen was hooked. From somewhere inside the sound of a famous broadcaster's voice giving the evening news came to Lee's ears as he rang the doorbell. He recognized the woman who answered his ring; she had been with Newton at the studio yesterday.

"Is Mr. Newton home?" Lee asked.

"What do you want?" The look in her eyes was hostile.

"I'm Lee Steadman from the Broadcast Cen—"

"I recognized you—"

"Maggie?" A man's voice called from somewhere in the house. "Who is it?"

"The young man who sings on the Logos Club," she answered, but did not unlock the screen.

"I don't want to see him—or anybody else from that goddamn place." The words confirmed Art Michaels' fears—and Lee's as well. "They're nothing but a bunch of quacks."

"You heard him," the woman said in a tone of deep resentment. "He don't wanna see nobody from the Center, not with his legs hurtin' the way they are."

"How long did the change that came over them yesterday morning last?"

"They were hurtin' again before supper. He's decided to let the doctors cut 'em off like they want to do."

"Perhaps I could pray with him," said Lee desperately. "Or he could see Brother Tim again."

Lee hadn't heard the wheelchair come into the front room until Oliver Newton, his legs extended on the wheelchair supports and his face contorted with pain and rage, appeared beside the woman standing behind the screen.

"Did Brother Tim send you?" Newton demanded. "Or is he too busy cashing in on a fake miracle to give a damn what's happening to me—now that he got all the publicity he wants out of it?"

"Brother Tim didn't know I was coming," Lee explained. "I—I was afraid something like this might happen after you left the studio, so I came of my own accord to see how you are."

"Well, take a look and then get the hell out of here." Oliver Newton jerked up the cuff of his pants to reveal the same bluish pallor of the skin covering his feet and legs they had shown yesterday. "Tell Brother Tim what he can do with his fake healing."

"I found a doctor who can help you," said Lee. "I just came from his office."

"What is he? Another faith healer?"

"He's a psychiatrist—Dr. Arthur Michaels."

"Good God, man! It's my legs that might develop gangrene any day, not my mind! Do you think I've got rocks in my head?"

"Please, Oliver, don't get so excited," the woman said. "It always makes your legs hurt worse later."

"They won't be hurtin' much longer because they won't be hangin' on me," Newton snapped.

"I just saw Dr. Michaels start the blood flowing through another man's legs the way yours flowed for a while yesterday," Lee pleaded. "Please let him help you."

"Go back to Brother Tim and tell him I'm going to let the world know what a fake he is!" the sick man shouted as he turned and sent the wheelchair hurtling back toward the rear of the house.

"He's been like that since his legs started painin' him again last night, Mr. Steadman," said the woman, on a note of apol-

ogy. "I guess you can't blame him either. He talked for days be-
fore he went to the broadcast about how he was going to make
Brother Tim heal him on the air. When it seemed like he had,
Oliver was like a new man. Then the color of his skin over his
feet and legs began to fade and the pain started in again—"
Her voice broke and she didn't finish the sentence.

"Try to convince him that Dr. Arthur Michaels at the University Hospital can help him," Lee begged. "I've already made
the arrangements. All you have to do is call for an appointment."

"Oliver won't listen to nobody now. He'd set so much store
on being healed by Brother Tim—"

"Give Dr. Michaels a chance, please. Mr. Newton doesn't
have anything to lose by doing that."

"I'll try," she promised, "but all he talks about now is what
he's going to do to expose Brother Tim. Thank you for coming anyway, but I don't think anything can change him now."

As soon as Lee got to his apartment, he telephoned Art
Michaels at the psychiatrist's lakefront home. "Oliver Newton
is in even worse shape than I'd expected," he told his friend.
"He's threatening to expose Tim."

"What about coming to see me?"

"He wouldn't hear of that either and ordered me away from
his house. I think his wife would like him to make one more
try at medical treatment, but he's determined to have the am-
putations because of the pain."

"Do you know what surgeon has been seeing him?"

"No. Would that information help?"

"I doubt it; surgeons are usually suspicious of biofeedback
and holistic medicine. If I had a chance to talk to whoever is
going to amputate, though, he might let me try a few treat-
ments first—on speculation."

"I'm sorry I couldn't talk Newton into it."

"You did your best. Are you going to tell Tim Douglas what
you found?"

"I guess the less said right now the better. Tim might try to
reason with Newton personally and someone in the neighborhood would be sure to recognize him and maybe call the
newspapers."

"You're probably right," the psychiatrist agreed. "Have a nice trip."

II

Asheville was lovely in late May and the Rock Creek Inn a pure delight. A delegation from the Christian Laymen's Guild sponsoring the appearance of the Logos Club team at the large convention center Friday and Saturday nights had gathered for dinner in one of the meeting rooms of the inn. Lee was impressed by the ease with which Alex Porcher took charge and by how many of those at the gathering the evangelist already knew. When the dinner was finished, Alex rose to speak:

"I brought with me from Weston today a man already known to any of you who listen regularly to the Logos Club broadcasts, our musical director, Lee Steadman."

There was a spattering of applause before Alex continued, "What you don't know is the degree of dedication this young man gives to our work at the Center. Not only is he a superb musician in his own right, as all of you who have heard him sing know well, but he is also a highly capable organizer and administrator. Not all of you, I am sure, can be classed as *aficionados* of the so-called gospel-rock type of music we use more than any other on the Club broadcasts, but there is a definite reason for it. I didn't tell Lee I was going to ask him to explain the appeal of this type of music. Instead, I'm going to let him speak for himself as one of the leading authors, arrangers and performers in this field. May I introduce to you the director of music for the Logos Club and the Gospel Broadcast Center, Lee Steadman."

"Alex wasn't kidding when he told you he'd given me no warning," Lee began. "Five years ago I was ending my sophomore year at the University of West Virginia with every intention of completing my musical training in college. I'd even planned to go back to Airmont, my hometown, and perhaps direct the choir in the First Presbyterian Church, teaching music on the side. Then something happened that brought me to a real 'high': Tim Douglas called me from Weston and invited me to act as director of music for the Gospel Broadcast Center."

"What gave you that 'high'?" a young woman in the front row below the speaker's table inquired.

"Frankly, I don't know," Lee conceded.

"Were you 'born again'?" the young woman insisted upon asking.

"I freely admit that I don't know exactly what the term means," said Lee. "I only know that something—and perhaps it was exactly what you're talking about—made me accept the invitation as soon as it was given to me. I had known Tim and Neeley while I was still a student. He was pastor of my church at Airmont and I suspect that, even then, Jesus was already in charge of my life, as He had long since taken charge of the lives of Tim and Neeley. I am sure, too, that it was the Master who directed me into the work in the Gospel Center at Weston. Anyway, I knew right away I had been called for the only cause that gave me certainty and the feeling of actual contentment in service."

"It was the Lord, Lee," said Alex from his seat beside the president of the guild. "He had already selected you for the task you're performing."

"Perhaps. I can only say that I'm glad it happened and I'm glad to be a part of bringing the new music to the work of the Center."

A young man in the crowd raised his hand and asked a question: "From what I've seen and heard during the concerts by the Gospel Troubadours and also on the Logos Club broadcasts, the new musical trends account for much of the appeal this form of evangelism has, particularly to young people. I wonder what your opinion is on that score."

"I presume that you're talking about what is sometimes disparagingly called 'gospel-rock,'" said Lee. "If so, I can assure you that it is one of our greatest tools in reaching the young people of the country, in spite of the prejudice so many older people have against it. Personally, I feel as much reverence while listening to something like Evie Tornquist's 'Mirror' as when I sing 'The Old Rugged Cross' on our own show. I would guess, too, that if you took a thousand young Christians today and asked them which music brings them most in tune with their devotion to Jesus of Nazareth, three fourths of them would name 'gospel-rock' as a major force in their religious experience."

"Isn't that going too far?" a gray-haired man in the audience asked. "As far as I'm concerned, the word 'rock' is synonymous with dope, drink and mortal sin."

"It is to a lot of people," Lee agreed, "but if I had the Gospel Troubadours here, I could convince most of you in a few minutes that a so-called rock tune can be a very beautiful experience. I suspect almost as much opposition was voiced to the introduction of instruments as accompaniments for Gregorian chant a long time ago."

Lee sat down to a spattering of applause, and Alex Porcher returned to the podium.

"I guess you can all see why we at the Gospel Broadcast Center think Lee Steadman is a powerful force in the success of our work," he said. "Now, let's get down to the business of saving souls. Your chairman tells me you have already organized yourselves, as we requested, into teams. Each team, too, has been assigned to a section of the convention center where the crusade will be held on Friday and Saturday evenings of the coming week."

"I'm not sure I like all this elaborate advance planning, Brother Alex," said one of the ministers at the head table. "To me, it smacks more of commercialism and public relations than the type of spontaneous born-again conversion that's the only force capable of saving this country—even the world—from the grip of Satan."

"I grew up in the old 'sawdust trail' school of evangelism like you apparently did, brother," Alex Porcher fielded the protest smoothly. "Even as recently as ten years ago, I would have agreed with you wholeheartedly, but working with Tim Douglas and the young people who are reviving our faith in a way stronger than any old-fashioned 'revival' ever did has taught me differently."

"The response you produce isn't spontaneous," the original

questioner insisted. "I can't see it as the sort of baptism of the Holy Spirit that can come only to the true 'born again' Christian."

"That's where I differ with you, brother." Alex's smile and the softness of his words managed to take any sting out of the rebuke. "I've seen the miracle of rebirth happen too many times —with just a little stimulation to get the troubled soul on the way to a full recognition of Jesus' love and His willingness to take control of a sinner's life—to doubt it anymore. Read again the first chapter of John's Gospel and you'll find it was Andrew who persuaded his brother, Peter, to listen to Jesus, and Philip who brought Nathaniel to the Master. All of you here are Christians. Many of you were 'born again' and baptized with the Holy Spirit in the true baptism that I pray will one day come to all who have not yet experienced the ultimate joy with Jesus. But is that any reason why you should not do as Philip and Nathaniel and Andrew did in leading their brethren to the secret of eternal life in Christ?"

The objectors seemed to have been quashed, but Alex continued: "Remember how difficult it was for each of you, when you first begged for the grace of God to be poured out upon you through His Son? And remembering, you can certainly realize that the man, woman or child sitting next to you while Brother Tim preaches, will be experiencing that same reluctance and that same holding power of a Satan unwilling to let go of any soul without a struggle.

"All you will be asked to do next Friday and Saturday nights is to take your assigned places in the audience." Alex continued, "When Tim Douglas and myself issue the invitation to be saved, you, too, can be a leader, as were Andrew, Philip and Nathaniel, by coming forward immediately and, even more important, by bringing that reluctant individual near you down to the altar with you."

There were a few more questions, all of which Alex answered easily and competently, before the dinner broke up shortly after nine-thirty.

III

A shaft of sunlight through the open window of his room in the Rock Creek Inn, next door to the suite taken by Alex Porcher, wakened Lee at about 6 A.M. Outside, birds were singing and the enticing aroma of spring flowers blooming on the mountainside gave such promise of a lovely day that Lee decided to take his morning run before the motel restaurant opened.

Pulling on the running shorts without which he never traveled and a T-shirt, he dropped the room key into the pocket of his shorts and opened the door. As he was about to step out into the corridor, he heard the faint squeak of the door to Alex's suite open, so he stepped back inside. Overcome by curiosity as to why Alex would be rising so early, however, Lee couldn't resist the temptation to glance out his own door a few seconds after he heard the other one close.

What he saw wasn't Alex, however, but the back of a woman hurrying down the corridor toward a door leading to the outside. She was a rather statuesque blonde wearing a dress much more suitable for an evening cocktail party than for six-thirty on a late-spring morning. What startled Lee even more than that she had obviously left Alex's suite was the fact that he recognized her. The hair, the figure and her movements on the high spiked heels were exactly the same as when he'd last seen her—teetering up the aisle of Jake Schiller's Temple in Atlanta, as she shepherded together the shills who would lead others to the platform for the healing service.

It was Eileen Stoddard.

IV

Lee had finished his run, showered, dressed and was ordering breakfast in the motel restaurant shortly after eight o'clock when Alex Porcher came in from the lobby, carrying a large manila envelope under his arm. The evangelist looked around and, seeing Lee, hurried over to his table.

"I called your room and, when you didn't answer, figured you'd be either out running or down here," he said.

"I ran earlier." Lee didn't mention having seen the blonde leaving Alex's room earlier that morning. "Won't you join me for breakfast?"

"Don't have time. I've got to take an early plane to Atlanta and will grab a cup of coffee and a danish at the airport or maybe on the plane. Can you meet in my place with the ministers of the counseling group here for luncheon at one o'clock?"

"Sure. What'll I tell them?"

"The Xeroxed instructions are in here." Alex put the envelope down on the table. "Just hand them out and answer any questions about the Center or about Tim that come up."

"That's easy enough. Anything else?"

"No. If they ask any questions you can't answer, just write them down along with the name of whoever asks; I'll write him a letter first thing Monday morning. You carry a Broadcast Center American Express card, don't you?"

"Yes. For paying hotel bills when we're doing concerts."

"Good. When the luncheon's over, just sign for all our charges here, including the luncheon today and last night's dinner. I'll tell the cashier you're going to take care of everything." Alex glanced at his watch. "I've only got a little over an hour to get to the airport and catch the plane for Atlanta. Hope the noise from my suite didn't keep you awake last night. Some old friends were at the dinner and we stayed up rather late afterward taking care of a lot of loose ends."

"I'm a sound sleeper. Didn't hear a thing."

"See you Monday morning at the broadcast, then," said Alex. "I've got to run."

Lee finished his breakfast leisurely, charged it to his room and turned his attention to the Xeroxed sheets in the envelope Alex had left him. The instructions were the same as others he had seen on the few occasions when the Troubadours had accompanied Tim and Alex on weekend crusades held in towns within a couple of hours' flight from Weston in the company plane.

The task of the counselors with whom Lee was to meet for lunch was to receive those who came forward at the end of the services, after Tim issued the call. Escorted from the auditorium itself by the counselors, while the choir was finishing the final verses of the invitational hymn, the new converts were to be gathered in rooms on either side of the auditorium. There they filled in forms for transmission to the churches selected by converts for their home church. If they had none, the counselors sought to shunt them toward their own. Because distribution of the plate collections taken up at every service during the crusade was made largely on the basis of the number of converts electing to join the different churches of the city, there was usually no lack of volunteer counselors from among the pastors of those churches.

One space on the card filled out by the counselors was particularly emphasized in the instructions. It contained the blank for the name and address of each possible convert, which then went into the Gospel Broadcast Center computer to become a part of its steadily expanding mailing list. Unlike most crusading evangelists, however, Tim Douglas' organization charged only expenses to the collection funds, a practice that made the pastors of local congregations much less reluctant to promote Brother Tim's crusades than with other evangelists.

The luncheon, scheduled for one o'clock in the dining room of the Rock Creek Inn, went off without a hitch—until Lee called for questions. Then a portly minister wearing an Italian silk suit that, Lee estimated, must have cost at least three hundred to five hundred dollars, stood up and said, "I've been through a lot of these crusades, from Billy Graham's to Oral

Roberts', and one thing I don't like seems to characterize all of them."

"What's that, sir?" Lee asked.

"If the advance teams have done their work and enough guides have been lined up from the regular congregations to lead the flock—"

"The term I use is 'Judas goats,' Joe," one of the ministers interrupted, to a wave of laughter.

"Maybe that's a better name for them than 'guides,'" the questioner agreed. "We know they're there for the purpose of starting sinners, once the invitation has been given, down what we used to call the sawdust trail. But getting back to what I was saying: If the preparations are made well and the evangelist is experienced in persuading waverers, a lot of converts do accept the invitation and are shepherded into the consultation rooms."

"What are you objecting to, Doctor?" Lee asked courteously, sensing that the questioner was losing the interest of part of the group—perhaps because they already knew what the question really was.

"Just this, young man. We work our asses off answering questions the evangelist didn't answer in his sermon. We take down a lot of names of would-be converts, too, so the next night the preacher can refer to the hundreds who answered the call the night before to accept Jesus. The trouble is that most of the potential converts get lost by the wayside somewhere. At least they don't turn up in my church very often for the instruction classes we require before people become church members, and I've got an idea the rest of you don't have any better batting average than I do."

A wave of applause indicated a similar experience by others at the luncheon.

"What I want to know," continued the original questioner, "is what happens to these 'one night' Christians, as I call them?"

"Perhaps they select other churches," Lee suggested.

"That's not the answer," a young minister objected. "The church rolls of this city have been going down for years, not up, as they should with all this preaching people hear on TV and

radio. I've only been associated with a few of these so-called
crusades, but I do know that right afterward you should expect
church rolls to increase markedly. The truth is that it just
doesn't happen."

"Hear! Hear!" echoed through the room.

"Why do we knock ourselves out talking our own church
members into serving as 'Judas goats' when most of them really
feel like they're duping the public by flocking down the aisles
at the first invitation from the evangelist?" the speaker continued. "And why take our own time with this counseling business when we could be evangelizing in our own churches? Instead, we waste time talking to people who've just been scared
half to death by an evangelist, when you know most of them
aren't going to join any church. For my money, these crusades
are just a waste of time—and money; money, incidentally, that
could be used to a lot better effect in the work of our own
churches."

An elderly minister stood up. "I can tell you why we do it
and why what we have to do has no part in bringing souls to
Christ—as we're always prating about," he said. "We *have* to
do it because these crusades—and I've been through enough of
them to know that 'charades' is a better word—bring in a lot of
money when those collection plates are passed. Even though
our share is small, after the expenses these big campaigns pile
up, it's still money. Old-time evangelists like Billy Sunday used
tin washbasins to take up collections because all that money
hitting them made a wonderful sound and encouraged people
to give more. Nowadays we may not be so crass, but we do
know that, even with the nonprofit associations these traveling
evangelists cloak themselves in to justify not paying income
taxes, they still manage to get their cut—and believe me,
brothers, except for Tim Douglas, it's a hefty one. Fortunately,
though, something is left for us and we're all going to grab for
it as often as we can."

"Actually, we're like the beggar named Lazarus Christ spoke
about in the Gospel of St. Luke," another interposed. "You all
remember the parable of the rich man and the beggar; to quote
Jesus himself—we desire '*to be fed with the crumbs that fell
from the rich man's table.*' Well, I for one am getting tired of

being the fall guy for these self-styled evangelists, who separate
the cream via television and leave us the skim milk and the
curd."

There was a chorus of general agreement and Lee finally was
forced to tap upon the podium to regain order.

Still another voice joined in what was rapidly becoming an
outpouring of dissent and even venom: "Even before we fill
out the form inviting the so-called convert, who's quivering
with fear from the threats of roasting in hell for eternity that
have just been hurled at him from the rostrum—if the evangelist takes the right text from the Book of Revelation—we're
required to make sure we've got his home address correct so
he'll go on the mailing list for Tim Douglas' Logos Club. I'm
not going to embarrass a fine young man like our host for this
luncheon by asking him how much money flows out of the mail
bags that arrive every day at the Gospel Broadcast Center—"

"I don't even know," Lee interrupted, hoping to stem some
of the avalanche of objections that had suddenly been un-
leashed by the first questioner.

"I read somewhere that it's more than fifty million a year,"
said the speaker. "I'd like to ask the rest of you what we could
do in home missions, in helping the elderly poor in our congregations with 'meals on wheels,' or by supporting our mis-
sionaries abroad, if we had control of that kind of money. Do
you realize that the take—and I use that word advisedly—
Brother Tim Douglas reaps every year would finance the entire
budgets of most denominations?"

"Gentlemen!" It was the portly minister who had started the
whole thing. "We have just been the guests at a very fine meal
of a young man who not only has a beautiful voice, which he
uses to sing praises to our God, but who also is himself a candidate for the ministry. We've responded by drowning him with
invective that we don't have the guts to get up and say from
our pulpits to our own congregations. I, for one, will welcome
Brother Tim Douglas to Asheville, because I think he's one of
the few really sincere TV evangelists living the Christlike life
today. I'll welcome him a second time, too, because the crumbs
I get from his table are worth considerably more to me than
what come from a lot of other evangelists. Say what you will,

Brother Tim pays his own way, even if he does get it back through the United States mail and a tax exemption. So let's thank Lee Steadman for a fine luncheon and wish him and the man he works for well."

The meeting broke up then and Lee, still a little shaken, not only by what he'd heard but also by the obviously intense feelings of the men who had spoken, went to the cashier's window of the motel. Shoving the American Express card of the Gospel Broadcast Center beneath the grille, he scribbled his signature on a bill for nearly five hundred dollars.

Only when he was in a taxi bound for the airport did Lee notice among the items he'd just signed for a notation under "room service" from the number of the suite adjoining his own modest room. The notation read "Champagne, two bottles—$20. Caviar, $15."

Chapter Thirteen

TRACY WAS READY WHEN LEE RANG THE DOORBELL OF HER DORMItory Sunday morning at nine-thirty. He had skimmed through the Sunday paper and was pleased not to find any reference to Oliver Newton's threat to attack Tim Douglas and the Center through the media. The day was warm and Tracy was wearing sandals, white slacks, a pale green blouse and had tied her hair back with a green ribbon. She carried a small bag, large enough to hold a bathing suit and cosmetics.

"How did things go in Asheville?" she asked as they were driving to the restaurant.

"We were busy. Alex had scheduled a one-o'clock luncheon Saturday afternoon for sponsoring ministers at the Rock Creek Inn, where we stayed. He had to leave for Atlanta early Saturday morning so I had to host the luncheon alone."

"With your usual efficiency, no doubt."

"I'm not too sure about that. The whole thing turned into a gripe session with a lot of the preachers sounding off against evangelists in general. Before they were through, my ears were burning, but I had to admit that most of their complaints were justified."

Breakfast at Mabel's restaurant finished, Lee carried the cooler with the food and drinks out to the car and they drove down to the pier extending out into the lake at the foot of University Drive. The Center's boat, a seventeen-footer with a powerful outboard motor and a half cabin, was moored near the end of the dock. Putting the food in the cabin, Lee checked the gasoline supply before casting off the mooring lines. Ski ropes were neatly coiled on the bottom of the boat at the stern, and three pairs of water skis were stored in brackets under the gunwales.

"The manufacturer donated this boat and motor to the Center," he told Tracy as she settled into one of the cushioned seats. "It was a bona fide charitable gift, but we do manage to print a photo of the boat in the Center magazine every now and then showing the name of the manufacturer painted on the stern. And we often use background shots during the broadcasts of some of the Troubadours skiing on the lake."

When Lee started the powerful motor, the boat moved away from the dock and began to pick up speed. For ten minutes or so, they roared down the lake toward the dam; then he cut back the throttle and allowed it to settle down to a slower pace where they could hear each other.

"This is the life," he said. "But then you must have a boat at home so you're used to it. I seem to remember seeing a large lake up near Lankashire from the air."

"My family owns a cottage on Lake Keowee," said Tracy. "We used to spend most of the summer months out there."

"Then you must be an experienced skier."

"I've been skiing since I was six but still love it."

"Any time you'd like to take a run, you can change in the head."

She trailed her hand in the water and shivered. "I think I'll wait awhile. You did say the water would be warmer down near the dam, didn't you?"

"It usually is, particularly on a bright, sunny day like today. Just say the word when you're ready."

"I'll change in a little while when we get down near the dam. By the way, my father's coming to Asheville next Friday for the crusade. He says he needs to talk to Tim about something concerning the Center. I want you to meet him while we're there."

"I'd like that," said Lee. "Do you mind if I tell him I want to marry you?"

She laughed. "He'd only tell you I'm over twenty-one and able to make my own decisions. Actually, if Dad wasn't coming to Asheville, I'd rather not go. I don't like Tim leaving Aggie when she's so sick. It doesn't seem right."

"I'm not sure I favor the weekend crusades either but for a different reason. That luncheon I presided over in Asheville Saturday was something of an eye-opener to me."

"How?"

"Practically everybody there complained that crusades like the kind Tim has in mind don't really bring many new members to their churches."

"But when the invitation is given on television evangelistic programs the cameras always show crowds of people going down the aisles."

"What they don't show is that a large part of those crowds are church members who've been drafted to set an example for people hesitating to take that step."

"That's cheating!" she exclaimed.

"Alex Porcher says the church members who go down are only helping the uncertain ones make up their minds and thus are also serving. But some of the men at the luncheon on Saturday had a different name for them."

"What was that?"

"Judas goats."

"That's terrible! Does Tim know about it?"

"I suppose so; he sent Alex to Asheville to make the arrangements."

"He depends a lot on Reverend Porcher, doesn't he?"

"More than I'm sure is wise, after that meeting we witnessed at the airport among Alex, Schiller, and Magda Sanderson. By the way, Hal Graham told me she was at the Chicago convention on Gospel Broadcast Center business, something about a seminar on donations by mail. Her presence on the same plane with Alex could easily have been merely a coincidence."

"I doubt it. That relationship looked a little cozy to me."

"Woman's intuition?"

She shrugged, and changed the subject. "If the pastors of the churches in the cities where the crusades are held don't like them, why do they help promote them?"

"Because of the collections. Part of what's taken in goes to the churches that participate."

Tracy was silent for a long moment. Finally she asked: "Why would Tim want to be a part of something that smacks of charlatanry?"

"I asked myself the same question coming back from Asheville yesterday. The only answer I got was that Tim sincerely believes it's his task to lead everyone he possibly can to follow Jesus Christ. Because of that belief, he's willing to use practically any legitimate method to accomplish his purpose."

"You may be right. You can't know him long without realizing how sincere he is, but does the aim really justify what my dad would call shyster methods?"

"If you're strongly enough convinced that you're doing the Lord's will, I suppose it could," said Lee. "Alex certainly approves. He says it's standard evangelistic practice."

"When did Tim develop this driving force?"

"He had it when I first knew him. Alex has written a biography of Tim, but it's more of a public-relations brochure than a real definitive study. Actually, you can't take everything Alex says in it about Tim as being exactly the way it happened."

"I've read it, but how can anyone learn the real truth?"

"I know most of it from my own association with Tim and what Neeley has told me," said Lee. "He grew up in West Virginia near where I did and, when he finished high school, got an appointment to the Air Force Academy. He graduated with honors as a jet pilot and was sent to Viet Nam almost immediately. Toward the end of his tour of duty there, he apparently became affected by the horror of bombing unprotected villages and strafing troop concentrations and developed a severe emotional depression. He had to be sent back to the States for treatment and, while he was in an Air Force hospital, struck up a friendship with a chaplain. Under the chaplain's influence, Tim had a charismatic experience—he was 'born again.' "

"I still don't understand what they're talking about," she confessed.

"Neither do I, because I've never experienced it myself, but I know those who do are never quite the same again. Their whole purpose in life afterward is helping others see the Light, as they call it. They become, in essence, disciples of Jesus

Christ, as the Twelve were, and devote the major part of their lives to following Him."

"I joined the church when I was twelve after going to an instruction class and being baptized like everybody my age was doing," said Tracy. "We were taught that being a Christian means living as nearly like Christ did as you can and believing He died to give you eternal life. I guess Kitty Lawson sums it up pretty well when she sings: *'I'm only four-feet-eleven, but I'm going to heaven.'"**

"You and I became Christians in what might be called the conventional way," Lee agreed, "but Kitty sums up the 'born again' way when she sings the line that goes: *'And that makes me feel ten feet tall.'* Those who claim to have had a real charismatic experience even say they see Jesus and talk to Him, especially when they receive what they call the 'baptism of the Holy Spirit.'"

"Is that when they speak in tongues?"

"Usually, but to me it sounds more like a child's babble when he's learning to talk. Art Michaels says speaking in tongues is really a retrogression into infancy or even a preinfantile state. He sees it quite frequently in some types of schizophrenia."

"Was that the kind of mental illness Tim had?"

"I doubt it. My own feeling is that sensitive and emotional as Tim naturally is, he was overcome by guilt for what he had to do during the war."

"Couldn't he have refused?"

"The service academies bear down pretty hard on loyalty and duty. Cadets are taught to go on obeying orders in wartime until they're either shot down, survive with scars that often never go away—or crack up emotionally. We're beginning to realize now that men who appear to have gone through the Viet Nam experience unscathed are actually so overcome with guilt at what they were forced to do in obeying orders that they have emotional troubles right and left. Art Michaels sees them all the time."

* Copyright © 1976, 1977, by Word Music, Inc. All rights reserved. International copyright secured. Used by permission.

She shivered. "Imagine having that burden of guilt hanging over you all your life."

"Art says it undermines their emotional stability until they find an outlet for their guilt in violence or other unlawful acts. With Tim, fortunately, it was the opposite. The chaplain at the Air Force hospital strengthened his basic goodness and helped him believe that, by following Jesus, he could do penance for what war had led him into. Maybe he was prepared that way for the born-again experience, or maybe he was just ready for forgiveness. The way he describes it, he was having a terrible dream one night, the sort that plagues so many Viet Nam veterans."

"I saw a movie about that. It was horrible."

"This dream had a happy ending, when a vision of Jesus of Nazareth came to Tim and promised him forgiveness if he followed the Lord thereafter. Less than a month later, the hospital discharged him as cured."

"Where was Neeley all this time?"

Lee had been expecting the question. "They were married the day Tim graduated from the academy and got his commission. The situation in Viet Nam was so bad then that they barely had time for a brief honeymoon before he was shipped out. Neeley taught school while Tim was in Viet Nam but, when he came back, she gave up her job and moved near the hospital where he was under treatment."

"She obviously loves him very much."

"They were childhood sweethearts," said Lee. "I'm convinced that Neeley's presence at the hospital, plus Tim's friendship with the chaplain, did more to help cure him than the psychiatrists were able to do. After his discharge from the Air Force, he used his GI credits to enroll at a fundamentalist seminary not far from Airmont, where he served as pastor of our family church during his last two years at the seminary. That's where I first got to know him."

"And patterned your life after him?"

"In a way, but I'm afraid I could never possess the absolute devotion that controls Tim. When I transferred to Weston and joined the Gospel Broadcast Center staff, Tim and Neeley got me a job playing the organ and directing the choir Sundays

at a small Baptist church just outside of town. What little they
paid me filled out my scholarship to where I managed to live.
The church I was playing at was near a largely black one and I
guess that's when I developed my love for gospel-rock and soul
music. When Tim started broadcasting on television pretty
soon after I came to Weston, I suggested that he let a small
combo I'd organized among the students furnish the music for
the Logos Club. That's the way the Troubadours got started."

"How many were there then?"

"Only a trio at first; Alice Turner, Kitty Lawson and myself
—with Jim Cates playing the piano."

"Was Alex Porcher with Tim then?"

"No. Jake Schiller had just left the Center, and Tim was
working alone. Jake is older than Tim and used to have his own
evangelistic program over radio from Charlotte. It never really
caught on very well and, when Tim started the Club, Jake
came to Weston and asked for the job of second banana—as he
called it. He wasn't really bad and he did a lot to develop the
publicity and organize the mail-collection system that kept the
station alive. By the time Tim woke up to the truth that Jake
was trying to take over the whole Center operation, he'd hired
new people loyal to him to operate practically every important
position and had almost taken control."

"How could he do that?"

"By buttering up the Board of Trustees, for one thing. From
what some of those who were working at the Center that far
back told me, Jake can be very persuasive. He soon gained a
faction among the trustees who weren't nearly as liberal in
their beliefs as Tim is. They'd favor anything Jake wanted to
do and turn thumbs down on Tim's ideas. Jake actually tried to
turn the program into a typical old-time evangelistic campaign
with daily services, direct pleas for money, healing sessions—the
whole bit. Tim went along for a while, when it appeared that a
lot of people were actually being helped."

"I'm sure Tim believes that today."

"So am I. Even Art Michaels admits that nearly two thirds
of the people who think they're sick, are really suffering from
psychosomatic illness. If you can bring them a certain amount

of peace of mind through religion, the physical effects are either going to be helped or go away."

"Nobody doubts that anymore."

"No, but Jake was bringing in people who actually make a profession of being healed and getting paid for it, the way Jeff Champion does now in Atlanta."

"Tim would never stand for that."

"He didn't waste any time cleaning out staff members who were working for Jake. By enlisting loyal supporters on the board, he managed to regain control and have himself reelected chairman. Your father replaced one of Jake Schiller's henchmen but there's still a small remnant of the board whose terms haven't yet expired, and they're as rabid about Tim's liberal tendencies as ever."

"Schiller certainly looked prosperous when we saw him in Atlanta."

"Jake's doing very well, with Jeff Champion managing the show. Jeff has a genius for showmanship; you could see that last Sunday. Jake's Temple—as he calls it—is located in a blue-collar area where I hear the Ku Klux Klan is pretty strong. When he isn't healing, Jake preaches a kind of Christianity that's antiblack, anti-Catholic and anti-Jew, the sort of thing that goes over big with a typically red-neck audience. Actually, I suppose it's about the nearest thing to a Nazi religion in the country, and Jake milks it for everything he can."

"If he's that bad, why would Reverend Porcher have been buddy-buddying with him?"

"I don't know but I certainly intend to find out." They were nearing the dam, and Lee swung the boat in a wide arc, leaving a towering wake. "If you like to jump the wake when you're skiing, I can really give you some big ones down here where the lake is at its widest."

"It looks like fun," she said. "I'll change and take a trial run, even though I haven't skied in almost a year."

II

When Tracy came out of the half cabin, Lee gave a low whistle of admiration that brought a flush to her cheeks. She was wearing one of the new-style, bright-blue maillots that fitted her like her own skin and was next to backless.

"I feel practically naked in this suit," she admitted. "Much more than I would in a bikini but the saleslady said that's what girls are wearing these days."

"She was right."

While Lee was breaking out the single ski used by experts, and tossing out the ski rope, Tracy dived in and swam with a strong, graceful crawl completely around the now-idling boat. When she reached the ski he tossed out to her, she treaded water while expertly slipping her feet into the two boots of the single ski and reached for the towing bar floating at the end of the long nylon rope.

"Ready when you are," she called out and he eased the boat forward until the ski rope was taut.

When he gunned the powerful motor, she came up like a graceful bird taking off into flight. She was an expert skier and he took her for a long, swift run up the lake, then back and forth in a series of sweeping curves that piled up waves several feet high behind the boat. Swinging far out until she was almost parallel with the stern, she came hurtling back like a bright blue streak, topping each wave of the giant V made by the wake and leaping clear of the water for a distance of several yards each time before landing skillfully.

For nearly half an hour, Lee took her back and forth across the lake above the dam until she indicated that she was ready to rest by tossing away the rope. Kicking off the ski, she treaded water while he cut the motor and pulled in the rope before idling back to pick her up. As she came up the portable ladder he lowered from the gunwale, he handed her a large towel and a smaller one for her hair.

"Why don't you change?" she said, dropping into one of the cushioned seats and wrapping herself in the towel. "By the time you're ready, I'll have enough breath back to drive the boat."

She was as skilled a pilot as she was a skier and Lee, too, enjoyed the long, swinging runs and the sensation of flying when he topped the waves on the single ski. When he pulled himself over the side of the boat without using the ladder, she had shed the towel and was combing the damp waves of her shoulder-length hair into place.

"Hungry?" he asked, drying himself with a heavy towel.

"Famished."

"While you finish your coiffure, I'll see what feast Mabel prepared for us. Would you like to eat on the forward deck in the sun?"

"That would be lovely. My hair should be almost dry by the time we're finished."

The cooler proved to be a veritable treasure trove of good things to eat: sandwiches, fruit salad in a plastic bag with plastic plates and liberal slices of icebox pie, along with Cokes buried in the ice.

"You're obviously a favorite of Mabel's, as you seem to be of everybody else's in Weston," Tracy assured him.

"Present company included, I hope." His tone was suddenly serious and, when she looked away and didn't answer, he added, "It should be apparent to you by now that I've gone overboard where you're concerned."

"Please, Lee! I like you very much but—" She stopped and didn't finish the sentence.

"There's somebody else?"

"I'm not quite sure."

"A fighting chance is all I ask."

She reached out to put her hand over his and squeeze it gently. "It would be easy for any girl to fall in love with you. In fact, you're about the most fall-in-lovable young man I've ever known."

"But you'd rather not be rushed? Is that it?"

She turned to look at him and he saw real concern in her eyes. "Can we leave it at that—for a while, at least?"

"Of course. After all, I'm going to be seeing you at least five days a week and you just admitted that I'm the kind of a guy who grows on people." He picked up the cooler and put the top on, carrying it back into the cabin where it would be sheltered from the sun.

"Know what I'd like to do?" she asked when he came back to the forward deck.

"What?"

"Spread out a towel on the roof of the cabin and take a nap in the sun before we change. We can use life jackets for pillows."

It was warm in the bright spring sunlight and, after the rather vigorous exercise of skiing plus the abundance of food, they fell asleep almost immediately. When Lee awakened, he saw by his watch that an hour had passed and turned to see Tracy lying on her side, looking at him with one of the towels thrown over her body.

"Did you get cold?" he asked, but she shook her head.

"I burn easily when I haven't been in the sun for a while. It's one of the penalties of being a redhead."

"Or the price of being beautiful. When I saw you come into the gallery that first morning a few seconds before the Club program started, you literally knocked me for a loop."

Tracy laughed. "I must say you didn't act like it. I read your mind as you thought: Here's another one with a voice better adapted to calling hogs, but I've got to listen to her screeching because her father's on the Board of Trustees and has put the bite on Tim Douglas for an audition."

"Then you sang one of the most beautiful songs ever written and I knew I had what I was looking for. What I didn't know was that I had also discovered a girl I could lose my heart to."

"Please, Lee. You'll have me crying in a moment because right now I can't love you the way you deserve to be loved."

"Don't let that get you down. As I said, I tend to grow on people and I'm going to be around you every day, so a miracle might still happen."

Chapter Fourteen

"ALEX SAYS YOU WERE A GREAT HELP TO HIM IN ASHEVILLE, LEE," Neeley said, when the Monday morning broadcast was over and the last of the gallery had departed. "Did you stay over? Asheville can be very lovely at this time of the year."

"I flew back late Saturday afternoon, in time for a picnic on the lake Sunday."

Neeley's eyes twinkled. "With somebody I know—I hope."

"With Tracy. We went skiing down near the dam where the water is warmer."

"She must have looked lovely with her red-gold hair and that gorgeous figure."

"She's also a champion skier. Made me look like an amateur."

"I've skied with you and doubt that. Have you told her you love her?"

"Yesterday, but she's not sure—of something."

"She will be, in time." Neeley's tone was serious now. "I've seen it happen before but they finally realize the truth, Lee, though sometimes not without experiencing quite a lot of pain. Help Tracy through this crisis and she'll eventually come to love you all the more because you were there with the kind of love every woman needs, if she's to fulfill her personal destiny."

II

Spying Art Michaels eating at a table when he came into the hospital cafeteria for lunch after the Monday-morning broadcast, Lee carried his tray across to where the psychiatrist was eating, while absorbed in a journal reprint.

"I called your house early this morning but you'd already left," Lee said as he placed his tray on the small table.

"I had what might be called an emergency in the biofeedback laboratory," said Michaels. "Your friend Newton called early this morning and insisted on seeing me right away. Ordinarily I wouldn't have seen him until regular office hours but I was afraid that, if I put him off, he might change his mind."

"I wish I'd known he was coming to see you," said Lee. "It would have saved me buying newspapers in Asheville and here to see whether the story of his attack on Tim had broken into print yet."

"I don't think there's going to be any attack on Tim from Newton."

"Thank God for that!"

"Thank Rabbi Metzger first. After you called me the other evening to say you'd struck out with Newton and he was determined to expose Brother Tim, I talked to Rabbi Metzger by phone and asked him to contact Newton. Being the kind of man he is, the rabbi went the second mile and had his wife drive him out to Newton's house. At first, according to the Metzgers, Newton didn't even want to talk to him, so he simply pulled up his pants legs, took off his shoes and socks and started thinking hot thoughts. When Newton saw Metzger's skin color change, just the way his own did when he dared Brother Tim to heal him, his attitude took a turn for the better."

"Why did he call you in such a hurry this morning?"

"I guess he started getting cold feet—speaking symbolically, of course. That made his pain worse so, being impetuous as he is, he grabbed for the phone."

"And you did a faith-healing job on him."

"*Touché*," Michaels said with a chuckle. "Actually, I put the sensors on him and showed him how to raise his own skin temperature a couple of degrees by increasing the blood flow. Fortunately, it worked beautifully and the physical changes were strong enough to convince him he should come into the hospital under my care. He's a good subject for biofeedback, so I think I can teach him how to control his own circulation. I also took the precaution of talking to his surgeon and he agreed to put off the surgery for at least a month, unless Newton loses faith in me before that."

"You just made an interesting observation."

"What?"

"Your exact words were 'unless Newton loses faith in me before that.' Faith in Tim—plus the healing power of faith in Jesus that Newton was convinced Tim possesses—brought about the dramatic 'cure' before the TV cameras, even if it was only temporary."

"Don't go making me a faith healer," Michaels protested.

"You are, nevertheless. My bet would be that, if you didn't inspire confidence in your patients to the point where you can literally accomplish miracles, you wouldn't be nearly so successful."

"I guess, when you come down to the nitty-gritty, that's what holistic medicine is all about," the psychiatrist admitted.

"Would you mind if I brought Tim to your next biofeedback session with Newton?" Lee asked.

"No, but what do you hope to accomplish? Your Brother Tim believes in religious miracles while I believe in scientific ones—and I'm afraid the twain will never meet."

"If they could, think what a combination that would be."

"I'll think about it," Michaels promised. "You know you're asking me to admit that I've been wrong about a few things, don't you?"

"Of course, but you're enough concerned about the welfare of the people who place themselves under your care to put personal prejudice aside."

"All right, but your boss is going to have to give a little, too, and I'm not sure he's broad-minded enough to do it."

"He is. You can take my word for it."

"How did the Asheville trip go?" Michaels asked, as they were depositing their empty trays and dishes on a moving belt.

"I learned a lot—a lot I suspect I might be happier not knowing in the long run."

"Don't believe it. A great man, Dr. William J. Mayo, once said: *'Truth is a constant variable. We seek it, we find it, our viewpoint changes—and the truth changes to meet it.'*"

III

Neeley Douglas came into the foyer of the Gospel Broadcast Center on Tuesday morning after the Logos Club broadcast, just as Tracy Ravenal was signing out in the logbook kept at the receptionist's desk for the staff.

"That duet you and Lee just did was out of this world, Tracy," she said.

"Thanks. Lee has a knack of giving you confidence."

"That's one of the many things that make him invaluable to the Center. I don't know how we'd do without him. Going to the university?"

"Yes. I have a class in half an hour."

"I'm going right by there with some stuff for the printers. Hop in."

"I'm a little worried about singing with the Gospel Troubadours during the crusade," Tracy confessed as they were leaving the parking lot. "It will be my first time before a large audience."

"You'll have a large one, all right. Alex says the auditorium will be packed but don't worry, you're going to come out fine."

"Lee and I had a picnic on the lake Sunday. Did some skiing down near the dam with the Center's boat."

"Everybody claims the water gets warm earlier down there in spring, but it's too cold for me, except maybe in June, July and

August. Lee spoke to me about your doing a duet each night
during the Asheville crusade and I gave it my enthusiastic
okay."

"I hope I measure up," said Tracy a little doubtfully.

"You will," Neeley assured her, as she shot out of the parking lot in a spatter of gravel. "Lee says you're tops as a lyric soprano and even somebody with a wooden ear like me can't
argue with him."

"You're very kind."

"You did 'How Great Thou Art' as a solo at vespers recently,
didn't you?" Neeley asked.

"Yes."

"It's one of my favorite songs. The director of the college
choir and his wife are friends of ours. When I saw him last
week at a luncheon, he was singing your praises. If you and Lee
are as good as I'm sure you're going to be, you'll be the hit of
the crusade."

"Are they so important—these out-of-town crusades?"

"I'm not too sure." Neeley's tone was serious. "Tim will be
going against such veterans as Billy Graham and he's no push-
over. The Graham organization has one goal, promoting Billy's
crusades, while we have to concentrate on the daily broadcast
of the Logos Club. Don't tell anybody I admitted it, but sometimes I'm sorry Tim ever got into the evangelistic crusade field
in addition to the Logos Club broadcasts."

"Couldn't you talk him out of it?"

"Not as long as I'm convinced that it's part of his calling,
too." Neeley laughed a little wryly. "You know the old saying:
'Behind every successful man, there's a woman—pushing.'
That's not exactly true in our case; Lord knows Tim's got more
energy, enthusiasm and pure creativity than any other man I've
ever known. But he's also got a childlike faith in the good in-
tentions of his fellow human beings."

"Would you want to change that?"

"Lord, no! It's one of the things everybody loves him for—
and me, too. Fortunately, Tim has an uncanny ability to project that faith and conviction to others, from the pulpit and
from the TV screen, as well as in everyday contact."

"I noticed it the first day. I hadn't particularly wanted to come to the broadcast, but I'm glad my father made me promise to come. It's opened a whole new world for me. I can't see very far into it as yet but it's certainly different from anything I've ever known."

"You can have a promising career—plus the love of one of the finest young men I've ever known in Lee Steadman."

"That troubles me, too," Tracy admitted. "I'm not sure I can return—" She stopped, but Neeley pretended not to notice it.

"Don't let it worry you," she said with her familiar chuckle and the gamin grin that endeared her to everyone. "One of the few cases of love at first sight I know of was between Tim and me. You can bet I took pains to let him see me at my very best after that.

"Actually," she continued, "I fell in love with Tim before I grew up to where I could understand much about the real world. Falling in love with a man who lives in a world dominated by tolerance and love for his fellow beings, whether they're in the gutter or the White House, can be quite an experience."

"I've never known anyone like him," Tracy confessed.

"He's the only one of his kind. After what happened last week when Oliver Newton was healed, Tim is absolutely convinced that what we saw happen to Newton's leg was as much a miracle as Jesus walking on the water. And if Tim really does have that power, he's convinced that it would be his duty to use it to help mankind."

"I certainly had no doubts when I was watching it."

"Sometimes I think I'm too much of a doubting Thomas," Neeley confessed. "Then I tell myself that if Thomas hadn't doubted—and our Lord hadn't resolved his doubts by letting Thomas touch the nail wounds in His hands and the spear thrust in His side—a lot of other doubters might not have learned to believe in Jesus and would have been lost."

They were turning in through the gates of the university campus. "Where can I drop you off?" Neeley asked.

"Anywhere here."

"Good!" Neeley pulled into a parking slot marked "Restricted" and brought the car to a halt. "I'm glad we had the chance for this little woman-to-woman chat, Tracy."

Tracy stood on the curb, waiting for Neeley to pull the small car out into the street again, before starting across the quadrangle toward the main building. As she walked, she rehearsed in her mind the conversation she'd just had. And the more she thought of it the more convinced she was that the older woman had intentionally suggested the duets to bring her and Lee closer together.

IV

Lee was on the way to his small office after the Tuesday-morning telecast, not certain just how to approach Tim with the request that the evangelist accompany him to Art Michaels' laboratory that afternoon, when Alex Porcher called to him.

"How did it go in Asheville after I left, Lee?" Alex asked.

"All right—I think."

"What happened?"

"The pastors at the luncheon were inclined to let their hair down. They're a little miffed that so few converts join their churches after a big evangelistic crusade in their city like we're going to stage."

"It's the truth. We can bring people to know Jesus but we can't force them to join the church."

"I wonder why."

"I heard much the same gripes when I was a young evangelist, learning the ropes as you are now." Alex gave Lee's shoulder a fatherly squeeze. "Back then we didn't give the churches much of a cut in the collections, so they had every right to gripe on that score. These fellows get a much better deal, though, especially the way Tim operates. Hal Graham tells me the Center barely comes out even, after expenses are deducted from our share of the take in a crusade outside Weston, but the local pastors still gripe. I hope you were able to quiet them."

"I didn't have to; one of the older ministers there gave them a fatherly talking-to. He said the failure of converts to come to their churches was a fact of life they'd just have to put up with. The important thing, he told them, was that their own budgets were swelled considerably by the lion's share of the collections that go to them."

"That sounds like Roger Peters; he's got a big downtown church and today most of them are losing members. Fortunately for Roger, a prominent Asheville family gave him enough practically to endow everything he does. If the average minister in the average church would make his message more appealing and organize enough outside activities to keep everybody in his congregation busy, especially the younger people, he wouldn't be complaining."

Alex gave Lee a slap on the shoulder in parting. "Many thanks for taking care of those fellows for me."

"I hear you preached in Jake Schiller's Temple at Atlanta," said Lee.

Alex gave him a startled look. "That was a last-minute invitation. How did you know?"

"The early news broadcast on our local religious radio station carried a mention of it this morning. Tracy and I attended a healing service at the Temple the Sunday after our concert in Atlanta. Jeff Champion, who seems to be Schiller's right hand, was a classmate of mine in college. I must say that between Schiller and Champion, they put on quite a show."

"That's Jake's forte, but you won't catch me performing in one of those healing services—I saw too many fake ones in the old days. Anyway, thanks for subbing for me last Saturday, Lee."

V

The door to Tim Douglas' office was closed but, when Lee knocked, Tim called, "Come in."

The evangelist was sitting at his desk, with a pile of papers

before him and the microphone of an office-type tape recorder
in his right hand. He looked up, smiled warmly and nodded toward the chair beside his desk.

"I was talking to Roger Peters in Asheville a few moments
ago," Tim said as he switched off the microphone.

"He came to my aid last Saturday at noon when the going
got pretty rough."

"Roger says you handled yourself well. We're going to have a
great crusade up there this weekend, Lee. By the way, Neeley
tells me you and Tracy are going to sing 'How Great Thou Art'
as a duet."

"The truth is, Neeley persuaded us."

"That minx I'm married to has been up to her old tricks
again, manipulating other people's lives. Anyway, it sounds like
a wonderful idea; Tracy has a fine voice." Tim's hand dropped
to the microphone he'd been using in an obvious signal that he
wished to end the visit. "Can I do anything for you, Lee?"

"I really came by to ask whether you could go with me to
Dr. Art Michaels' laboratory at the University Hospital this afternoon."

"What time?"

"Would five o'clock do?"

"Fine. I go by to see Aggie about that time every afternoon.
Any particular reason why you want me there?"

"Just something Art Michaels is working on that I think
you'll find interesting. I'll meet you at five in the hospital parking lot."

Chapter Fifteen

LEE WAS WAITING WHEN TIM DROVE INTO THE HOSPITAL PARKING lot promptly at five. Together they took the elevator to Art Michaels' laboratory.

"You're still keeping this a secret until the last moment, aren't you?" said Tim. "It must be something very important."

"I think it is," said Lee as the door was opened by Art himself. "I believe you know Dr. Michaels."

"We were on a TV panel once; tore each other apart," said Art as he shook hands with Tim. "Glad you could come, Reverend."

"It's Tim," said the evangelist.

"Fine. Tim Douglas, meet Rabbi Metzger, a patient of mine."

"*Shalom*, Rabbi," said Tim, shaking hands. "I read in a newspaper about a year ago that you had been forced to retire because of ill health, but you certainly look healthy to me."

"I owe that to Dr. Michaels," said the smiling Metzger. "He's a miracle worker."

"I forgive you for muscling in on my field, Dr. Michaels, but you have an advantage over me," said Tim. "My healing has to be done through television and what people write me about their cures, while you can see yours happen."

"As long as you don't start sending healing cloths through the mail and having people put their hands against yours on the TV screen, like one clown I sometimes see during breakfast

Sunday mornings, I won't hold your practicing medicine without a license against you," Art Michaels promised.

"I do have a license," said Tim. "You'll find it in the New Testament—Matthew 10:8 and Luke 9:2 and 10:9."

"In Ecclesiastes 3:3," said Rabbi Metzger, "the preacher says: 'A time to kill and a time to heal; a time to break down and a time to build up.'"

"Dr. Michaels has a patient I think you'll be interested in seeing, Tim," said Lee. "His name is Oliver Newton."

"Newton? Wasn't that the name of the man I healed with poor circulation in his feet and legs last week?"

"Yes."

"Then why—"

"What Lee's saying is that Newton's cure wasn't quite as complete as it seemed to be on the TV screens and in the newspapers," said Art Michaels.

"Are you implying that it was faked?" Tim's voice was suddenly sharp.

"It was real enough—at the time. Unfortunately, it didn't last."

"I think you'd better explain, Doctor." Tim's voice hadn't changed.

"Gladly," said Michaels. "I happen to be experimenting with biofeedback. Are you familiar with it?"

"Only by name."

"It's a method of teaching people to control involuntary functions—those covered by the autonomic nervous system—voluntarily."

"Such as circulation or digestion?"

"Among others. The dramatic changes in Oliver Newton's condition recorded by the TV cameras during your broadcast last week was one of the most impressive proofs I've ever seen that autonomic function can be controlled. When I saw the pictures in the newspapers the next morning, I asked Lee to come by and watch the same effect in the case of Rabbi Metzger."

"The same effect?" Tim's voice was curt.

"I'll leave that up to you," said Art on the same somewhat belligerent note.

"Six months ago the circulation in my feet and legs was just as bad as that in the case of Mr. Newton," the rabbi interposed soothingly. "I'd even been advised to have them amputated by one surgeon but fortunately my wife insisted upon a second opinion. The second surgeon we consulted happened to be familiar with Dr. Michaels' studies in biofeedback."

"I think we might look at some films now," said Art Michaels, moving to the switch that controlled the curtains.

The two films Lee had seen were shown—before and after. When they were finished, Rabbi Metzger stretched out on the table and Art applied the sensors to demonstrate temperature and blood flow. As the delicate instruments on the wall recorded the dramatic changes being reflected in the color of the skin over the patient's feet and legs, the evangelist watched in silence.

"That's the most remarkable thing I've ever seen," Tim admitted when the demonstration was completed. Then he added with a wry smile, "I feel like a fool proclaiming to have accomplished a miracle, when only a simple physiological process was involved."

"Physiological, yes—but far from simple," said Art Michaels. "Lee tells me that when Oliver Newton challenged you to cure him that morning, he was very aggressive and obviously in a state of considerable emotional excitement, all adding to what might be called an emotional charge. Fortunately, your obvious concern and sympathy for him, plus your faith, channeled the nervous energy of that emotional charge into the part of the autonomic—automatic is probably a better word—nervous system that controls the size of the arteries of the body, particularly those that make them larger. The result was what you and the cameras saw."

"A miracle of faith, Brother Tim," said Rabbi Metzger. "Without your own faith and your ability to stir an answering faith in Mr. Newton, nothing would have happened."

"You give me too much credit, Rabbi," said Tim. "The faith was in Christ, not in me."

"As a psychiatrist, I suspect the two are very close—if not identical," said Art Michaels. "Unfortunately, when Newton left you, he left most of the source of his faith behind. Doctors soon learn to view dramatic symptoms of any kind with suspicion and, when I saw those photos, I wondered whether anything so startling could last very long. That's why I put a bug in Lee's ear, hoping he would investigate."

"I went to Mr. Newton's home that same afternoon," Lee explained. "The effect you observed in the studio lasted only a few hours, Tim. I found Newton in a rage, threatening to go to the press and expose you as a charlatan. The best I could do was tell him something of what Art here has been doing and beg him to call for an appointment."

"Why didn't you tell me?" Tim demanded.

"I was afraid you'd go to see Newton and he would—"

"Spill his guts—along with a lot of venom—to the press," said Art Michaels. "He was still ready to do that when he called me, which is why I saw him early Monday morning instead of waiting until my normal office hours."

"With what results?" Tim asked.

"I can show you more than I can tell you," said the psychiatrist. "My technician has had Newton connected to the feedback recording instruments in an adjoining laboratory for the past fifteen minutes or so, and I think you'll be impressed. Fortunately, Mr. Newton is a very emotional man and reacts quickly."

II

"Brother Tim! I never expected to see you here!" Oliver Newton was sitting on an examining table with his legs extended and the small sensors connecting him to the delicate recording instruments on the wall in place. Although the skin of the patient's feet and legs was far from the almost vivid pink tint it had exhibited in the television studio at the Center, the color was still much nearer normal than when he'd first sent his wheelchair hurtling up the ramp to the stage.

"I'm glad you took my advice, Mr. Newton, and called Dr. Michaels," said Lee.

"You can thank my wife for that, young man. She threatened to leave me if I didn't give the doctor here a chance to help me." He turned to the evangelist. "But I do owe you a lot, Brother Tim, for sending Mr. Steadman to check up on me."

"I didn't send him, Mr. Newton. When you left the studio, I was so certain that Jesus had performed another miracle—with me as his agent—it never occurred to me that the effects might not last."

Once again Lee found the right words to say at the right time. "Except for what Brother Tim here did, you would never have found your way into Dr. Michaels' hands, Mr. Newton. That's the real miracle here."

"You're doing better, aren't you?" Tim asked Newton.

"A lot better, as you can see—else I'd've been on the amputation table before now. Dr. Michaels tells me I'll soon be able to jog like Rabbi Metzger does."

"But not very far," said the rabbi, who had followed them into the laboratory. "I just thank God for being able to get around as much as I do without pain."

"The Lord is curing you and teaching me modesty at the same time, Mr. Newton." Tim held out his hand, and the other man shook it vigorously. "I'll be praying for this good work to continue," he told Art Michaels. "When you've taught Mr. Newton to increase his circulation to where the TV cameras will show it once again, I'd like to have both of you on one of the Logos programs to explain how it all happened."

"I wish I could be sure of the exact mechanism myself," the doctor admitted. "That's why I've been pestering the hospital administrator to set aside a dozen beds for a deeper study of holistic medicine."

"Holistic," Tim frowned. "If I remember correctly, the word comes from the Greek *holos,* meaning whole."

"I believe so," said Michaels. "It's somewhat of a new expression for an old concept, one the family doctors of long ago knew very well, that unless you treated the whole man—both soul and body—you couldn't really achieve an effective cure. My father tells me that when he was a medical student at Johns Hopkins in the twenties, Dr. Adolf Meyer used that concept in treating people with mental diseases. He called it 'psychobiological integration,' but I'm afraid few of the students knew what he was really talking about."

"This feedback?" Tim asked. "Is it part of what you call holistic medicine?"

"A tool, and a very valuable one. If you can spare a few minutes more I'd like to put the sensors on you and show you how biofeedback really works."

"For that I don't mind being late for dinner. Call Neeley while the doctor is getting me ready, Lee, and tell her I'll be maybe a half hour late."

While Art was applying the sensors to Tim's right hand in the adjoining laboratory, Lee called Neeley from the adjoining office. "Tim wants me to tell you he's going to be half an hour late for dinner," he told her.

"So what's really new? If that husband of mine ever got to a meal on time, I'd collapse at his feet. What is it this time?"

"We're at Dr. Michaels' office—"

"Is anything wrong with Tim, Lee?" Her voice was suddenly anxious. "I keep telling him he's working too hard and he doesn't pay me any attention."

"Nothing like that." Lee gave her a quick rundown on why they were at the hospital.

"So Mrs. Newton pulled the old Lysistrata routine on her husband." Neeley was her old bubbling self again. "Works every time—even after twenty-five hundred years."

"Art's demonstrating how biofeedback works—with Tim as the subject. He's fascinated with it and with holistic medicine."

"Whatever that is but don't tell me now; Tim will be talking of nothing else for days. Before the week's out he'll know more about it than the whole faculty at Weston Medical School. Tell Tim I've got to go back to the studio and record the puppet show, then I'm going to the hospital to stay with Aggie until bedtime. We can have a bite together in the snack shop off the foyer."

"Is there any change in Aggie's condition?" Lee asked.

"None I can see, though Dr. Thorpe assures me she's holding her own."

"Neeley wants you to wait for her in Aggie's room after you finish here," Lee told Tim when Lee came back into the adjoining laboratory. "She has a recording session scheduled to-night for the Punch and Judy show but is going to the hospital as soon as it's over and wants you to have a snack with her there in the coffee shop."

"Thanks, Lee." Tim was watching eagerly the slowly moving needle of a recorder on the wall. "Look at that! I've already raised the temperature of my index finger by two degrees. This whole concept is absolutely fantastic. I can see that its possi-bilities are unlimited."

"I wish you'd convince the hospital administration and the executive staff of that," said Art Michaels.

"I'll do even more! If the idea taking form in my mind be-comes a reality, we're going to be working very closely together from now on, Dr. Michaels. Working for the betterment of mankind where sick are concerned."

"Unfortunately, my wife isn't nearly as liberal as yours when it comes to my being late for dinner," said Art as he started removing the small sensors from Tim's skin.

"Tell her not to plan anything for next Tuesday evening," Tim told him. "I hope you can both come to dinner at my house, along with Lee and his beautiful girl friend and some other people. By that time, the idea I just mentioned should be almost full grown and I'd like to try it on for size with the rest of you."

"Alix will be happy to escape the chore of cooking," Art Michaels assured Tim. "Besides, we've both been anxious to see that house of yours ever since we visited Fallingwater last summer.

"Is your boss always that enthusiastic about new projects?" Art Michaels asked Lee as they were leaving the laboratory after Tim had gone on to the isolation ward.

"Only those he really believes in—but you certainly con-vinced him this afternoon."

"I guess I've always sold him short before now," said the psy-chiatrist. "We see a lot of cases where preachers try to inter-vene in the lives of people with serious emotional problems. Sometimes, with every good intention, a minister can literally commit emotional mayhem, so it's hard to believe one of them could be as completely unselfish as your Brother Tim appears to be."

"There was one, a long time ago. Unfortunately, the world of that day wasn't ready for His teachings."

"Is it any more so today?"

"I used to wonder, but since working with Tim, I find much of my faith in mankind coming back."

"He *does* have that quality. I don't suppose he has many enemies."

"Maybe not, but he's got plenty of enviers and that can be almost the same thing."

"What do you mean?"

Lee gave Art Michaels a quick summary of the events of the past weeks. When he finished, Michaels' expression was concerned. "This fellow Schiller. Do you believe he really thought he could marshal enough votes at the fundamentalist convention to censure Tim Douglas?"

"It appears to have been more of a skirmish, sort of testing out Tim's strength when he wasn't there to defend himself."

"The dagger-in-the-back principle," Art Michaels commented. "Schiller didn't get anywhere, did he?"

"I'm not too sure of that either. The vote against Tim was a lot stronger than I would have expected."

"Why do you think it went that way?"

"I don't suppose anybody really knows the whole answer. Today, competition in the evangelical arena is pretty vicious. A lot of TV preachers are in serious trouble financially."

"I thought they were all busy raking in the dollars by mail."

"They are, compared to the collection plates in the regular churches, but a lot of the stars of the 'Electric Church' appear to have been convinced that the goose would always lay the golden eggs—by mail—no matter what they did with the money. Some started building extravagantly expensive churches. Others are building fundamentalist colleges that will have trouble getting themselves accredited by regional and national associations."

"How could that happen?"

"Their students get fired up with religious enthusiasm and enter college, then halfway through find the curriculum so restricted it hasn't trained them to be anything but a preacher in a small country church or a Bible teacher, jobs that don't pay enough to live on. If they transfer to a state college, they usually find half the courses they've taken aren't accepted and after two or three years in a so-called Bible college, they're still rated no higher than a freshman or a sophomore, even if they've got a degree."

"It would take a lot of religious faith at that point not to believe somebody had sold you down the river," Art Michaels commented.

"That's exactly what's happening. Several of the new fundamentalist colleges have had to halt construction. One or two healing-oriented evangelists have found themselves with half-constructed hospitals, even medical schools, in areas that are already overpopulated as far as doctors and hospital beds are concerned. One tried to build a complete religious-oriented retirement community and wound up with a big mudhole."

"So what's going to happen?"

"Much of what the public calls the 'Electric Church' has found its voltage dropped to where it can barely operate, while a lot of others are already in the red. Tim has escaped that by not building any farther than the Christian Broadcast Center and employing a top-notch administrator in Hal Graham to operate it efficiently. The Center markets products like the Logos Club that sell like hotcakes in the religious TV and radio market—entertainment."

"With an almost subliminal religious message." Art Michaels whistled softly in admiration. "The more I see of that employer of yours, the greater respect I have for him."

"Unless I miss my guess, you will soon be seeing a lot more of him. Don't ever make the mistake of selling Tim short, either, particularly with Neeley there to put on the brakes."

"I'll be interested to hear what he comes up with next week." They were at the elevator leading to the lower floors where the medical wards were located and Lee asked, "Is there any chance that I might look in on Aggie? I'm her godfather and she means a lot to me."

"Sure," said Art. "I'm going to stop by the isolation ward myself to check on her before I leave the hospital."

Masked and gowned according to the rules for visitors to isolation cases, Lee and Art Michaels let themselves into Aggie's
room, but stopped just inside the door. The little girl lay on the
bed without moving, except for the faint rise and fall of the
counterpane covering her. The nurses had prepared her for
Tim's daily evening visit, however, by brushing her hair and
tying it back with a blue ribbon. With her cheeks slightly
flushed by fever and the collar of a frilly pale blue nightgown
tied by strings of ribbon at her throat, she looked almost ethe-
real and more beautiful than Lee had ever seen her.

Tim stood by the bed, holding Aggie's left hand and looking
down at his daughter's face. His lips were moving in a whispered prayer, but it was the look on his face that startled Lee.
A father would naturally feel anguish at seeing his only daughter lying there in a coma—from which the attending physicians
would give no hope of her ever recovering. Instead, Tim's face
was transfigured by a light Lee could characterize in no other
way than one of glory, a light remarkably like the one that had
illumined Tim's eyes that morning when he'd thought he had
cured Oliver Newton with a true miracle.

Lee nodded to Art Michaels that he wanted to leave and the
psychiatrist was reaching behind him for the doorknob when
Tim spoke. "Don't go, please." His voice, too, like his face, almost seemed to be overflowing with happiness. "The Lord has
just revealed to me that my daughter will soon be well and I
want you to share that revelation with me."

"I'm sorry." Art Michaels' tone was genuinely sad. "You see,
I don't believe in faith heal—"

"Oh no! You don't understand! This will be no miracle of
faith, beyond my own faith that it will happen, as Jesus has
revealed to me that it will. Aggie's healing will be a result of
medical science."

"But—"

"I know you can't see any chance of that now," Tim continued in the same quiet tone. "But you will, and soon."

"God knows I hope you're right, Dr. Douglas." Art Michaels'
voice was hoarse with emotion. "I hope it more than I can ever
remember hoping anything else in my life."

"So do I," said Lee quietly.

"Then take my word—the word of Jesus—that it will."

There was no more to say, so Lee and Art eased the door open and moved out into the corridor to shed their caps, masks and gowns. Neither spoke until they were going down the steps to the walk that led to the parking lot.

Art voiced their common thought: "Do you suppose my demonstration of feedback with Oliver Newton and Rabbi Metzger convinced him that his daughter will be cured?"

"I don't know. Has every means you and Dr. Thorpe know of been tried already?"

"Everything. Continuous spinal drainage was our last hope, but the virus is so entrenched in her body proteins that even that procedure couldn't wash it out."

"At least you know you've done all that could be done."

"Medically, yes. But if I've started a false spark of hope burning in a father's heart, when there's no reason to believe it can ever become a flame—"

The psychiatrist didn't finish the sentence. He didn't need to. Even Lee felt some of the guilt his friend was experiencing, for he had played a part, too, in the events of the afternoon— by bringing Tim to Art Michaels' laboratory.

Chapter Sixteen

"DID YOU RECOGNIZE ANY OF THE CHURCH PEOPLE YOU RECRUITED among those answering the invitation tonight and pretending to be new converts?" Tracy asked Lee as they were leaving the stage of the auditorium in Asheville for the motel where the crusade personnel were staying.

"They were there in force—and those not yet convinced followed them, just as Alex said they would. I've seen a lot of revivals but people never poured down those aisles to answer the invitation like they did tonight."

"And much of it due to advance work."

"Most, I'd say. What did you think of the sermon?"

"I was entranced," she said. "This was the first time I'd ever heard Tim preach except on the tape from the National Cathedral. He's very effective."

"The secret of Tim's success, I'm sure, is that he's careful to be the same sort of person in the pulpit that he is during the Logos Club broadcasts. The fact that everyone hearing him can't fail to recognize his complete sincerity makes him even more successful. By the way," he added as they came out into the warm summer air, "your solo of 'In the Garden' was absolutely tops."

"Thanks, but I liked our duet better. Knowing you are there to back me up gives me confidence," she assured him.

"Before we left the Center this afternoon, Neeley told me she'd like to schedule Tim's interview with you, the one I spoke to you about the other day, on a Club program next week. Alex has to be away Thursday and Friday, I believe, and Neeley asked me to fill in by taking part in the interview."

"I like your being there for that, too," she told him. "With both you and Tim, I won't have so much stage fright."

"There's nothing to be afraid of," he assured her. "Neeley does want a solo just before the interview, though. If you'll tell me what you'd like to sing, I'll help with the rehearsal after the morning broadcast the first part of the week."

"I really don't know what to choose," she confessed. "What would you suggest?"

"One of the gospel-rock songs."

"Why that? I'd say it's probably my weakest place."

"Neeley and I both think you can be another Evie Tornquist, if you'd really like to do it. This broadcast would be the proof of that."

"But our duets together are so beautiful. Why can't we sing one of them and then go into the interview?"

"Being a principal guest on the Logos Club will mark your debut as an individual performer, so it wouldn't be right for you to sing anything except solo. Besides, Neeley wants to send the tape to Word or Leeds, and I wouldn't be surprised to see you get a recording contract."

"But you and I sing together as well or better than I ever could sing alone. Why wouldn't they want you under contract, too?"

"Male leads are not nearly as effective in the TV evangelical field as beautiful female sopranos."

"I'm not sure I'd want a recording contract," she objected. "Wouldn't it take me away from Weston a lot so I couldn't continue to sing with you and the Gospel Troubadours?"

He understood what was troubling her and it did nothing to raise his spirits, although he had felt very pleased by the success of their duet tonight.

"Suppose we're offered a recording contract together—as a gospel-rock team?" he asked. "Would you like that?"

They had reached the lobby of the motel and in the brighter lights there he saw that her eyes were troubled.

"Forget I asked that." He reached out to take her hand. "I was just hoping—"

"I'm sorry, Lee." He saw that she was close to tears. "I can't help what happened that first morning at the studio, but now, just being there—near him—means more to me than anything else in my life."

"But—"

"I know it's hopeless and I hate myself for feeling the way I do about someone who has no inkling of it at all—and would probably be horrified at the very thought."

"Neeley knows and she doesn't condemn you any more than I do."

"But I feel so guilty about allowing you to make all these plans." Her voice almost broke. "Maybe I should just go away to Lankashire or even back to Switzerland where I wouldn't complicate the lives of wonderful people like you and Neeley."

"Stop worrying. Did your father get here in time for your solo?"

"No. He telephoned from Hendersonville just before I left the motel to tell me that he was having some car trouble and didn't expect to get here much before midnight."

"That's a shame," said Lee. "But he will be here tomorrow night, and you'll be singing just as well."

"I hope so," she said. "Dad wants us to have breakfast with him at the Rock Creek Inn tomorrow morning, if you can make it."

"I'd love to meet him—if you think I can stand inspection," said Lee with a smile.

"You're Dad's kind of person," she assured him. "He likes his breakfast early, though. Can you be ready by eight-thirty?"

"I'll make it. Do you want me to call your room?"

"Please—about seven forty-five. We can drive over to the Rock Creek Inn in the Porsche."

II

The telephone was ringing in Lee's motel room when he came in, and he hurried to answer it.

"This is Jack Feagin, Mr. Steadman!" said the caller. "I'm an A and R representative for Word Music in Waco. Did Neeley Douglas tell you I'd be in Asheville?"

"She thought you might be."

"Thought?" Lee could hear Feagin's chuckle over the phone. "She practically threatened to stop using our music on the Logos Club and blacklist our artists if I didn't show up."

"That's our Neeley."

"And one of the many reasons why we all love her. I've got to catch an early plane to Atlanta in the morning. I know it's late and you've had a busy evening, but could you possibly meet me in the coffee shop for a few minutes?"

"Sure." Lee hesitated. "I might be able to bring Miss Ravenal, if you'd like me to."

"Not this time," said Feagin. "I gather that you're sort of managing her career."

"Not as much as I'd like to, but she usually follows my advice."

"Good. See you in five minutes."

Jack Feagin was redheaded, with an infectious grin that made Lee like him immediately.

"Let me say first off," he said as the hostess was showing them to a table, "that I'm glad Neeley made me come to Asheville. Music is my business and I've rarely heard as professional a backup group as you have in the Troubadours."

"Thank you. They'll appreciate hearing that."

"I already knew your electric-bass player and he tells me you're responsible for their expertness."

"We all work well together."

"That goes without saying," said Feagin. "I liked Miss Ravenal's solo very much and also your duet with her. She has a lovely voice that fits your baritone very well."

"She's in her third year of voice at Weston and working very hard."

"I was late in calling you tonight because I wanted to talk to a friend with the Leeds Music Corporation, who heard both you and Miss Ravenal sing at your Atlanta concerts," said Feagin. "Has she had much experience in gospel-rock?"

"Only what she's had since she joined the Troubadours. Why do you ask?"

"My friend in Atlanta has recommended to the Leeds organization that they sign her to a contract as a soloist. But after hearing the two of you together tonight, I'd be more inclined to offer you both a contract."

"I'm not sure Tra— Miss Ravenal wants a musical career."

"So Neeley Douglas told me, but she intimated that Miss Ravenal would follow your advice."

"Does that mean you'd be willing to sign me, too, in order to get her?" Lee asked bluntly.

"Whatever gave you that idea?" Feagin asked.

"I'm afraid *you* did."

"There I go putting my foot in my mouth again! A religious TV station in Waco carries the Logos Club and we've actually been watching you for six months, long before Miss Ravenal came on the scene. When we saw her and learned how quickly you'd trained her in gospel-rock, when her musical background had been largely operatic before—"

"How did you discover that?"

"A friend on the Weston music faculty acts as sort of a spotter for us in this area. When I heard Leeds was interested in Miss Ravenal, I had him check into her musical background. Obviously, as beautiful as she is, she can have a career in popular music if she wants it. What we're really looking for, though, is a girl who can become a top star in gospel-rock, the hottest new field in music today."

"She could do it," said Lee.

"With you coaching her," Feagin agreed. "Anyone who could train a group the way you've trained your Troubadours is an expert in the field, besides being blessed with a magnificent voice, as you are. As soon as I can get back to Waco, I'm going to try to convince our top brass that, since you and Miss Ravenal can do both solos and duets, you're a double threat. In addition, you can train her to be one of the top female stars in the gospel-rock field."

"If she decides that she wants that kind of a career."

"Sure." Feagin hesitated, then added, "I hope I'm not prying but you're in love with her, aren't you?"

"I've asked her to marry me but she's—I suppose you could say—taking the question under advisement."

"That's always a woman's prerogative but either way you're both going to stay with Tim Douglas, aren't you?"

"For the time being, at least—where Tracy's concerned. I'm committed for at least another year, and perhaps longer."

"If we sign either or both of you, we'll be happy to have you stay with the Logos Club and continue your concert work," Feagin assured him. "Nothing could give an artist any more exposure than you'd get through the Club, and that always sells records."

"Suppose you can't convince your top management in Waco that Tracy Ravenal has the potentialities you think she has in gospel-rock and needs more experience."

"If she's with you, we know she'll be getting the best possible training, as well as the exposure that could make her a top star. What worries me most, and frankly the reason why I wanted to talk to you before I discuss this whole question with my bosses in Waco, is the possibility that Leeds may offer Miss Ravenal a contract before we can."

"She wouldn't accept without asking me about it."

"I'm sure of that, just as I'm pretty sure you'd advise her to take it—even though that decision would take her out of your life."

"You're right there," said Lee. "I know your company has a fine reputation but a contract with Leeds means MCA would be behind Tracy, too, with all the backing and know-how both companies have."

"I guess that's that, then, until I can get back to Waco. Let's hope nobody at Leeds is smart enough to realize the potentialities of having both you and Miss Ravenal as a team. I'm certainly not going to tell them."

"They may find out before long anyway," Lee warned him. "Tracy Ravenal is going to make her debut, so to speak, as a gospel-rock soloist Thursday or Friday of next week on a Logos Club broadcast, prior to being interviewed by Tim. That religious station in Waco you spoke of takes the Club broadcast live off the satellite we use to bounce programs to other stations all over the country. Unless I miss my guess, every record company in the business that sees and hears her sing that day is going to offer her the moon."

"Possibly without Lee Steadman," Feagin warned. "Have you thought of that?"

"I'm going to be too busy rehearsing with her next week to worry about my own career. One thing you can be sure of, though, when Tracy Ravenal sings on a Logos Club broadcast next Friday, she's going to be in top form, so you'd better get your bid in early." Lee stood up. "Good night, Mr. Feagin, and thanks for the vote of confidence."

"Good night. I've just met someone I never expected to meet, after twenty years in this business—a completely unselfish artist."

III

Tracy sounded sleepy when she answered Lee's call to her room the next morning. "I never could understand why my father always got up so early," she complained.

"Look outside and you'll see," he told her. "It's a beautiful late-spring morning. I've already run about five miles."

"Don't tell me you ran into Eileen Stoddard again."

"Not this time, but I wouldn't have been surprised. Apparently, she helped Alex organize this crusade."

"Or something. I'll be ready in thirty minutes. It's no more than a fifteen-minute drive to the Rock Creek Inn."

Tracy was wearing a bright-colored summer dress with a light sweater across her shoulders, and Lee was sure he'd never seen anything more beautiful. "After we have breakfast with Dad," she said as she got into the Porsche, "do you suppose we could drive south along the parkway as far as Clingman's Knob? I haven't taken the path to the top in ages and the view from there has always been fabulous."

"Sure. We can have lunch on the way back at Mount Pisgah Inn. I set the rehearsal for tonight's songs at four so everybody would have most of the day to themselves."

"You always think of the nicest things." She settled back in the bucket seat as he started to drive away from the motel. "Will there be as big a crowd as last night?"

"Probably more. Saturday night is the time of celebration in southern towns, and a big revival meeting is considered a form of recreation." Briefly he debated telling her about his conversation with Jack Feagin last night but discarded the idea, lest knowing that her gospel-rock performance on next Friday's Logos Club broadcast could earn her a recording contract might make her less assured.

"I've been thinking about what I'd like to sing on Friday," she said.

"You must have been reading my mind. What have you selected?"

"Of all the songs we've done in that field, I like 'If Heaven Never Was Promised to Me' best. Would that do?"

"Perfectly. We'll start rehearsing first thing Monday, and by Friday you'll be letter perfect. I'll go over the sheet music tomorrow afternoon back in Weston and see whether I can make some changes in the arrangement to fit your range better than the way it's written."

At the entrance to the dining room of the famous inn, Tracy gave her name to the hostess. "Your father came in about ten minutes ago, Miss Ravenal," the woman said. "He's out on the porch reading a paper with a cup of coffee."

Caleb Ravenal was of medium build, his face sun- and wind-burned, while his hair was just beginning to start turning gray. As they crossed the porch to his table, Lee estimated that Tracy's father must be close to sixty, and when he got to his feet, Lee saw that Ravenal was actually taller than he looked sitting down. In fact, he appeared to be exactly what he was, the epitome of a successful businessman.

"This is Lee Steadman," said Tracy after greeting her father with a kiss.

"I've seen you on the tube enough to recognize you, Lee." Caleb Ravenal's handshake was firm. "The morning paper says the music at last night's revival service was outstanding."

"The Troubadours, especially Tracy, did a fine job, sir. I was very proud of them."

"The way I hear it, a lot of the credit belongs to you."

"We all work together. I couldn't have made them into such a fine group if they all weren't excellent musicians. We owe you a debt for sending Tracy to us."

"When I wasn't at all certain I wanted to go," she added.

"In a little over two weeks she's become our top performer, Mr. Ravenal." They joined the textile magnate at his table on the porch. "If you want to hear her best performance, be sure to watch the broadcast of the Logos Club Friday morning. She's going to make her debut then as both star performer and guest."

"I figured if I could ever get her into something she really loved doing, she'd be a success," said Ravenal. "None of us gives up very easily and Tracy tells me you're cut from pretty much the same cloth."

"I'm afraid my heritage isn't quite as distinguished as that of the Huguenots who came to America," said Lee. "The first Steadman was an indentured servant to a farmer in Maryland. He served his seven years and then went West about 1750, when the Wilderness Road was opened from Lancaster, Pennsylvania, into what is now West Virginia. We've been there ever since."

"The first Ravenal to land on the South Carolina coast was a weaver journeyman from Paris. I guess that's why we naturally went into textiles when we got to the New World. I haven't ordered—"

"My father will have ham and eggs and so will I," Tracy told the waitress. "What about you, Lee?"

"Sounds fine, with some hash browns on the side. I get a little hungry after running five miles."

"Every morning?" Caleb Ravenal asked.

"Five times a week, at least. I do some of my best composing while I'm running. The rhythm sort of sets the notes moving in my brain."

"You should hear some of Lee's songs," said Tracy. "They're lovely."

"Never had much of an ear for music myself," Ravenal admitted, "but nothing's wrong with my sense of smell. Do either of you two have any idea what's going on at the Center?"

"What do you mean?" Tracy asked.

"Last week this blonde turned up at the office—"

"Medium height, maybe 130 pounds, and wearing very high heels, sir?" Lee asked. "Named Eileen Stoddard?"

"That's the name she gave. Said she came on business for the Center, or I would never have let her in the office."

"I hope you turned your recorder on," said Tracy. "A handsome widower like my father is always being pursued by conniving women," she explained to Lee. "Before I left home, I had him add a secret switch and microphone to his office dictating machine—for his own protection."

"It's kept me out of trouble more than once, too," said Ravenal with a chuckle.

"The blonde works for Jake Schiller in Atlanta," Lee told him.

"The faith healer?"

"Yes."

"Lee and I saw her at one of Schiller's services there," Tracy volunteered. "The next weekend she was here in Asheville with Alex Porcher, arranging for this crusade—among other things. Lee spotted her leaving Alex's room at six-thirty in the morning."

"Didn't Brother Tim throw Schiller out of the Center some time ago?" Ravenal asked.

"It happened before I came to the Center," said Lee. "Schiller tried to take over when it became pretty obvious that the Center was going to be a success. He was giving false information about Tim's operations to some of the trustees, and Tim fired him. I'd be very much interested to know what Miss Stoddard told you, sir."

"She said she represented a group of board members who aren't entirely happy with the way Brother Tim is running the Center. When I tried to pin her down about the nature of their complaints, she was pretty vague. Mostly they involved matters of doctrine that don't mean much to me anyway."

"Did you read where Schiller attacked Tim in Chicago, sir?"

"Yes, but the report also said your man, Porcher, defended the Reverend Douglas there. If Porcher has been working against Brother Tim, as Tracy suggested the other night over the phone, why would he defend him at the convention?"

"We don't know the answer to that, but Tracy and I are pretty sure someone is trying to destroy Tim and the Center. The one person who would profit most, if he could gain control of our TV network, would be Jake Schiller. He already has a small one of his own."

"Apparently Eileen Stoddard was sent to sound you out, Dad," said Tracy, "and possibly influence your decisions by giving out false information against Tim at the next meeting of the Board of Trustees."

"Which is liable to be pretty soon from what she said," Ravenal commented. "This group she represents is going to demand a call meeting; I looked up the bylaws after she left and she was telling the truth. If enough trustees make a formal demand in writing, they can call a special meeting with only a week's notice."

"Did she say how many trustees are involved in the move against Tim, sir?" Lee asked.

"I tried to pin her down but she was vague enough in her answers to make me think they're not quite ready to make their play," said Ravenal. "Did you know Brother Tim has been talking to the president of Weston University and the dean of the Medical School about establishing an institute for some special type of medicine? I forget the name Miss Stoddard used, but I'd never heard it before."

"Was it 'holistic,' sir?" Lee asked.

"That's the word! What does it mean?"

"Studying the whole person instead of just the disease."

"That makes sense. Why would they hold that against Tim?"

"A faith healer would—that's why we think Schiller is involved, along with some other reasons," said Lee. "Tim's daughter, Aggie, is still very sick. Ten days or so ago, Tim thought he'd performed a miracle—"

"The man whose legs were going to be amputated?"

"Yes, but the changes that showed on TV and in the newspapers didn't last. Mr. Newton was going to denounce Tim publicly as a fake until I talked him into going to a doctor who specializes in holistic medicine at the Medical School. Dr. Michaels taught Newton how to use his emotional tension to dilate the blood vessels going to his legs. When Tim saw the demonstration I'm afraid he went overboard for the idea of combining religion with holistic medicine."

"Is that why he's been exploring the idea of a research institute with the top brass at the university?" Ravenal asked.

"We didn't know he'd gone that far," Lee admitted. "Tim's invited a number of people to dinner at his house Tuesday night, though, and I believe he's going to make some sort of an announcement. It will probably be about the institute."

"They couldn't call a meeting of the trustees and stop Tim before Tuesday night, could they?" Tracy asked.

"Actually," said Lee, "they'd probably prefer to let Tim make the public announcement—"

"Mind telling me why?" Caleb Ravenal asked.

"The medical profession isn't sold on the idea of holistic medicine completely, and neither is the evangelical community. After all, most evangelists pray for the sick and, quite frequently, the results are rather spectacular, though usually only for a little while. Faith healers naturally look on doctors practicing holistic medicine as muscling into their act, too. If Tim sponsored such an institute here at Weston, it would almost certainly be tied in closely with the Center."

"Why?" Ravenal asked.

"A lot of money would have to be raised."

"Did Eileen Stoddard mention that?" Tracy asked.

"It was part of the spiel," said Ravenal. "Here comes our waitress with breakfast; suppose we resume this discussion afterward. Right now I'm too hungry to do much productive thinking."

The food was delicious and disappeared rapidly. When the dishes had been taken away and their coffee cups filled a second time, Tracy looked at her father quizzically. "All right, Caleb—as Mother used to say—" she said with a smile, "what did the blonde do—besides talk?"

"Oh, she propositioned me—subtly. Suggested that we have dinner together, the whole bit—but it didn't work. I've seen her kind too often hanging around the gates to the mill, waiting for the three-to-eleven shift to get off work. No matter how much finesse they use, it's still the same old pitch."

"I'm surprised that she went that far, sir," said Lee. "The two times I saw her, she looked like a much smoother operator."

"I was surprised, too, which may mean the group she's working for is pushed for time," said Caleb Ravenal. "Fortunately, I've got it all down on tape."

"Hold on to it, please," said Lee. "From the way the plot is developing, I'm convinced that this whole business will be coming to a head soon. That tape could be important evidence of just how far Schiller and his backers are willing to go to discredit Tim."

"Keep it for your own protection anyway," Tracy urged. "I'd have no objection to your bringing home the right sort of stepmother one day, but I'm darned if I'd accept a washed-out blonde like Eileen Stoddard."

"Tracy and I probably know more about this conspiracy—if that's what it is—than anyone else connected with the Center, Mr. Ravenal," said Lee. "Do you think we should tell Tim Douglas what you've just told us?"

"Not yet. We don't have anything concrete to go on so far, just suspicious actions, and they're not enough."

"That was our feeling. As you say, we don't have very many hard facts but I'm sure the group means to damage Tim in any way they can."

"You're pretty sharp and Tracy's pretty well endowed with woman's intuition—got it from her mother," said Ravenal. "Why don't we all sit tight for a while? If I hear any more about the called meeting of the trustees, I'll let you know."

"I'll keep you informed about anything that happens in Weston," Tracy promised.

Caleb Ravenal looked at his watch. "I've got to run over to Gastonia to see about a mill that might be for sale there, but I'll be back in time to hear Tracy sing at the service this evening."

"You'll be proud of her, sir," said Lee. "And so will I."

Chapter Seventeen

BACK IN WESTON SUNDAY AFTERNOON, FOLLOWING A THIRD SERV-ice earlier that day in Asheville for young people, the hospital reported no change in Aggie's condition. The Monday- and Tuesday-morning broadcasts were uneventful, too.

"Don't forget that we're going to Tim and Neeley's house for dinner tonight," Lee told Tracy Tuesday morning, when they finished rehearsing "If Heaven Never Was Promised to Me," which Tracy would sing before the Logos Club interview on Friday. "I'll pick you up about seven-thirty."

Promptly at seven forty-five, Lee brought his car to a stop back of the Douglas residence where a parking area had been cleared atop the cliff almost on a level with the roof. As he and Tracy started down the steps to the front door, Art Michaels' car pulled into the parking place, and the two waited for the Michaels to join them. Alix Michaels was dark-haired, fair skinned and vivacious, although a little on the plump side after bearing three children.

"Tracy Ravenal, Alix and Art Michaels," said Lee.

"I saw and heard you on the Logos Club the other morning, Tracy," said Alix. "Neither the camera nor the sound really did you justice."

"Thank you," said Tracy. "I'm still not quite used to the cameras, but the Club programs are fascinating."

"Everybody loves Brother Tim," Alix agreed as they went down the curving stairway carved from the rocky cliff. "And Neeley's a real doll."

Tim opened the door and greeted the newcomers warmly. Since it opened directly into the broad expanse of the living room, they could see that a half-dozen guests—Hal Graham, the Center business expert, with his plump wife, Sarah, and Ray Jowers of the *Weston Chronicle*, with his wife, were looking out on the lake, where darkness was just beginning to fall. Lee was surprised to see Dr. Edward MacMahon, dean of Weston University Medical School, and his wife, Mary, professor of child psychiatry on the school faculty. All the other guests already knew each other so there was no need to introduce anyone except Tracy. By the time the introductions were completed, dinner was announced.

"This is strictly an informal affair," Neeley told the guests. "Fill your plates in the dining room and find seats in the living room. You'll see some card tables located here and there so you won't have to balance your plates on your knees. By all means, come back for seconds if you'd like."

Tim gave the blessing, and the group started around the table, which was loaded with typical southern fare: chicken, roast beef, potatoes, green peas, string beans, and piping-hot biscuits right out of the oven. For a while the guests devoted themselves strictly to eating and conventional chatter.

"I've been reading a biography of Kathryn Kuhlman," Alix Michaels said in the midst of the chatter. "It's fascinating, but what surprised me most was that she never claimed to heal through any power she possessed herself. She always gave the credit to the Holy Spirit."

"I read that in Dr. William A. Nolan's book called *Healing*," Hal Graham agreed. "Nolan investigated a number of cases where a miraculous cure was claimed by the Kuhlman organization but he wasn't able to find one in which there appeared to be a true miracle."

"The doctors who operate the government clinic at the shrine of Lourdes in France have examined thousands of so-called miracle cures," said Lee. "They found less than a hundred they couldn't explain medically."

"Brother Tim performed a true miracle just last week," Graham's wife objected. "I was watching the broadcast that morning and saw it happen."

"You saw *something* happen," said Tim. "Unfortunately, you didn't see the miracle you thought you saw—and I was convinced I had performed."

"Do I smell a story here?" Ray Jowers asked.

"You'll get your story in good time, Ray," Tim assured him. "First I want Dr. Michaels to tell you about some miracles he's been performing lately in his laboratories."

"I didn't know medical men believed in faith healing, Dr. Michaels," said Jowers.

"We don't," said Art, "but we'd be the last to deny that such emotions as religious faith can have a quite dramatic effect upon many of mankind's ills."

"Are you talking about psychosomatic medicine?"

"A form of it. I got interested in it during the two years I spent in Viet Nam with a small and highly mobile hospital."

"Like 'M*A*S*H' on TV?" Tracy Ravenal asked.

"I wish it had been, particularly the fun and games, but we weren't quite so lucky. One thing we did learn, though; we couldn't cure some illnesses that in civil life respond very quickly to medication. Our experience wasn't new, either: Doctors in World War II weren't any better off at curing them than we were. Take peptic ulcer for an example."

"You can't tell me anything about that," said Hal Graham. "I had one for five years until this new drug came along. My doctor put me on it and I was cured in two weeks."

"Don't give all the credit to the drug," Art Michaels advised. "Some of your cure may have arisen from a change in your life pattern or your outlook."

"It was about the time I came to the Center," Hal Graham admitted. "Just associating with Brother Tim here went a long way toward giving me a faith I never had before."

"That probably deserved as much credit as Cimetidine," Art told him. "The only way we could cure a soldier with an ulcer in Viet Nam was to get him out of there. It was the same with a complication of athlete's foot that World War II doctors used to see called neurodermatitis or, more graphically, jungle rot. The worst-looking patients suffering from that often got well while their papers were being processed, after a medical

board had given them the Certificate of Disability Discharge
called a CDD."

"Was that the reason for your interest in holistic medicine?"
Lee asked.

"Holistic?" Ray Jowers asked. "What's that?"

Art Michaels gave a brief description of the new tendency to
treat the whole patient instead of simply his disease and, at
Tim's insistence, a brief case report on Oliver Newton and
Rabbi Metzger.

"What you're saying all sounds reasonable," the newspaperman agreed. "You don't even have to know anything about
medicine to feel that way."

"It's bound to be the new wave of the future as far as healing sick people is concerned," said Tim. "A combination of
religion and medicine to cure man's physical ills relieves the
emotional conflicts that cause so many diseases."

"By religious faith?" Ray Jowers asked.

"That—and other things."

"Does that mean you're getting back to faith healing again?"
Jowers asked.

"Only as part of a new program," Tim explained. "You don't
have to go beyond the New Testament to discover that Jesus
told many of the people He healed that *thy sins be forgiven
thee.*' The phrase appears in all of the Gospels in regard to the
miracles of healing our Lord performed."

"Among ancient people, healers and priests were one and the
same," said Dr. MacMahon. "So what you're talking about is
going back to ancient medicine?"

"Not back." Tim's voice rose in his enthusiasm. "Forward—
to a new union of medical science with religious faith. Right
here in Weston we have one of the best privately endowed
medical schools and hospitals in the South, perhaps in the
country. Why shouldn't it also be the first to have an institute
of holistic medicine?"

"Are you planning such an institute?" Jowers' newsman instinct was obviously aroused.

"I'm considering it," said Tim. "Dr. MacMahon and I have
been discussing the possibility."

"Where would the money come from?"

"In the beginning, from the Center," Tim admitted. "Organizations like ours frequently take in considerably more money through mail contributions than they need to finance their routine activities. Most of the larger ones have been putting very large amounts into special schools."

"Like Pat Robertson's '700 Club'?" Alix Michaels asked.

"Yes. He's built a school at Virginia Beach for developing communication techniques, particularly in religious broadcasting," said Tim. "The 'PTL' started what they call a 'total living center'—"

"And nearly got drowned in a financial morass," Hal Graham pointed out.

"The last I heard, it's pulling itself out of trouble—with the help of an administrator. Fortunately, I've got you to ride herd on me, Hal. I brought you into the Center organization when I realized that I could get worked up about a particular idea to the point where I might be biting off more, financially, than I could chew."

"Hear! Hear!" said Neeley with some force, and a ripple of amusement went around the room.

"This project of yours for an institute," Ray Jowers insisted. "How much would it cost?"

"I don't have any idea," Tim admitted. "At my request, though, Dean MacMahon and Hal Graham have been looking into the finances involved. They haven't given me a report, but even I could see that it will take millions."

"More than you could imagine," Hal Graham said, a little grimly.

"I did insist on one thing," Tim continued. "If the institute I hope to see takes form here at Weston, Dr. Art Michaels must be the head of it."

"Don't make me an administrator," said Art Michaels fervently. "Just let me labor in the vineyard—"

"As clinical director then."

"That, perhaps, but no higher in the pecking order. I've had too many unpleasant experiences in the groves of academe already."

"One thing is certain," said Dean MacMahon. "This new dream of Dr. Douglas' could be one of the most important advances in medicine in years. No other medical school has anything exactly like it."

"I certainly agree with your enthusiasm for the project under the sponsorship of the Center, Tim," said Hal Graham, "but I don't want us to incur financial obligations that might destroy what you've already built up here."

"Neither do I; that's why I'm going to proceed cautiously," said Tim. "If we don't get started soon, though, the whole thing will die aborning and that could be worse than not being born at all."

Ray Jowers glanced at the clock on the wall. "Good heavens! It's almost eleven! Our baby-sitter's parents will be having a fit. One more question before we go: Are you ready to make a public announcement of the project?"

"That was the general idea of inviting all of you here tonight," Tim conceded. "I plan to make the announcement over the air on Thursday's Logos Club broadcast."

The reporter looked at Hal Graham. "I haven't heard any estimate of the cost, Mr. Graham," he said. "Without that, my whole story would fall flat."

"So far, we're talking in terms of ten million for the institute," Graham admitted, somewhat reluctantly. "Operating costs could be even more."

"That's what I need," said Jowers. "Is it all right if I break this story in the Thursday-morning paper, Brother Tim, at the time you make your announcement on TV?"

"It sounds like a perfect arrangement."

"Did you see Aggie before you left the hospital, Art?" Neeley asked as the party was breaking up.

"Yes, but there's no change."

"It will come," said Tim confidently. "After all, she's been washed in the blood—"

Lee saw Art Michaels go suddenly rigid. "What did you say?" he asked Tim.

"In the first Epistle of John, verse seven, it is written: *'But if we walk in the light, we have fellowship one with another, and the blood of Jesus Christ his Son cleanseth us from all sin.'* Aggie has been baptized—symbolically 'washed in the blood'—

and so is without sin. The Lord has promised me not to take her life away from us."

When they reached the parking lot at the top of the cliff upon which the house stood, Lee caught Art by the arm before he could get into his car.

"Something Tim said just now—about being washed in the blood—caught your attention, Art," he said. "Mind telling me what it was?"

"I just remembered one important treatment we haven't used on Aggie yet—plasmapheresis."

"Come again?"

"Follow us over to Mabel's and we'll talk about it over a cup of coffee. I can call our baby-sitter's parents from there and tell them we're held up for a little while."

At the small restaurant, the four of them crowded into a booth. "We don't know too much, even yet, about how viruses attack the body," Art began. "What we do know is that they go for the proteins, even to the point of insinuating themselves into the DNA chain and damaging the blocks of which body proteins are built."

"So what?"

"The first diagnostic sign that proved Aggie has viral encephalitis was an increase in the proteins of the spinal fluid. No doubt those proteins were pretty well infested with the virus of encephalitis and those of the blood plasma only a little less so. If we remove the proteins of the plasma, those in the nervous system will migrate into the bloodstream to fill the void, so to speak, hopefully taking the virus away from the brain, where it's doing the most damage."

"Can you do that?"

"We do it all the time in our blood bank. Dr. Jim Taylor, the Professor of Hematology and head of the bank, uses a continuous centrifuge to spin the heavier blood cells out of the liquid plasma. Then he draws off the plasma and uses it in cases where plasma is needed, reinjecting the cells that carry oxygen. That way, a donor can give much more often than where the cells themselves are removed."

"Isn't taking all that blood dangerous for such a sick patient as Aggie is?" Tracy asked.

"You don't remove much blood at a time," Art Michaels explained, "because plasmapheresis is a continuous operation. Blood is taken from one arm, its elements separated in the centrifuge and the plasma drawn off. The red cells are then reinjected, mixed in saline, into the other arm."

"Washed in the blood," said Lee thoughtfully. "I've heard that phrase a thousand times in evangelical preaching but it has never had more than a symbolical meaning to me."

"If Jeremy Thorpe and Jim Taylor agree—and I'm sure they will—we'll work it out with our blood bank and hematology laboratory," Art promised.

"When would they do it?"

"The sooner the better—tomorrow if possible. The longer that virus remains concentrated in Aggie's tissues and bloodstream, the more danger there is of permanent brain damage."

II

When Lee brought the car to a stop before Hubbard House on the university campus, Tracy didn't immediately make a move to get out. "What do you think about what we heard tonight, Lee?" she asked.

He saw in the light of the lamp on the pole near where they were parked that she was seriously concerned.

"I've been half expecting something like this ever since I took Tim to Art Michaels' laboratory," Lee admitted.

"Do you approve?"

"Of the concept, yes; after all, I've actually seen it at work twice. But when the cost is considered, I wonder whether Tim can pull it off."

"So do I."

"One of his greatest attractions is his tremendous enthusiasm and his sympathy for human problems. Heretofore, he's believed they could all be solved by faith in Jesus and service to His Kingdom. But his enthusiasm for holistic medicine is practically the first time I ever heard him admit that anything other

than religious faith needs to be included in the solution of
human problems."

"And human ills?"

"Of course. Obviously, the two go hand in hand."

"Do you really think this project of Tim's for a special institute will work?"

"None of his projects have ever failed—"

"But he's never undertaken anything so large—and so expensive."

"Maybe not, but don't forget that he bought a rundown
radio and TV station here in Weston with less than a thousand dollars and turned it into a going concern."

"I still wish he wouldn't risk everything, especially when so
many people are trying to bring him down right now."

"Tim believes implicitly that the Lord will always guide him
in the way he should go," said Lee. "And Art Michaels' seizing
on that idea of washing Aggie's blood to remove the virus may
prove he's right."

"Why do you say that?"

"Tim says the Lord assured him that medicine itself will find
a way to save Aggie. He didn't just base that conviction on
religious faith but told Art and myself in Aggie's room that
medical science was what would cure Aggie. If what Art pro-
poses to do does that, then no one could deny that Tim really
was speaking the will of God when he said it."

"Oh I hope so," said Tracy, opening the door. "If Aggie
should die, the people fighting Tim will have just that much
more ammunition to use in trying to bring him down and that
certainly could shake his faith."

III

When Lee knocked on the half-open doorway to Neeley's office
after the Logos Club broadcast Wednesday morning, she called
a cheery "Come in," and smiled when she saw him.

"That duet you and Tracy sang this morning was beautiful

beyond belief, Lee," she said. "Hearing it, and watching you two as you sang, nobody could deny that you're made for each other."

"I hope you're right," he said fervently. "Do you think Tim would mind if we used some more recent tunes in the next crusade—perhaps one of the new gospel-rock hits?"

"He'd love it and so would I. A lot of those waiting to come forward are bound to be depressed and a rousing hymn would cheer them up." She gave him a probing look. "But you didn't come in here to hear me say how wonderful you and Tracy were just now, did you?"

"No. Something's bugging me a little."

"I could see that last night. I think we're both a little bit leery of the turn toward a healing ministry Tim has taken lately. We've both known him long enough to be familiar with his sudden bursts of enthusiasm for special causes and so far he's been right about the possibilities of most of them. This is the biggest project he's ever conceived, though, and as much as I believe in it, I wonder if he can bring it off without endangering what we've accomplished here."

"I don't have as many doubts about the holistic institute as you do," Lee told her, "perhaps because I'm more familiar with Art Michaels' work and have so much confidence in him. Do you mind if I close the door?"

"Of course not. This sounds serious."

"It may be—or again, it may be nothing at all."

"Obviously, you'll feel better if you get it off your chest anyway."

Lee gave Neeley a quick summary of his and Tracy's visit to Atlanta, where they'd dined with Jeff Champion and had seen Eileen Stoddard.

"I remember Jeff," said Neeley. "Both Tim and I have known ever since Jake was forced to leave the Center that he'd take the first opportunity that came his way to damage us."

To Lee's surprise, Neeley didn't seem to be shocked when he told of seeing Eileen Stoddard leaving Alex Porcher's room in Asheville.

"The Stoddard woman isn't Alex's first conquest," she told him. "There have been others and I've known of the running affair between him and Magda Sanderson for months. Alex is all male, a fact that comes across on the TV screen with a powerful impact, especially to women viewers."

"Nobody could deny that. He's very handsome, too."

"And as such, he's the perfect foil for Tim who, bless him, is the epitome of human goodness and concern for his fellows, just the way I'm sure Jesus was. On camera, Alex and Tim's images sharpen each other by contrast." She laughed. "Maybe I should let my hair down and admit that what I'm talking about is sex appeal—which I'm sure sounds sacrilegious in work like ours."

"You're being frank, at least."

"I'm being pragmatic, Lee. A woman looks for one of two things in a man she's interested in, whether as a savior or as a lover."

"This is revolting—but fascinating."

Neeley laughed. "I'm a pragmatist, so I try to see life as it really is. I realize that women adore my husband, whether they see him on the screen, meet him here in the Center as visitors, or during one of the weekend crusades. They see in him the gentle, understanding lover who, as the father of their children, could combine the sex and satisfaction they need with the spiritual enrichment every woman longs for—and rarely finds."

"You only have to read a few of the letters that pour into the mail center every day to know that."

"Alex is another kind of man altogether—with a different but still powerful appeal to many women," Neeley continued. "It's largely physical, so they don't make very good husbands; Alex himself has been married several times. When he first came to the Center, he even made a short-lived play for me. Such men feel obliged to try with every woman they meet who's not a hag, and a saucy little redhead like me was a natural target."

"Don't tell me he—"

"Nothing physical, just a preliminary warmup to see what the possibilities were. When he saw they didn't exist, he backed off, but he's had several affairs since he's been here besides the one with Magda."

"The new preacher and the choir leader syndrome?"

"It's been called that—and it happens more often than you might think."

"I guess I'm too strait-laced."

"Stay that way, darling," said Neeley. "I didn't hear you say too much last night about this new project of Tim's; when he's really enthusiastic about something, it's hard not to be carried away by his own enthusiasm. How does it look to you in the cold light of the morning after?"

"The idea is still good so I can't understand why something about it—something I can't explain—troubles me."

"In what way?"

Briefly, Lee considered telling Neeley about his breakfast in Asheville with Tracy and her father, then decided to honor his promise to Caleb Ravenal to wait and see what developed.

"That's just the difficulty," he said. "I can't pin anything down."

"I have the same feeling, but my concern is mainly over the financial impact," said Neeley. "I don't want us to make the same mistake some others have made and spread ourselves too thin. Besides, I've been too worried about Aggie, in spite of Tim's faith that medical science will cure her, to have much time to think about anything else."

"Has Art Michaels discussed plasmapheresis with you and Tim?"

"Yes. You know it's scheduled for this afternoon, don't you?"

"I didn't, but I'm glad he could arrange it so soon."

"Dr. Michaels wants us to watch from the gallery of the operating room where they're going to work. Tim's blood matches Aggie's, so they'll be taking his plasma in another room to give her during the procedure. Would you mind coming along to hold my hand?"

"I'll be there," he told her.

"Watch—and pray, Lee," said Neeley soberly. "Tim has always wanted children, and my not being able to give him any more is a heavy burden. If Aggie dies—" Her voice suddenly broke, and when he reached across the desk, she took his hand in both of hers, but was still unable to speak for a long moment.

"If that happens," she said finally, "I pray God to give me the courage to give Tim up to some other woman who could give him the child—or, better, children—he wants and deserves."

Chapter Eighteen

THE CLOCK OVER THE DOOR OF THE SPOTLESS TILED OPERATING room said two in the afternoon when Neeley and Lee Steadman entered the glass-walled observation gallery and took seats at the front. Located some ten feet above the floor of the large room below, the gallery allowed visitors to observe every detail of an operating procedure without need for wearing the gowns, caps and masks required of those in the operating theater itself and with no chance of bringing infection in from the outside. As they took their seats, Aggie's bed was being pushed through the wide doors into the center of the room.

"She looks like Sleeping Beauty," said Neeley. "How can she be perhaps fatally ill and look so normal?"

"I made the same remark the first time I saw her in her room," said Lee. "Art Michaels told me the fever heightens the color in her cheeks."

In the operating theater below, several gowned and masked people had been setting up the complicated apparatus which, it was hoped, would save the little girl's life. In addition to nurses and technicians, Lee recognized Dr. Jeremy Thorpe, the pediatric neurologist in charge of Aggie's case, and Art Michaels. A third doctor appeared to be in command and Lee judged him to be Dr. Jim Taylor, the hematologist who was director of the hospital blood bank, which was also responsible for plasmapheresis procedures. Art Michaels, he saw, was wearing a small microphone by which he could communicate with those in the gallery, where several medical students and residents had joined Lee and Neeley.

"What you are about to witness is a rather recent development in the treatment of disease involving the bloodstream," Art's voice came through the speakers in the gallery. "In this case, what we seek to do is to remove as much blood plasma from the patient's circulation as possible.

"The theoretical justification for the procedure is the assumption that most of the virus of encephalitis in her body is now attached to her blood proteins, as well as those in her brain and nervous system. Admittedly, this is an experimental procedure, but if the proteins of the blood plasma are removed with the virus attached, the amount of that virus in her body can be substantially decreased. Then, hopefully—though probably more than one plasmapheresis procedure will be needed—the immunity her own body automatically develops to combat the virus may be able to overcome it."

The nurses had wheeled a complicated-looking machine to the foot of Aggie's bed and were now busy connecting it up to a power source.

"The machine you see," Art continued, "is called a continuous-flow centrifuge, or blood-cell separator. Somewhat similar to the artificial kidney machine, the centrifuge that is its main component spins at a rate of 750 revolutions per minute. When blood taken from a vein in one arm is introduced into the centrifuge bowl, the spinning action separates the plasma, or colorless portion, from the cells. These can then be pumped back into the body through a vein in the opposite arm. In this case, the plasma which, we believe, contains a large amount of the virus in her body, will be discarded. Meanwhile, in an adjoining room, plasma is being taken from the patient's father, Dr. Douglas. It will be added to her circulation at the end of the procedure to give needed strength, plus the immune bodies all people who reach adulthood develop."

"That must be why they've been giving her immune globulin," said Neeley.

"It is," Lee confirmed. "Art Michaels explained that to me the first day I came to see her."

"The day Tim was given divine assurance that she will recover through medical treatment?"

"Yes."

"I wish I could be as sure of the Lord's will as Tim is,"
Neeley confessed. "I even wonder sometimes if Aggie's sickness
could be a punishment for my lack of faith."

"The God you and Tim trust could never do that," Lee assured her.

While Art had been speaking, Dr. Taylor had been inserting
large needles into veins in both of Aggie's arms, connecting
them by plastic tubes to the now-humming centrifuge machine.

"It is our hope that removing the plasma, with its proteins to
which the virus of encephalitis has attached itself," Art continued, "will cause similar proteins with their virus components to
migrate from the tissues of the patient's brain and spinal cord
into the bloodstream, thus decreasing the concentration of infection in the tissues themselves. If that happens, the chances
that her body's own immune forces will be able to attack and
destroy the virus will be greatly increased."

"It sounds like magic," said Neeley in a voice tinged with
awe.

"Scientific magic, Mrs. Douglas." The nameplate pinned to
the pocket of the resident's white jacket said, "Dr. Sam Jenkins." "My little girl always watches your puppet show so I
feel I know you already as a friend."

"Could you explain what's happening in a little more detail
than Dr. Michaels is doing, Dr. Jenkins?" Neeley asked.

"Of course. You see, the blood is composed of four major
components. The white blood cells fight infection. The red
blood cells carry oxygen and are therefore vital to the body.
Platelets are very small cells that control clotting, and plasma is
the colorless portion containing the bulk of the protein in the
blood. Because each component has a different density, it will
separate from the others in the centrifuge, the way we used to
separate cream from milk in my father's dairy farm back in Virginia. Red cells, which your daughter has to have in order to
carry the oxygen that keeps her alive, are the heaviest and are
thrown down to the bottom of the centrifuge bowl, where they
can be drawn off and reinjected into her circulation. Plasma,
the least dense component, remains at the top and can also be
drawn off separately from the rest. Plasmapheresis is widely
used to obtain plasma without permanently removing the red

blood cells so a donor can be used at more frequent intervals."

"In this case, won't the plasma be discarded?" Lee asked.

"That's what Dr. Michaels said," Jenkins answered. "It's an ingenious theory and might just work."

" 'Might just work'?" Neeley's voice trembled. "Is that all the hope you can give us, Doctor?"

"It's never been tried before in viral encephalitis to my knowledge, Mrs. Douglas, but the theory is ingenious," Jenkins admitted.

In the operating room below, everyone had been moving with a quiet confidence and efficiency that was immensely reassuring. When the plasmapheresis was about two thirds finished, the door at the back of the visitors' gallery opened and Tim Douglas came in. He took a seat beside Neeley who promptly gripped his hand with her free one while continuing to hold on to Lee with the other. Except that he appeared to be a little pale, Lee could not see that the removal of Tim's own plasma for injection into Aggie's veins had affected him.

"How's it going?" he inquired.

"Art hasn't indicated any hitch," said Lee, "so I suppose everything is okay."

"The fact that her cheeks have remained pink indicates that they're getting the major part of her red cells back into the circulation through one needle as fast as the blood is being taken out with the other, roughly a rate of fifty cubic centimeters a minute," said Dr. Jenkins. "Plasmapheresis is so widely used nowadays in blood-bank operations that it shouldn't bother her at all."

"That's what they said in the other room; certainly losing over a pint of my own plasma didn't," said Tim. "How long would you estimate it will take before we can tell whether or not it will be effective, Doctor?"

"If the theory Dr. Michaels has described is correct, virus-containing proteins should already be moving out of her nervous system, where they're concentrated, into the bloodstream from which the virus has been removed. In addition," the resident assured him, "your own plasma undoubtedly contains some degree of immunity, which will help combat the virus."

Art Michaels and Dr. Jeremy Thorpe met Lee, Neeley and

Tim as they were leaving the operating-room floor, after Aggie's bed had been wheeled out.

"Everything went beautifully," Michaels assured them. "We should know in another twenty-four hours whether removing the plasma proteins will cause those in the nervous system to migrate toward the bloodstream."

"What then?" Tim asked.

Michaels looked questioningly at Dr. Jeremy Thorpe. "Anything that causes improvement is worth repeating again, probably in about four days," said the neurologist. "Do you feel all right, Dr. Douglas?"

"Ready for a big steak," said Tim. "They told me in the other room I should have one for dinner."

"I'll stop by the store and get the biggest one the butcher can cut," Neeley promised. "First, though, I'd better pick up the late-afternoon mail."

II

Lee drove Neeley to the Center and went in with her. Lying on the desk in his own tiny office was a letter to Tracy in his care, left there by the mail clerk. Putting it into his pocket, he started for the door to the staff parking lot but stopped when Neeley called to him from across the hall. The tone of her voice told him something was wrong and, when he stepped through the door, he saw that she was breathing quickly, her face red with anger.

"Jake Schiller and his crew didn't waste any time," she said tersely as she handed him a letter. "Look at that."

The letter was brief, a demand over the signature of the secretary of the Board of Trustees of the Center notifying Tim, as chairman, that more than one third of the board's members had petitioned for a special meeting to be held the following Wednesday afternoon, a week away.

"They couldn't have chosen a worse time to stir up trouble," said Neeley. "Tim has enough to worry about with Aggie so sick, without having to defend his plan for the Institute for Holistic Medicine before the board. Did you read the bottom paragraph?"

"Not yet."

"It's the worst of all." Neeley took the letter. "Listen to this: 'In order that requirements of the bylaws of the corporation may be strictly followed, the chairman is duly notified that a resolution removing him from his position and the election of a new chairman will be proposed.'"

"Jake didn't lose any time," said Lee, "but it could be worse."

"How?" Neeley was close to tears after the strain of the afternoon at the hospital and now this peremptory notice.

"The enemy doesn't know we're aware of Alex's part in this. When the meeting's held, Jake, Jeff Champion and Eileen Stoddard will probably be in Weston preparing to celebrate their victory. What they don't know is that I'm also a witness to the early stages of their preparations and will be glad to testify and reveal their part in the whole plot."

"Dear, dear Lee." Neeley had regained her composure and could think rationally now, as her next words revealed. "Why don't we keep what we know under our hats until the actual meeting. If we throw a bombshell into the middle of the attempt to gain control of the Center, the shell fragments just might hit some of the enemy and bring out things we haven't discovered yet."

"I'm with you all the way." Lee glanced at his watch. "Right now I'd better get to my late-afternoon class. See you in the morning."

"Thanks, Lee, for everything."

At the door, Lee turned back. "This isn't going to affect Tracy's solo and interview on Friday, is it? I asked Jack Feagin with Word Music to have their people listen to her that morning."

"The program's already set up, but you'd better not tell her about the meeting next week. It might disturb her too much."

"I won't," he promised. "You'll hear 'If Heaven Never Was Promised to Me' sung Friday morning as you've never heard it before."

III

Lee's final class ended at five and, knowing Tracy usually spent the hours from four to six in the rehearsal room she'd rented, he stopped by the Music Department. He reached the rehearsal room in time to hear her sing the last chorus of the song she was to feature on the Friday-morning broadcast.

"You've got it down letter perfect," he told her. "I came by to take you to dinner."

"I've got a sorority meeting at seven-thirty."

"No sweat. We'll eat at Mabel's."

"How did Aggie's operation go?"

"Beautifully, but it's not really an operation. That crew at the hospital made it look simple."

"I'm glad. Did they use Tim's blood?"

"Only the plasma. It didn't bother him at all, either. Dr. Thorpe said they may have to repeat the procedure, though, before they can hope to see much effect."

"H-how did Neeley take it?"

"Like the trouper she is."

"She loves Aggie very much—and Tim, too."

"More than you would imagine," said Lee soberly as he helped her into his car and went around to open the door.

"What do you mean?" she asked.

"The fact that she can never have another child has troubled Neeley ever since Aggie was born. She's steeling herself now to make a sacrifice if Aggie shouldn't recover from encephalitis."

"Sacrifice? I don't understand."

"Neeley loves Tim enough to bow out of their marriage and let him marry again, to a woman who could bear him a child, or children."

Tracy's eyes went wide with shock. "She told you this?"

"After the morning broadcast. I guess that's the greatest sacrifice any woman could make for the man she loves."

For a moment she didn't speak, then she said, a little

hoarsely, "Do you mind if we don't have dinner, Lee? I—I don't feel like it."

"Of course." Then he remembered the letter for her and took it from his pocket. "This came for you with the second mail—in my care. I almost forgot it."

She took the letter and opened it, her movements almost robotlike, as had been her voice when she asked him to take her to her dormitory instead of to dinner. "It's from Leeds Music Corporation. They're offering me a recording contract."

"That's great! I thought they would."

"But you're not included—"

"It's *your* voice they want. In the religious-music field, beautiful girl singers are almost worth their weight in gold, while male baritones are a dime a dozen."

"But before you auditioned me that first morning, I was just another music major."

"Not just *another* music major but a very *special* music major." Lee managed a laugh he was far from feeling. "You're making me out to be a Svengali or something and we both know that's not true. I chose your songs and taught you something about gospel-rock music, but your own very beautiful vocal cords produced the sound."

They had stopped before Hubbard House and she opened the door but did not get out. "I—I don't have to do anything about this contract offer right away, do I?" she asked.

"A day or two won't make any difference but, as your manager, I advise you not to delay much longer. Leeds has the whole Music Corporation of America behind them and the way they can promote new girl singers could out-Cinderella Cinderella. See you in the morning for the Club broadcast. I've scheduled a duet for us, after your solo, one of those we did at Asheville, but you won't need more than just a few minutes' rehearsal before the Club broadcast begins. Good night."

"Good night, Lee." To his surprise, she suddenly leaned over and kissed him—one of those feathery-light kisses to which he'd become accustomed—before pushing open the door and getting out. She ran up the short walk to the steps, but turned back to wave good-by and, in the glow of the light above the entrance, he was certain he could detect, even at that distance, the sheen of tears in her eyes.

IV

Neeley was humming at her desk when Lee came into the Center Thursday morning, an hour before the Logos Club broadcast was to begin.

"Dr. Thorpe telephoned this morning after he'd made rounds," she called through the open door of her office. "Aggie's temperature has dropped and her sedimentation rate is much nearer normal."

"How soon does he plan to do another plasmapheresis?"

"Probably on Sunday, but he won't take any plasma from Tim then; he says it's too soon after Tim gave yesterday. Dr. Thorpe is cautiously optimistic, though, and that's the best news we've had since Aggie got sick."

"Aggie can have my plasma," Lee assured Neeley. "I'd be happy to give it. By the way, how did Tim take the letter from the secretary of the board?"

"He was mad, madder than I've ever seen him."

"Can he prevent the meeting?"

"Not according to the bylaws. Besides, Tim wouldn't try to evade a showdown on something as important as a revolt within the board."

"Did you tell him what we already know?"

"Yes—except the suicide episode; it's hard to make him believe even Jake Schiller could stoop so low. Knowing Alex's part in it hurt Tim very much, too. It was all I could do to keep him from calling Alex last night and having it out."

"Tim's going along with our plan to let the other faction make their play first, isn't he?"

"Yes—but he wants you to be his advocate."

"I'm not a lawyer," Lee protested. "Wouldn't it be better to have one? The bylaws allow legal representation for anyone against whom proceedings for removal from office are being brought."

"You brought the scheme to light, Lee. But for you, we'd have no chance to prepare a defense. Tim needs you in his corner at the meeting."

"I'd be there anyway, of course, but—"

"He and I both insist that you play the dominant role in his defense, too. We're counting on you to keep the opposition off balance and make them reveal both their plan and their strength. Once we know who supports them on the board, we can fight more effectively."

"You can depend on me," said Lee grimly. "Did you know Tracy's had an offer of a recording contract from Leeds?"

"Leeds? I've been working on Jack Feagin and Word in Waco—for a contract that includes both of you."

"Feagin's tackling it from that angle, too; we had a long talk in Asheville after the first service of the crusade. He thinks Tracy still needs someone close to bring out her full potentialities, though, and likes our duets, too. He promised to give me a decision after Tracy's debut on tomorrow's Club program."

"How does she feel about Leeds?"

"She's still stunned. Last night she said she'd refuse to sign a contract without me, but if Word doesn't come through by Monday, after hearing her sing on Friday's broadcast, I'm going to insist that she sign the Leeds contract."

"I guess, being you, that would be the only thing you could do—even if it meant losing her."

"I doubt that I ever had much chance there anyway," he conceded wryly. "Besides, I certainly wouldn't want to do anything to block the kind of musical career Tracy can have, if she wants it."

"Does she really want it, Lee? If I were in her place, being married to you would be worth more than all the recording contracts in the world."

"She might have both, if she wants them. Jack Feagin said that if Word does offer us a contract as a duo, they'd want us both to stay right here, at least for a while. He says singing with the Troubadours in the Logos Club broadcasts could give us both an exposure we'd never hope to get anywhere else. Besides, we could always fly down to Waco weekends for the recording sessions."

"Tim and I would like that; I'll pray that it works out," said Neeley. "Meanwhile, be thinking of what we can do to weaken Jake Schiller's support among the trustees."

V

Watching, and hearing, Tracy sing on the Friday-morning Logos Club broadcast, Lee knew she had never been in better form. In the interview that followed, she was poised and completely assured as Tim did his best to bring out her natural charm and patrician composure. When it was over and a recorded break came on between the two sections of the program, the whole crew and staff crowded around to congratulate her. Afterward, when they sang their duet in the last thirty minutes of the program, Lee knew their voices had never blended into a more perfect harmony. When the station and network logo came on at signoff, he took her hands in his.

"I guess you know you outdid yourself this morning," he told her.

"Only because I knew you were there backing me up. You should have been able to tell that from the duet."

"Everything was just perfect." Neeley had come onstage. "You two are made for each other—musically and in every other way. Don't let him get away, Tracy. They don't make them like Lee very often."

"I know," she said quietly. "That's why I decided right after our duet just now that I'm not going to take the contract Leeds offered."

"I thought you'd make that decision," Neeley told her with a quick kiss on the cheek. "I'm sure you'll never regret it."

"You could be making a mistake," Lee warned as they were leaving.

"I'm still going to turn down the offer."

"Don't do anything before Monday anyway, and be thinking

about it over the weekend. By the way, Aggie's a lot better and they're going to do another plasmapheresis on Sunday. Dr. Thorpe thinks she has a good chance of coming through okay."

"I hope so," said Tracy and he wasn't surprised to hear a note of resignation in her voice. "I really hope so."

"I'm sure you do," he told her. "Just as I'm more sure than ever that I love you and want to marry you. Shall I see you tonight?"

"Give me a rain check," she said, and smiled. "After all, a soprano who's just been proposed to by a handsome baritone needs time to herself—to think. Besides, I have to practice tonight for Sunday vespers."

Lee was surprised to receive a telephone call that evening as he was watching a production of *Kiss Me Kate* on the local PBS station. It was Caleb Ravenal.

"I called Tracy earlier to tell her I thought she was wonderful on the program this morning," said the textile magnate. "You both were."

"Thank you, sir."

"She also told me you've asked her to marry you."

"I hope you gave your approval, sir."

"I told her she'd be nuts not to and I think she halfway agreed, but it has to be her decision. By the way, is this recording contract she's been offered on the up and up?"

"Leeds is one of the biggest and best in the business, sir. I advised her to sign it."

"She says she's not going to accept any proposition that doesn't include you."

"I think she would be making a mistake. Leeds can promote her into becoming a star, not only in gospel-rock but in other fields of music as well. You heard her sing this morning so you know she doesn't need me any longer."

"*She* needs you, and *I* need grandchildren, but I really called about something else. A fellow by the name of Jeff Champion came to see me this afternoon—from Atlanta."

"He's Jake Schiller's right-hand man there."

"I thought I remembered you and Tracy mentioning his name when we had breakfast together in Asheville."

"Jeff's clever enough to use Tim's interest in holistic medi-

cine as a weapon to create uncertainty in the Board of Trustees
and promote Schiller's attempt to take over for himself."

"That's the way I figured it, too. From what Champion said,
a majority of the board is afraid of Brother Tim's new project
and doesn't want to risk damaging the financial future of the
Center."

"He might be right there," Lee conceded, "though I don't
think so. We figure only a small minority, not more than a
third, would actually vote against Tim and the project to estab-
lish the institute. What we don't know for certain is just how
many trustees are involved in the plot to damage the confidence
of the board in Tim."

"There's a way to find out."

"How's that, sir?"

"I read the bylaws again. They say the chairman can declare
in advance that the meeting will be open to the public."

"I noticed that provision, but didn't see how it would help
our cause."

"Judging by the sneaky way the opposition has been waging
this campaign, I doubt that very many of them would like to
have their finagling exposed to the newspapers and on TV,"
said Ravenal. "Logically, then, their first move would be a motion to close the session. When that comes up for a vote, we
can tell right off who's for us and who's against us."

"That's good thinking, sir," said Lee. "You didn't happen to
reveal any of what we already know about the plot to Champion, did you?"

"Not a word." Ravenal chuckled. "In fact, I did the best I
could to lead him off on a wild-goose chase. Will you ask Tim
about declaring an open meeting?"

"I'll request it and I'm sure Tim will go along," said Lee.
"Actually, he's asked me to conduct his defense."

"He couldn't have put it in better hands," Ravenal assured
him. "Another thing: You don't need to call me 'sir,' even
though I'm old enough to be your father. If Tracy's got the
sense I think she has, I hope you'll soon be calling me 'Dad.'
Good night, son."

VI

Jack Feagin called from Waco Saturday morning. "I couldn't get a decision from the brass who watched your Friday-morning program until last night," he said, "but figured it was too late to call."

"What's the verdict?"

"Word Music, Inc., is prepared to give you and Miss Ravenal a standard recording contract, both individually and as a team."

"I'm glad you didn't wait until Monday," said Lee. "She was offered a contract by Leeds Wednesday afternoon."

"Without you?"

"My name wasn't mentioned in the letter. She hesitated to take it because of that but, if you hadn't called, I think I could have convinced her that it's best for her to accept it."

"Will she accept ours?"

"I think she will but there's something you ought to know before we sign anything. I remember your saying in Asheville that Word would want us to remain with the Logos Club because of the exposure we get on the programs."

"Everybody here is agreed on that."

"An attempt is going to be made Wednesday afternoon by a faction among the Board of Trustees to unseat Tim Douglas as chairman. If it succeeds, it will be only a matter of time until I'm fired and Tim is eased out, too."

"Why would anybody want to do that?"

"Tim has a new project for an Institute for Holistic Medicine—"

"I've been reading about that and it makes sense. Can he finance it?"

"Tim thinks so and I agree. He'll need ten million but we've raised that much more than once with a telethon."

"Brother Tim's a genius at raising money," Feagin agreed. "I'd bet on him but I'll have to talk over the possibility that you and Miss Ravenal may not be singing with the Logos Club much longer. I take it that she'd pull out, too, if the opposition took over and you were fired."

"Almost certainly, even though I'd advise her against it."

"When did you say the showdown will occur?" Feagin asked.

"On Wednesday afternoon of next week at three o'clock. We're pretty sure we can make it an open meeting. If you're up this way, you can watch it for yourself."

"I may just do that," said Feagin. "And just in case Brother Tim wins, I'll have the contract for you and Miss Ravenal in my pocket."

VII

Lee attended the Sunday-afternoon vespers concert. Tracy was in the choir but didn't sing a solo.

"You took a rain check on dinner last night," he told her when she came out of the robing room. "Any chance of my collecting on it tonight? It's sort of a special occasion but I'd rather not tell you about it until after dinner."

She smiled. "Anything that mysterious must be important enough for a steak. I studied for a test all morning and then took a catnap and barely woke up in time to get to vespers, so I'm starved."

"How does Barney's suit you?" The popular steakhouse was located on the lakefront, about five miles away on the road to Greenville.

"Fantastic! Maybe we can get a table on the porch overlooking the water."

They reached the steakhouse ahead of the regular Sunday-night crowd and were given a table in the corner to themselves, with the broad expanse of the lake before them, its surface taking on a metallic sheen from the rays of the setting sun. The steaks were perfect, as was the dessert, called "grasshopper pie." Over fragrant mocha coffee, Tracy leaned back in the tall wicker chair that almost engulfed her and gave a deep sigh of satisfaction and pleasure.

"Did you hear how Aggie's plasmapheresis went today?" she asked.

"Fine. I was the donor."

"Did your blood match hers?"

"Plasma doesn't have to be matched," he explained. "After they separated my red cells from the plasma, they reinjected the cells. It didn't bother me a bit. Tim and Neeley were there and, when they wheeled Aggie out of the operating room, she looked ready to wake up any minute."

"I hope she does. I really hope so." Once again Lee was sure he heard the same note of resignation he'd noticed in her voice once before.

"I heard from Word Saturday night, but wanted to wait until a special occasion to tell you. They've offered us a contract to record as a duo and also individually."

She turned to look at the lake, where dusk was rapidly turning the broad expanse of the water into a dark pool of mystery, before she spoke. "You want me to accept, don't you?"

"Of course, but there's a hitch."

"Like what?"

"I told Jack Feagin they should wait until after the meeting of the board on Wednesday before making the offer final."

"Why?"

"I'm going to represent Tim before the board. If the vote should go against him, it's just a matter of time before the other side will have me fired."

"And if they couldn't be sure we would continue to sing on the Logos Club broadcasts, Word wouldn't want us?" she asked.

"They'd still want *you*, or you can always go to Leeds. I certainly wouldn't want my not being there to stand in the way of the kind of musical career you can have for the asking, not only in gospel-rock but in other fields as well."

"I don't want a musical career without you to back me up," she said simply.

"Don't give up a chance like this out of consideration for me," he pleaded. "If Tim should lose, Jeff Champion would probably soon be in charge of the Logos Club broadcasts and he'd be certain to keep the Gospel Troubadours intact. You could go on singing with them until we both get our degrees a year from now; then I could be your manager."

"Managing my career would still mean giving up your own."

"I wasn't thinking of myself."

"I know." She reached across the table to take his hands. "You never do, which is another reason why everybody loves you."

"Especially you, I hope."

"It wouldn't be hard to do. Will you give me a little more time?"

"Of course. Fortunately, your father's on my side; so is Neeley."

He knew he'd said the wrong thing when she withdrew her hands and turned to look out across the lake, but the words had been spoken and there was no way to withdraw them.

"Do you mind if we go now?" she asked. "I really should study some more for that test tomorrow afternoon."

"Of course. The meeting Wednesday afternoon will be open to the public, and Jack Feagin is coming up from Waco for it. We'll talk to him about the contract afterward."

She didn't answer, but rose to go.

VIII

After the Monday-morning broadcast was over, Hal Graham came into Lee's office while Lee was making out the requisitions for the next week's sheet music. The business manager's expression was grim.

"Can you run up to the control room with me?" he asked. "I've got some filmstrips you'll be interested in seeing."

Henry Waterford was waiting for them in the control room. Taking two rolls of videotape from a locked drawer, he threaded one into a projector. When the picture appeared on a small monitor, Lee saw that it covered part of the mail-opening room with the small camera centered on Magda Sanderson.

"I had one of the video technicians rig the closed-circuit camera nearest to Magda so it would stop for a few moments on each round but not long enough for her to know it," Hal explained. "The two strips you'll see were recorded last Thursday and Friday, while the mail was being opened."

With the moving camera stopped briefly, the picture was distinct and its meaning unmistakable. Each time Magda Sanderson came to an envelope that contained cash, she swiftly extracted the bills, slipped them into her pocket but did not touch the adding machine at her elbow before going on to another letter. The checks removed from most envelopes she piled separately, carefully adding the amount they showed to the total she was making with the calculator. The picture was so clear that Lee could even read the denominations of most of the bills being purloined. The second filmstrip was almost identical with the first.

"I counted five hundred in cash not recorded on the first strip, and four hundred on the second," said Hal. "I know Tim has put you in charge of his defense at the meeting, and her taking cash might have something to do with the plot against him. Shall I have her arrested for theft?"

"I think you're right about the money, but let's wait awhile." Lee turned to Henry Waterford. "Can you rig a videotape projector and a monitor screen at the back of the platform in the chapel where the trustees will meet by Wednesday afternoon without calling a lot of attention to what you're doing, Henry?"

"Sure. But why? The evidence is right there; no court would refuse to accept it."

"We'll come to that later," said Lee. "This will be an open meeting, with press coverage. I think those two tapes are going to be valuable evidence in revealing what's behind this attempt to discredit Tim."

"Will do," said Waterford.

"If I'm right about where that money's going, it will be interesting to see one observer's face when that picture flashes on the screen," said Hal Graham grimly. "Talk about Caesar and Brutus. Shakespeare would have loved this little drama."

"What about the plans for the institute?" Lee asked as they were returning to Hal Graham's office.

"Tim and I have had two conferences with Dean MacMahon and one with the university Board of Trustees," said the business manager. "They're anxious to have the institute here for the prestige it will give the Medical School, but Tim will have to raise the money."

"How much?"

"About what I guessed when we had dinner at Tim's house —ten million. He's going to put a proposal before the trustees Wednesday for a thirty-six-hour telethon sometime this summer to raise it. If they approve, we'll start planning right away."

"That makes it all the more important that we win our case at the trustees' meeting," said Lee.

"How do you figure Tim's chances?"

"The enemy may have some surprises for us, but I'm hoping to have some surprises for them, too—like those two tapes Henry has locked up in the control room."

Chapter Nineteen

THE SMALL CHAPEL WHERE THE STAFF MET EVERY MORNING FOR a brief reading of Scripture and prayer by Tim or Alex could hold nearly a hundred people. As Tim's representative, Lee had telephoned an announcement to the newspapers the day before that the meeting would be open and the main subject to be discussed would be the proposal to build and operate an Institute for Holistic Medicine in connection with both the Gospel Broadcast Center and the university Medical School. As a result, the chapel was about half full, many of the visitors newspapermen or photographers. Representatives of TV stations in Spartanburg and Charlotte were also there with the inevitable TV minicameras, each with its own battery-powered light source.

At Lee's suggestion, Tim had also notified all trustees by telegraph, in his capacity as chairman, that the meeting was to be open to the public, which meant, of course, the press as well. As a result, he was anticipating the motion to close the meeting Caleb Ravenal had suggested as a way to get a straw vote on the strength of the opposition.

The small rostrum barely held the twelve chairs for the trustees, plus a table with four chairs at the front for the presiding officers and the recorder. All seats were diagonally placed so the cameras of the newspapers and TV photographers could record the faces of both trustees and officers at any time.

By five minutes to three, all of the four chairs behind the small table were occupied except one. At one end sat the re-

corder, her stenotype machine in front of her. Next came the
secretary, a minister from Spartanburg named Alexander. The
third chair was vacant since Tim Douglas had not yet appeared. In the fourth sat the vice chairman, a hatchet-faced
minister named Lemuel Tyler from a small Carolina town.

Lee wasn't surprised to see Jeff Champion and Eileen Stoddard in the second row of seats on the floor of the chapel. Sitting alone at one end of the front row was Desire Halliday,
whose address Lee had been able to get through the hospital
record with the help of Art Michaels. He'd had some trouble
persuading her to come to the meeting until he threatened her
with prosecution for conspiracy in her role during the fake suicide scene. At the other end of the front row of seats, Alex
Porcher was sitting, chatting with Magda Sanderson. Just before
the clock struck three, Lee saw Tracy come in at the back of
the chapel and take a seat there.

Lemuel Tyler had been watching the clock and promptly at
three moved to the seat reserved for the chairman and lifted
the gavel.

"The meeting will come to order," he announced with obvious relish, giving the table a determined whack. "In the absence of the chairman, the bylaws provide that the vice chairman will preside."

"Mr. Chairman." Lee spoke from where he was sitting on the
front row of the gallery. "Brother Tim has asked me to represent him in the matters before the board today and I respect-
fully request a brief delay in starting the meeting."

"On what grounds, Mr. Steadman?" Tyler asked sharply.

"Brother Tim and his wife went to the University Hospital
shortly after noon, where their daughter, Agnes, has been
gravely ill for several weeks. The doctors in charge are performing an important procedure, which was scheduled to be finished
by now. Something must have delayed them but they should be
here any minute."

"Request refused," Tyler snapped. "The chair will entertain
a motion to close the meeting."

The motion was made and seconded immediately and the
chairman called for a voice vote. To Lee, the responses seemed

about equal but Tyler ruled, "The 'ayes' have it. The meeting will be closed. All spectators are request—"

"Mr. Chairman!" It was Caleb Ravenal. "I move a tally of the house with a recorded roll call."

When the motion was promptly seconded, the presiding officer had no choice except to have the roll called and the vote of each trustee recorded. This time the "nos" won by a margin of nearly two to one, much to the chairman's chagrin, and the spectators were allowed to remain. Watching Alex Porcher, Lee thought he detected a fleeting look of apprehension, but couldn't be certain.

The meeting then proceeded normally. Minutes of the previous session were read by the secretary and approved. Promptly after that vote was announced, a known supporter of Jake Schiller, who was not present, demanded a reading of the call for the meeting, including the stated purpose of removing Tim Douglas from his position as chairman. Before any action could be taken, however, Tim appeared, with Neeley, who took a seat in the gallery beside Lee.

"How's it going?" she asked in a whisper.

"We won the first round," he told her, "but the opposition is strong."

"Thank you for taking charge in my absence, Brother Tyler." Tim's voice had its usual note of warm humor. "I presume that you opened the meeting with prayer."

A moment of stunned silence greeted his words, then Lem Tyler mumbled, "No, we didn't."

"Let us pray then."

Tim had obviously taken charge of the situation, and the prayer that followed was brief but eloquent. When it was finished, he took the chair Tyler had occupied and calmly reached across for the gavel.

"First, let me apologize to all of you for being late and putting you to an inconvenience," he said. "Some of you may not know that my daughter, Agnes, has been in a coma for almost two weeks with encephalitis. For a while, we feared for her life but God answered our prayers by enabling medical science to overcome the infection. This afternoon for the first time, while the doctors were performing a delicate procedure called plas-

mapheresis, she became conscious and recognized both myself
and her mother. As in the first treatment a week ago, the doctors used my own blood plasma today, and the delay was
caused when the machine was slow in delivering my red blood
cells back to me."

"Then she's going to recover?" Caleb Ravenal asked.

"The doctors assure me that she will, without complications,
but God had assured me early in her illness that medical science would be able to cure her." Tim turned to Tyler. "How
far had you gone with the meeting, Brother Lem?"

"The call had just been read," Tyler admitted.

"Then no action has yet been taken on the demand by a
group of trustees that I be removed from the position of
chairman?"

"No."

"In that case, I will now entertain such a motion."

Promptly a plump minister named Ayers rose to his feet. "I
move that Timothy J. Douglas be removed from the position
of chairman of this board and that a new chairman be elected."

Before the proposer of the motion could sit down, Lem
Tyler, now just another member of the board, seconded it, and
the plump minister remained standing.

"You have the floor, Brother Ayers," Tim said pleasantly. "I
take it that you wish to speak on the motion."

"I do, on the grounds that you have proposed changes in the
operation of the Gospel Broadcast Center that are against the
function of the Center, as defined by the bylaws."

"Could you be more specific?" Tim asked in the same pleas-
ant tone.

"Is it not true, as has been announced in the press, that you
propose to make the Center a minion of the medical profession
in order to enhance their status with the public?"

"That certainly is *not* true, Brother Ayers." Tim's tone was
even but firm. "However, I am proud to be able to state that
God has revealed to me how, through a joint effort of medicine
and religion, many people can be cured of illnesses that neither
has, hitherto, been able to attack."

"You are denying the existence of miracles, then," said Ayers
on a note of triumph. "Surely such a denial is an act of blas-

phemy, when Holy Writ specifically describes many such performed by our Lord, Jesus Christ."

"I do not for a moment deny that miracles of faith have brought healing, even recovery from near death, through medical science and sometimes outside the field of medicine," said Tim. "The same Holy Writ with which you would condemn me, Brother Ayers, repeatedly tells us in all three Gospels that Jesus did not claim to heal except by faith. When a woman with an issue of blood touched the hem of our Lord's garment, He told her, '*Thy faith hath made thee whole.*' And again when a blind man was healed, Jesus told him that *his* faith had made him whole."

"Those were real miracles," Ayers shouted. "You are condemning yourself and denying the power of Christ Himself when you say doctors must be involved in healing."

"I do not deny the power of Christ to generate faith, Brother Ayers, nor the fact that this same faith can help doctors to cure," said Tim. "The basic principle of holistic medicine, the study of which I hope to promote through the institute that I will shortly ask all of you to approve, is that peace of mind such as religious faith brings may be the most important tool doctors can use in their profession."

"Would you deny true healers the right to cure the sick and afflicted, simply because they do not have medical degrees?"

"Not at all," said Tim. "What I do deny is the existence of any healing power by man, except through faith. Less than a month ago, on this very stage, I was convinced that I had performed a miracle of healing that many of you no doubt witnessed on television or read about in the newspapers. Yet, a few days later, I realized I had failed when I saw that same man healing himself through learning to control his own emotions and direct them toward curing his legs. What we will seek to do in the Institute for Holistic Medicine is to help people generate the faith that will make them whole, by working as partners with medical science. The whole principle is that simple, Brother Ayers, and I hope I can enlist your support in making what is admittedly a dream come true."

"Humph!" Ayers negated that hope with a snort and sat down.

Questions followed from several sources. Some were about cost. Others questioned the mechanisms of holistic medicine and the implied downgrading of faith healing. In all, they continued for close to half an hour, but Tim answered them with the same logic and good humor he had used in blunting the charges hurled at him by Brother Ayers.

When it seemed that the other side had no more ammunition, they suddenly changed their tactics. The attack came when a large man in the back row who gave his name as Reverend Elmer Schneider took the floor. Lee thought he looked familiar, but could not place him until a note, in what he recognized as Tracy's handwriting, was passed down to him.

"Schneider is one of Jake Schiller's assistant ministers," she wrote and, with his memory jogged, Lee remembered seeing the large man directing the ushers who had taken up the collection that Sunday morning in Atlanta.

"You have claimed in literature sent out from the Gospel Broadcast Center that through your intervention on television, people have been dissuaded from suicide," Schneider charged. "Yet you personally paid a woman recently to pretend suicide so you could plead with her over television until you could summon a rescue squad and make it appear that she was saved by your prayers."

Tim was obviously taken aback by the question, and Lee was sorry they had not told him before about Desire Halliday. Before Tim could try to answer the attack, Lee rose to his feet.

"Mr. Chairman," he said, "may I have the floor briefly to make a statement about this charge?"

"You may," said Tim.

"By what right does he speak?" Schneider demanded angrily.

"Mr. Steadman is an associate of the Center; to be exact, the director of music," Tim explained. "Since he has been looking into the background of the charge of unfitness made against me by those who called this meeting, I asked him before this meeting to represent me here."

"What can he do?" The burly speaker had obviously not realized that Jeff Champion was frantically trying to signal him not to push the charge, having noted the presence of Desire Halliday.

"I can produce the person you claim was paid by Brother Tim to pretend suicide," said Lee calmly. "She is sitting in the visitors' gallery." Without waiting for the accuser to answer, he said, "Will Miss Desire Halliday please stand."

"Mr. Chairman!" Lem Tyler snapped as the blonde rose to her feet. "I protest this irregularity."

"'Irregularity,' Brother Tyler?" Tim's voice was suddenly like a sharp-edged sword. "Or 'plot'?"

Tyler's stunned silence as he sank back in his chair was as much an admission of guilt as was the expression of controlled fury on his face.

"Miss Halliday," Lee said quietly, for she was obviously quite nervous, "were you hired a few weeks ago to pretend suicide and then call the Logos Club number displayed on the screen while a broadcast was going on?"

"Yes, I was."

"Then you did not actually try suicide?"

"Me kill myself?" she said indignantly. "I get too much enjoyment out of life to even think of such a thing."

"May I ask how much you were paid to pretend?"

"I was to get five hundred for the job, two-fifty before I left Atlanta and another two-fifty when I got back. It was worth every nickel, too. Those firemen damn near killed me with the stomach pump, and that stuff they gave me to keep me quiet at the hospital was worse than castor oil."

"What did you take to make it appear that you had tried suicide?"

"Oh, a few downers," she said. "I bought a bottle of 'em at a drugstore but I only swallowed a few, enough to get a mild high. The rest I scattered on the floor to make it look like I gulped down a lot of 'em."

"By 'downers' I presume you mean Seconal capsules."

"That's right."

"Now I want you to answer my next question carefully, Miss Halliday. Is the person who hired you in the studio?"

"Y-yes."

"Would you point him out?"

Lee had expected her to point to Alex; instead she directed an accusing finger at Jeff Champion. "It was him."

There was a sudden stir of interest among the spectators, especially the newsmen. Flash attachments flared and the powerful light of a TV reporter's portable camera was centered on Jeff Champion, almost blinding him.

"Let the record show that Miss Halliday has indicated Mr. Jeff Champion as her employer for the incident in question," said Lee. "Now, Miss Halliday, will you tell us how you came to be employed by Mr. Champion?"

"Well, I've worked a few times as a shill in Reverend Jake Schiller's Temple in Atlanta during his healing services."

"A shill? Would you explain?"

"Everybody knows what 'shill' is—an old sideshow barker term. You know, the one that's let win at a skin game to encourage the marks. I guess preachers wouldn't be expected to know about things like that either, but a mark is a sucker who's being set up to be taken to the cleaners."

"I think we all understand what you mean," said Lee. "Please go on."

"Well, I'm an actress, so I can fake almost any sort of a complaint when I come up on the platform to be healed. I was pretty good in gymnastics in high school, too, so I know how to fall when I'm 'slain in the Spirit.' Anyway, Mr. Champion knew I could fake almost anything so he offered me the five hundred to suck Brother Tim in on a suicide try."

"Did you get the five hundred, Miss Halliday?"

"Not the second two-fifty. Jeff Champion got real mad when I called to tell him the paraldehyde the doctor gave me in the hospital had got me so high, I'd accidentally let you and your girl friend know I was being paid. You see, I was supposed to hold a press conference the day I got out of the hospital and accuse Brother Tim Douglas of paying me to fake the suicide. But with you and your girl friend knowing the whole thing was a fake, Jeff couldn't take a chance with the papers and called the press conference off. He threatened to take me to court if I came back to Atlanta, though, so I stayed on here in Weston."

"Are you absolutely certain it was Mr. Champion who paid you the two hundred and fifty dollars and was supposed to pay you the same amount after you denounced Brother Tim Douglas to the newspapers?"

"It was him, all right. I've done enough jobs for him in the healing racket to know him."

"Thank you, Miss Halliday." Lee turned back to the group of trustees. "Would any of you like to ask the witness a question?"

Nobody answered and Tim's voice was stern when he spoke directly to Elmer Schneider, who had made the accusation. "Since you're an associate of Mr. Champion and Reverend Schiller in Atlanta, Mr. Schneider, I imagine you already know Miss Halliday."

"I never saw the woman before in my life," Schneider blustered.

"He knows me, all right!" Desire Halliday said. "Practically every Saturday night when I'm in Atlanta."

Schneider sat down abruptly, his guilt written on his face.

"Brother Tim," said Lee, "I believe in all fairness, Mr. Champion should be given a chance to defend himself."

"Of course," said Tim. "You have the floor, Mr. Champion."

"We lost that round," said Jeff Champion with a shrug. "But there'll be others."

"Does anyone else have a charge to make against me?" Tim asked.

When there was no answer, he turned to Lee. "Since you are in charge of my defense, Lee, do you have any more evidence to present?"

"I do, Mr. Chairman," said Lee. "It should be obvious by now to all of you that a rather elaborate plot has been developed to damage Brother Tim Douglas in the eyes of the public so his effectiveness in the work of the Gospel Broadcast Center would be irreparably damaged. I don't think we need to identify the source of that plot any further, but to prevent it from continuing, I would like to show you how its financing was probably achieved. If you will direct your attention to the rear screen, we will show you two very revealing sections of videotape taken in the mail-sorting room right here at the Center with the closed-circuit-camera system."

The studio lights were darkened from the control room by Henry Waterford, and the videotape of Magda Sanderson began to roll. Seen on the large screen, it was even more revealing than when Lee had first seen it on the monitor in the control room upstairs—and equally damning. As the second tape appeared, a sob came from Magda Sanderson, and a man's voice suddenly sounded from the audience.

"You don't need to show any more, Lee," said Alex Porcher. "Mrs. Sanderson was only obeying my request when she took money from the mail. What she took was delivered to me each day and forwarded to Jeff Champion in Atlanta to be used in what you have correctly called a plot to discredit Brother Tim Douglas. Not one cent of it was kept by her."

The studio lights came back on and the picture of Magda Sanderson faded as the powerful glare from the spotlight above one of the TV reporters' minicameras picked Alex Porcher out where he stood amid the crowd in the gallery.

"I couldn't believe what I was hearing when Lee told me about the tapes, Alex," Tim Douglas' tone was eloquent with pain and disappointment, "so I had Henry Waterford run them for me. What have I done to you to deserve this kind of disloyalty?"

"I had no idea those who were trying to unseat you would go this far," said Alex. "I hope, too, that you know I would never stoop to such a tactic as hiring Miss Halliday to pretend a suicide attempt."

"I don't see any difference between that and using Magda Sanderson's infatuation for you to obtain money from the Center itself to finance the plot to discredit Brother Tim," Lee said sharply.

"You're right, of course, Lee. In fact, looking back on what has happened in the past month or two, I'm not even sure anymore of my own motives. I have always believed in the inerrancy of the Bible, Tim. When you seemed to heal the man whose legs were threatened with gangrene a few weeks ago, I was really convinced the Lord was performing a true miracle through your hands, just as I still believe Jesus has healed thousands through our efforts on the Logos Club programs."

"I'm convinced of that, too, Alex," Tim said quietly. "The only difference between us is that I have come to realize the actual mechanism by which such healing takes place. I want to help promote a greater knowledge of that mechanism and, more particularly, the strong faith in God that will promote its operation."

"I should have understood that," Alex said, in what had now become a dialogue between him and Tim Douglas, with the observers seemingly forgotten. "But when you stated that our Lord had revealed to you that Aggie would be cured by medical means, after your prayers and mine for her life had failed, I was convinced that your concern for someone you loved had made you deny the power of God to heal. And when you announced your intention to build an institute for combining healing by faith with healing by medical science, I was sure you were denying the power of God and His Son, in itself an act of blasphemy."

"I would never deny that God is all-powerful, Alex," said Tim. "You should know me better than that."

"I do now and I fully realize the degree of my disloyalty to you."

"How long ago did this disloyalty begin?" Lee demanded. "Surely not just in the past few weeks."

"No," Alex confessed. "Looking back on it, I can see that it began at least a year ago, when Jeff Champion offered to make me the host on the television program he planned to build around the present Logos Club, once Tim was ousted."

"For which I freely forgive you," said Tim.

"I would expect that forgiveness from you, but my own conscience will not allow me to be absolved of guilt so easily," said Alex. "When the plot by Jeff Champion and Jake Schiller, with the help of a minority among the Board of Trustees, to discredit you before the world was first proposed to me I refused to have anything to do with it. Only after you appeared to deny the power of God over human life did I agree to help them and ask a woman I love to steal money to finance their campaign. The guilt there is mine, not hers, and I hope she will suffer no harm because of her love for me."

A sob from Magda Sanderson interrupted him and he reached down to take her hand before continuing:

"Only now, when the extent of my guilt has been revealed and you have been magnanimous enough to forgive me, do I realize that my reasons actually went far deeper than I have confessed. Throughout my ministerial career, I have always found myself playing a secondary role—I suppose 'second banana' would be the show business term that best describes it. Your success in the field of television evangelism—"

"For which you are considerably responsible," Tim assured him.

"That may be true but I realize now to what degree envy gradually eroded my loyalty to you. Without that erosion, I would never have convinced myself that any other reason justified the part I have played in the plot revealed here today. Of that I can only be ashamed and ask your forgiveness."

"As I said, it's freely given."

"Thank you, but it cannot absolve the degree of my sin. For that I must do penance and I shall begin by tendering my resignation, effective immediately."

As Alex Porcher sat down, Caleb Ravenal immediately rose to his feet. "Mr. Chairman," he said, "I believe there is more to this plot against you than has been revealed. I would like each trustee recently visited by Miss Eileen Stoddard, who is sitting beside Mr. Champion and I am certain is a part of this plot, to raise his hand."

Nearly half of the board raised their hands, and Caleb continued. "I won't ask each of them whether his interpretation of Miss Stoddard's behavior while in his office was the same as mine. For my part, I am convinced that she was trying to seduce me and thus compromise me into voting against Brother Tim Douglas at this meeting."

"Knock it off!" said Jeff Champion sharply. "I sent her to do a job and she did it well. We've lost a few rounds here but the fight isn't over."

"I think it is, Mr. Champion," said Caleb Ravenal. "The vote recorded during this meeting will show who was a party to this plot. *They* already know and, unless those involved want to risk legal prosecution, which I will gladly undertake at my own expense, I suggest that they hand their resignations to the secretary as they leave the meeting. To bring this contemptible plot to a close, I move the previous question."

"The question has been moved, so there can be no discussion," said Tim. "Those in favor say 'aye,' those opposed 'no.'"

The "ayes" prevailed by a large majority on putting the question and the "nos" by an equally large majority on the motion to replace Tim Douglas as chairman of the board.

"I further move," Caleb Ravenal added, "that a committee of this board be appointed to examine the feasibility of establishing an Institute for Holistic Medicine, as a joint venture with the Weston University Medical School, and launching a funding drive to implement this project."

That, too, passed with a large majority followed by Ravenal's motion to close the meeting, which was seconded and passed easily.

"Thank you, Caleb," said Tim. "We will close the meeting with prayer."

II

Occupied as he was, Lee had not noticed Jack Feagin when he came into the visitors' gallery during the latter part of the meeting and took a seat beside Tracy. As the trustees filed out, Tracy and Feagin came down the steps to where Lee was being hugged by Neeley Douglas, before she went to embrace Tim.

"You missed your calling, Lee," said Feagin with a smile. "You should have been a prosecuting attorney."

"This was my first and only appearance in that role—I hope."

"It looks like you and Miss Ravenal will be singing on the Logos programs for another year at least, until you both graduate. I hope that means you'll be recording for Word."

"I leave such decisions to my manager," said Tracy. "Right now, I'd better thank my father for helping save Lee's job and mine."

"Why don't we have dinner tonight—Mr. Ravenal, too, if he's available—to celebrate the start of a recording career for you and Miss Ravenal?" Feagin asked. "Say at Hotel Weston about seven?"

"If your expense account can stand it, I'd like to include Neeley and Tim," Lee suggested.

"That's even better," said Feagin. "Miss Ravenal's father can witness her signature, and Brother Tim and Neeley, yours. See you there at seven."

Caleb Ravenal and Tracy crossed the stage as Feagin was leaving. "My daughter tells me you and she will soon be recording stars, Lee," Caleb Ravenal said. "I know I'm going to be very proud of both of you."

Lee was surprised, when he went out to his car, to find Jeff Champion standing in the parking lot beside his Jaguar. "I waited to congratulate you, Lee," he said. "You licked us fair and square."

"What I can't understand is why you ever tried."

"Actually, I advised against it but Jake hates Brother Tim and rather fancies himself in the role of David attacking Goliath. Schiller pays me a very handsome salary, along with a cut of the take, so I had to go along and give it my best. We'd have had a good chance, too, if that bitch Desire Halliday hadn't gotten high on the paraldehyde they gave her in the hospital and let you and Tracy in on the plot. Obviously, after that we couldn't stage the press conference claiming Tim Douglas had paid her to fake the suicide."

"Eileen Stoddard didn't help much, either. Caleb Ravenal suspected what was up from the first."

"I should have realized how sharp he is and told her not to try to involve him, but don't sell Eileen short. She scored with a few of your trustees and the voting would have gone our way if you hadn't spooked them from the start by revealing the suicide try as a fake."

"What now?" Lee asked.

"Back to work. There's plenty of gold for everybody in what's coming to be called the 'Electric Church.' I've been telling Jake for months he should give up the healing pitch and let me build a better mousetrap for him. Too many con men are working that street already, and the big money never was there anyway."

"So you're staying with Jake?"

"Why not? He's the kind of platform orator who can have

the rednecks following him in droves but we're not going to stop there. The real money lies in lining up middle-class America behind us with a theme of salvation in Heaven and conservative politics here at home. I know where we can hire a couple of smart sermon writers who can whip people to a frenzy over communism, socialism, sex in television and the marketplace, and corruption in government. With prices going up and inflation eating away at the dollar, we'll be campaigning against Godlessness in America. We'll carry our campaign right into government, too, by threatening the politicians where it really hurts, with a campaign to deny them votes by organizing Christians all over the country into a political as well as a religious force."

"It won't be easy," Lee warned. "One or two men in the 'Electric Church' movement have tried that ploy and failed."

"You never heard Jake really get going on sin in high places. Give him the right words and rehearse him a few times, and old Jake can turn into a raging tiger. Women love it, too. Don't think those 'slain in the Spirit' on the platform when he's conducting a healing service aren't driven as much, or more, by a yearning for Jake himself as for healing and salvation. We've got nine TV stations now but by using the 'Americans for God and Morality' ploy, we'll have ninety this time next year and nine hundred the year after. This country is ripe for a revolution combining religion and politics, Lee, and Jake is the general who can lead it."

"With you pulling the strings?"

"Who else? Jake was down and out when I took over managing him and look how far he's come in a few years. If we hadn't struck a little bad luck this time, we'd be on the verge of taking over the Christian Broadcast Center right now. Fifty million a year pouring into that mailroom ain't hay, brother, and it would have all been ours."

Lee shook his head slowly. "I won't deny that you're smart in ways I could never be, Jeff, and you certainly gave us a scare. But there's something hard to believe about a movement toward righteousness and against sin led by you and Jake Schiller."

Jeff Champion whooped with laughter. "Stick to your singing, Lee," he said, when he was able to speak. "You're a genius there and, with that contract Jack Feagin just told me you and Tracy are going to sign, you'll go a long way. But leave the real promotion of the greatest religious movement in history to fellows who know how to give it the full Madison Avenue treatment." He held out his hand and, after a moment's hesitation, Lee took it.

"Good-by, sucker," said Jeff. "I've got to get back to Atlanta and start writing the sermons old Jake's going to be preaching in the Temple and over the rest of the South in the next few months."

The engine of the Jaguar roared, its tires spurting gravel as Jeff Champion left the parking lot. For a long moment after it disappeared into the adjoining street, Lee stood watching. A half hour ago, he'd been elated at winning the contest against Jeff and Jake Schiller. But if through that victory he had given Jeff the argument that would turn Schiller's tremendous energies and undeniable personal appeal in another, and very dangerous, direction, he couldn't help wondering now whether he hadn't done a disservice to the element of sincerity he knew to be in the 'Electric Church' movement.

Tim Douglas was, at the moment, the acknowledged front runner because he, more than anyone else on the airways, was the living epitome of that sincerity and the teachings of the gentle Nazarene upon which it was based. But if Jeff Champion and Jake Schiller ever got their movement really going the way Jeff planned it, the TV cameras could be the weapons that would destroy what Tim and the Man he served really stood for.

Chapter Twenty

THE THIRTY-SIX-HOUR CHRISTIAN BROADCAST CENTER TELETHON to raise ten million dollars for the Douglas Institute for Holistic Medicine was in its thirty-fourth hour—still a half million dollars short of its goal. When the marathon broadcast had begun with the start of the Logos Club program at ten o'clock on a Friday morning, everyone had been fresh and enthusiastic. Now weariness had begun to sap both enthusiasm and confidence that the goal could be reached in the final hour and a half.

Months of preparation had passed since the climactic scene in the Center chapel, when the enemies of Tim and Neeley had been bested through Lee Steadman's revelation of the chicanery by which they had sought to unseat Tim from control of the Center, and their carefully planned campaign suddenly shattered. After the resignation of Alex Porcher, Tim and Neeley had insisted that Lee take over Alex's duties, including both the interviews and the music. Following up on the recording contracts signed with Word Music, Inc. that same evening, Tracy had flown to Waco a few weekends later to record two gospel-rock songs on a single record that was already starting to rival some of Evie Tornquist's most popular recordings in the field.

Busy with preparations for the crucial telethon that could determine whether the institute ever came into being, Lee hadn't been able to go with Tracy. Now he was sitting with her at a table just out of camera range with a half-empty coffee cup before him. Both were tired and a little hoarse from the dozens of songs they had sung during the telethon—together, alone and with the Gospel Troubadours.

In the preceding 34½ hours, a steady procession of famous people in both the religious and secular areas of show business, as well as many figures in the vast "Electric Church," had passed across the Logos Club stage and set. There the telethon was being devoured by the insatiable hunger of the cameras and flung from broadcast towers to listeners all over the world.

The flow of pledges through the fifty telephones had started in the first few minutes after Lee's usual opening musical statement, "He's Alive!" swelling to a flood that seemed to have no crest as the early hours passed. After that first flood, however, it had gradually trickled to a steadily lessening stream as the final hours ticked themselves away.

"We're not going to make it." Lee looked at the huge thermometer at the other side of the stage where the level of pledges was being recorded. The red column had seemingly come to a standstill at nine million, five hundred thousand, a half million short of the announced goal.

"Surely the lack of just five hundred thousand couldn't sink the whole project," said Tracy.

"The five hundred thousand couldn't, but the failure of the telethon to reach its goal could."

"How?"

"The figures up there represent pledges, not money. If the campaign fails to reach its goal, a lot of people who pledged will have second thoughts about the project and Tim's ability to make it everything he wants it to be. When that happens, they'll start reneging on their pledges and, before you know it, the endowment fund won't be large enough to start building the institute."

"It would be an awful disappointment for Tim to have come so near and still fail."

"Especially when it's the first project he's ever put his heart into that wasn't carried through."

"Maybe there's still a way." Tracy reached for the telephone on the table and started dialing. When he heard Caleb Ravenal's voice in the receiver, Lee realized who she was calling.

"Dad," said Tracy, "are you watching the telethon?"

"Ever since it started, except when I nodded off a few times."

"If I remember the way you look at TV, that would be a lot of times."

"How about you and Lee? Can you still croak?"

"Not much more than that, at least for my part. Lee's right here. You can say hello, if you wish," she told her father, "but he may not be able to croak back."

"You and Tracy have been doing a fine job the past thirty-odd hours, Lee," said Ravenal. "I've been awake enough of the time to see and hear a lot of your songs."

"Thank you, sir—"

"I told you months ago to leave off the 'sir.' "

"I guess it's got to be a habit, unless I can change it the way you want it."

"What was that all about?" Tracy took the phone back and asked her father.

"I told Lee in Asheville I hoped he'd start calling me 'Dad' soon, but I haven't seen any sign that it's likely to happen."

"Haven't you got five friends who could pledge a hundred thousand each if you gave them a call in the next half hour?" Tracy asked. "It would let us go over the top."

"I guess I could put the bite on a few who could afford a hundred thousand," Tracy heard Caleb Ravenal say. "But first, I want you to answer one question for me."

"What's that?" Tracy asked.

"When are you going to marry that fellow I want to start calling me 'Dad'?"

When Tracy didn't answer immediately, Lee followed her gaze to the set where Neeley and the puppeteers were busy with their familiar routine. Tim was sitting in the front row of the visitors' gallery, with Aggie—still a little pale from the long illness but otherwise well and free from any sequelae—beside him. As the black puppet came out with one of her pert rejoinders, both of them burst out laughing and Tim put his arm around his daughter's small waist to squeeze it and kiss her cheek.

"Tracy!" Caleb Ravenal's voice sounded again in the earpiece of the telephone she was holding. "Are you there."

"I'm here," she said, with just a touch of the wistful note in her voice Lee had heard there before, when she was watching Tim.

"You didn't answer my question," Caleb insisted.

Tracy turned to look at Lee and there was no regret in her eyes or her voice when she told her father: "The answer is the next time he asks me."

"Which is right now," said Lee loud enough for the listener at the other end of the connection to hear.

"Then get off the phone so I can start calling for that last five hundred thousand," said Caleb Ravenal.

"Okay, Dad," said Lee and Tracy in the same breath.